**PALM BEACH COUNTY
LIBRARY SYSTEM**

**3650 Summit Boulevard
West Palm Beach, FL 33406**

Blood Thinners

Blood Thinners

A Love Me Dead Romance

Heather Novak

TULE
PUBLISHING

Dedication

To MS, who can do anything in heels. To Amber for loaning me the courage to write this book. To Katie for keeping us safe. Chris, I miss you and wish you could've read this one. And as always, in loving memory of my mom.

Chapter One

MY HEART WAS still thundering with adrenaline as I pulled my wooden chopstick out of the dead vampire's heart. I eyed the makeshift weapon with apprehension, realization dawning that no amount of dish soap would be enough for me to eat with it.

"Great. Now I'll have to eat dinner with a fork!" I glared at my dead attacker, a middle-aged man in a disheveled, bloodstained suit. I dropped the chopstick to the ground, then crouched and shoved at one hundred and ninety pounds of literal dead weight. Thank god I hadn't worn a skirt today.

"Get...under...there!" I huffed, pushing him inch by inch under my SUV. A pillar hid part of my car, which would hopefully also hide the vampire until I called in a disposal team. All I needed was my nosiest neighbor, Doris, seeing a dead body and flipping out. Although, it would give me a reason to sedate her...

With one last herculean effort, I got the vamp underneath the vehicle. I leaned my right side against my truck, gripping my left shoulder, which was more metal than bone. It throbbed with each breath, reminding me it was going to take time to get back into the swing of things. Today had been my first day back in four months, and it could not have gone worse.

I took a step toward the passenger door and nearly face-planted when my shoe's heel broke off. "Dammit!" I caught myself on the handle and closed my eyes, taking a deep breath. It did nothing to calm me down. Careful to keep the vampire goo away from my takeout, I nabbed the bag and limped toward my apartment building.

Home, haunted home.

I burst through the front door, choosing to ignore the group of ghosts trying to hang a "Congratulations, Mina!" banner in the common area. Startled, they broke their concentration. The fabric drifted through them to the floor. Very apropos, seeing how I didn't get the promotion they were so eager to celebrate.

"Mina! What happened?" Dani, the mother figure of the group, called.

"Stray vamp," I muttered, leaning on the handrail as I limped up the stairs to my second-floor dwelling.

My plans to mope *alone* with a glass of wine were drowned out by the unmistakable sound of Celine Dion's "My Heart Will Go On" echoing down the hallway. Ghosts were such assholes. I jammed the key into my lock and flung my door open. "My dudes!" I yelled over the noise as I walked in, dropping my take-out on the counter and kicking my shoes toward the garbage can. "What did I say about reenacting *Titanic* at full volume?"

My ghost roommate Sebastian and his best friend Reggie were standing on my curbside-acquired green plaid couch, pretending they were on the bow of a doomed ship. Reggie had tied his sweater backward around his waist (to make it look like a dress) while Sebastian stood behind him. Reggie was Guatemalan-American, with dark hair and tawny skin, and Sebastian could almost pass for a young Leonardo DiCaprio. After he froze to death.

Sebastian's eyes grew wide. "Mina! You've arrived early!"

I muted the music streaming from the television and crossed my arms. "Seriously? You trying to get me another noise complaint? If I get a third one, you know Doris will try and get me evicted, and I swear I will move far enough away so you two couldn't see each other as punishment."

Sebastian smirked at me. "You would do no such thing. We are delightful."

Reggie groaned. "It's just getting good!"

"Oh, so you haven't gotten to the part where you take the cushions off the couch to make a door?"

Sebastian pushed Reggie, who crashed through the coffee table with the force of a shadow, then popped back up with his hands on his hips. "Rude."

Sebastian stepped down with a smirk, smoothing his shirt. "We're intelligent enough to share the door."

Reggie grabbed Sebastian's forearms. "I'll never let you go, Seb."

I pinched the bridge of my nose. "Host a ghost agent, they said. It'll be fun, they said." It's not that I didn't love *Titanic*—back in the nineties—it's just that they'd been doing this three times a week for the last three hundred and forty-eight days. "You both would've died anyway!" I called over my shoulder as I trudged toward the kitchen while pulling off my now-ruined button up, leaving me in a ripped tank.

I balled up my shirt and threw it into the nearly overflowing trash can. An open-concept apartment was nicer on paper than reality. I couldn't hide my dirty dishes behind a wall if there was no wall.

Sebastian clicked off the TV and straightened his cravat. He had broken his neck in a drunken carriage-racing accident on the way home from a ball and was forever doomed to wear his Regency-era evening attire. "I'm a duke with a large inheritance. I would've survived," he called after me in his posh British accent. His arrogance was impressive for a guy who had died over a century ago and had no more substance than a benzodiazepine hallucination.

"Were a duke!" I reminded him. "Your great-great-great nephew is now the duke."

Reggie laughed. "She got you, amigo."

I needed an entire bottle of wine. Or a new apartment building. There were way too many ghosts here, and especially in this apartment. "I'm getting tipsy and watching Netflix tonight. If you don't like it, go to Reggie's." Reggie lived with his divorced, older (living) brother, who also worked for SHAP.

"No se puede. Lola is staying the week and you know she's afraid of ghosts," Reggie explained. "She tried to perform an exorcism last time, my own sobrina!" He shook his head in disbelief.

"Oooh, an exorcism! That sounds lovely," I shot back. "Think your niece'll let me help?"

Sebastian gasped. "After all I have done for you, a simple tradeswoman? We wouldn't even be acquainted had we met when I was alive."

I snorted. "If only. And you need to get over this duke thing. You still expect staff to clean the apartment." Sebastian pretended he couldn't do much more than push buttons and flip switches as if he were a baby ghost, though I'd seen him refold my entire linen closet because he was bored. Useless housemate.

"I provide encouragement while you labor."

"You provide migraines." I finished washing the goo from my hands, then grabbed a paper towel and wiped the sweat and blood off the back of my neck and forehead. After tossing a bag of frozen vegetables on my shoulder, I pulled the cork out of my open bottle of wine, not bothering with a glass. A half dozen ghosts standing in a pyramid greeted my return to the living room.

"No," I told them. "Whatever this is, no."

Reggie made a cutting motion across his neck at the group, then sat on the couch with an innocent face when they disappeared.

Sebastian's eyes narrowed. "Why are you in such a foul temperament? I thought you were getting promoted to a desk job today."

"Regional director is not a 'desk job.' It's a necessary step if I want to take over when Dad retires." Sure, it meant more time at my desk and less time kicking ass, but regional director, or RD, meant being in charge of all the agents and their missions in southeast Michigan.

If I snagged the promotion before my thirtieth birthday this November, I'd be the youngest agent ever to receive the honor. One step closer to everything I'd been working toward my entire life. I wanted to be the first female Territory Director at SHAP, and it was only three more promotions away. Well, four now.

I had already been the youngest active agent in history, starting my career at fifteen. While most of my friends were bagging groceries or making pizzas, I was hunting down dangerous supernatural creatures. I was basically Buffy the Vampire Slayer, but without the end of the world and falling in love with morally ambiguous vampires. This probably explained why my only friends were ghosts or coworkers. It was easier—no one to worry when I didn't come home.

SHAP, or Supernatural-Human Accountability Partnership, was the company that kept humans and supernaturals from killing each other by utilizing a series of strict agreements. Or they tried to, anyway. I kinda broke one of those agreements about ten minutes ago.

"Is the blood part of a hazing ritual?" Reggie leaned in, trying to wipe blood out of my blond hair. My head went right through his hand, leaving me chilled. "Mierda. I keep forgetting." Reggie had only died a year ago and was still learning his ghost ropes, so to speak. If he kept trying, *unlike Sebastian*, he'd be able to open and close doors by December.

I rubbed at my forehead. "Never stops being weird."

Sebastian crossed his arms, as if he were my older brother about to go to bat for me. "Where's the blood from, Mina?"

"Small scuffle with a vampire." I needed to talk to the complex about more security. This was the second attack in as many months, and for what I paid in rent for this tiny scrap of a place, I should have my own personal security guard. Of course, I'd probably be a better protector than whoever they hired, injured shoulder or not.

I slumped into an admittedly hideous scratchy orange armchair and propped my feet on the coffee table. Sebastian hated when I disrespected my furniture, but I'd gotten it at a garage sale for five bucks. It wasn't some heirloom piece that had been in my family for eight generations.

"I didn't get the promotion today, but whatever... How was your day? Haunt anyone to death?" My voice caught on the last word, my eyes stinging. I blinked hard. I didn't cry. Emotions made me drop my guard, which would get me killed.

Reggie winced. "I better go call off the flash ghost mob. Nos vemos mas tarde." *See you later.* He disappeared.

Sebastian sat on the arm of my chair. "Love, what happened?"

I lifted my hands and let them fall against my lap, staring at the bright red scratches across my pale skin, remnants from the fight. I didn't want to put the moment into words. It was a level of mortification I didn't need to relive.

The conference room had been so hot and the number of people who'd gathered to welcome me back to work after my short-term disability had been overwhelming. My partner Jake had stood by my side, ever the supportive best friend. Sure, moving to RD would mean breaking up our duo, but this had been my dream since I was a shy twelve-year-old watching her father become the leader of the United States branch of SHAP. I wanted him to look at me with the same pride I felt for him.

It was in my blood, and we had all known what was coming; the sheet cake (even though I hated cake; pie was far superior) in the break room that read "Congratulations,

Mina!" was the final touch. It wasn't nepotism. I was really that fucking great at my job. When Dad—Director of United States Operations—stood to make his welcome back speech, everyone waited with their hands on their water glasses to make a toast.

The toast never came.

When I cornered him in his office afterward, he had simply said, "Last mission was too reckless."

"I did what I had to do to catch the bastard!" Catching a serial killer wizard who had been operating for decades had made the accident that destroyed my shoulder worth it. A high-speed chase during an ice storm wasn't ideal, but I had forced him into the concrete barrier before I rolled my truck. As they loaded me into the ambulance, I'd stayed conscious long enough to see him locked into a transport van.

Sure, I had *almost* died in the process, but it was the biggest win of my career. I had earned that promotion.

My dad just looked up at me over his reading glasses and said, "Reckless. Prove your responsibility next case."

Sebastian murmured my name, pulling me out of my spiraling memory. I swallowed hard against the lump in my throat. "Gotta do another case."

He stared at me for a long moment and tilted his head. "Are you prepared for that?"

I frowned. "What do you mean? I'm done 'convalescing.'"

"Dancing with death changes a person. It's acceptable to not want to partake in another mission so soon."

I waved him off. "I'm fine and no, I don't want to talk about it anymore. Tell me about your day?"

"Well, I had to do *something* to distract myself from this atrocious decorating." He grimaced while looking around. "My casket was more appealing, and it was cast iron." A laugh snuck up on me. SHAP had assigned Sebastian to this neighborhood two years ago and in a moment of weakness, I had agreed to his residency. He had yet to stop complaining that my place wasn't up to his standards.

Ghosts were something not even SHAP could explain—either why they appeared or why only some people could see them—but the general consensus was they were leftover energy from a human's life that didn't dissipate. Or maybe they just had unfinished business and couldn't cross over until it was resolved. Only about half of SHAP employees could communicate with ghosts, but it was a requirement for all field agents and upper management. Ghosts were extremely tuned in to the space around them and an asset to any agent. Which is why I put up with this one.

"And, I had quite the day," he continued. "I dueled with a pair of demons trying to invade the Andrews' place. You should have a talk with them about their hobbies. Last month, I had to deal with a bushel of poltergeists, which was just preposterous."

I pinched the bridge of my nose. "I'm going to drop off groceries later this week. I'll make sure to have a chat." Last time, Amber Andrews had been "accidentally" crocheting summoning spells into her sweaters. Accidentally, my ass. Amber may look like a grandma from a made-for-TV movie, but there was a sharpness behind her watery eyes and wrinkly smile.

Applechester, Michigan, was a supernatural hotspot,

which included the Countryside Village apartment complex. Resurrected from an old hotel that had been turned into a hospital during the 1918 influenza pandemic, these walls held as many secrets as my old journal. While the gray paint, wood floors, and ornate staircase suggested a safe and cozy environment, I practically had a second job trying to keep the demons, wendigos, and vampires from sneaking in.

Many of my neighbors worked for SHAP, human and supernatural alike. While most humans outside of the town limits didn't know supernaturals existed, everyone here just rolled with the unexplained events.

"Did you report the attack yet?" Sebastian asked.

I took a sip of wine. "Nope." I had no desire to report it. Zero. Zilch.

He crossed his arms. "In my opinion—"

"Which, you'll notice, I didn't ask for—"

"It falls under your employment agreement to report any and all vampire attacks. Pray tell, how did you dispose of the…carcass?" He said the word as if it offended him.

"It's in my garage. Shoved him under my car."

He grimaced. "It's July. Remember the zombies?"

I cringed. Three zombies had stolen a Cadillac last summer to go on a joyride, hit a pothole, and—zombies being very fragile creatures—lost control of the car when the driver's arms fell off. They crashed into a tree and rotted for four days before someone reported it. I could still remember the smell.

I groaned. *Fucking vampire.* Sebastian was right though. It was still eighty-nine and humid even with night approaching. Last thing I needed was the dead vampire smell to seep into my new truck.

This was going to be the cherry on top of the shit evening ice cream sundae.

List of things I hated, in order:

1. Giving Jim Summers bad news
2. Demons
3. Cucumbers
4. Vampires

Giving Dad bad news was not for the faint of heart. I'd had men twice my age beg me to give him a message. Newsflash: he didn't like hearing it from me, either. "Can't you report it for me? Isn't that your job?"

"I only make reports on demons, fairies, and other spirits," he said, as if I didn't know. God forbid he do me a solid. "Do you want to explain to your neighbors why the garage smells like a dead pheasant left in the sun for a fortnight?"

"If you report it, I'll let you watch *Titanic* as many times as you want this week."

He adjusted his cravat. "If I become so desperate, Mina, I'll simply meander next door for my entertainment. My tether stretches ten miles, and Dr. Brady in 4B works evenings."

When a house ghost was assigned a base residence, their essence was tied to an object from their past that SHAP encased in an unbreakable box for safe keeping. The relic allowed the ghost to be tethered to earth, instead of floating off into the ether, or wherever they went. Sebastian's was, unsurprisingly, his flask. He (and his flask) had been found at an estate sale out in Boston about five years ago, having come to America by some collector.

"I hate you." But I grabbed my phone from the pocket and pressed my top contact. *Please go to voicemail. Please go to voicemail.*

"Summers." No greeting, of course. What did I expect? He only ever answered his phone by identifying himself.

"Hi...Dad." His response was loaded—judging silence. I looked at Sebastian, who motioned for me to get on with it. "Got a vampire situation. At my place. Well, more precisely my garage."

"Explain."

I went into a quick recap: It approached from behind. I killed him with the chopstick from my takeout, left him under my car. "I checked for an identification device but couldn't find one."

All potentially harmful supernatural species residing within cities were required to have identification devices, a peace offering from the supernaturals after a coven of witches had completely decimated a town during a spell gone wrong. It had been the most human lives lost to a single supernatural incident in the last century. To find a vampire attacking within city limits, potentially without a device, was a serious issue. Hopefully they'd discover one during the autopsy.

"Injuries?"

Wow. He really did care. "None sustained." *Lie.* My shoulder was throbbing, and I had vampire goo *in my hair.*

The gelatinized substance was typically only found in very fresh vampires; the older ones at least had the decency to keep themselves self-contained upon permanent deanimation (or super permanent death). If I was really lucky, they'd be ancient, burst into ash, and disappear on the breeze. Sadly, I rarely got to kill the old-ass ones, as most were "too civilized" to drink directly from humans anymore, and preferred reusable blood bottles. Environmentally friendly vegetarian vampires were all the rage.

"Protocol is capture alive," he reprimanded.

I sucked in a steadying breath. "I know you'd prefer them alive, but I was too busy trying not to die to be super gentle."

"Roger." He hung up.

I stared down at the phone, somehow expecting it to explain his plan. Not that I needed it. He'd send some agents over for cleanup and investigation, then send me an email confirming the details of my report. We'd continue like this until my birthday, when he'd utter two words to me instead of only one.

I tossed my phone on the coffee table and stood. "I need to shower before the troops get here."

Sebastian smiled, a rakish grin that once had likely made every debutant in a ballroom swoon. "Do you desire company?"

"Why are you hitting on me?"

He shrugged one shoulder. "Flirting with you is one of the few pleasures I have left."

I laughed. "I'm bisexual, not spectrosexual." I gave him a once-over. "How would that work anyway? You're not exactly…" I waved my hand.

"Hard?"

"Corporeal." I shook my head. "You've got twenty minutes to Celine it up. Keep the volume down."

"What will you do if I disobey? Punish me? That, my dear, is not a deterrent."

"Exorcism!" I called back over my shoulder, then paused. "Wait…hold up. You planned a ghost flash mob?"

Sebastian just winked.

Chapter Two

TUESDAY AFTERNOON, I sat inside Café Eleonora, an eclectic noshery next to SHAP headquarters. Lots of protein-packed salads and veggie-based shakes on the menu; although they also had a loaded pastry case I was having a hard time not licking. That would be unsanitary.

Despite the lunch rush, no one bothered to ask if the seat across from me was occupied. If I was in the café during business hours, it was for a meeting, a sentiment that didn't help my social life. It's what made me a great agent and a terrible friend.

When my dad's assistant, Sienna, walked in, I set down my mug of black coffee and sat up straight. She smiled, her blood red lipstick almost as intimidating as her golden werewolf eyes. Despite being at least ninety years old, she could easily pass for forty. "I'll bite him for you, if you want," she offered.

I lifted an eyebrow as she sat down across from me. "You'd risk your job because he didn't promote me?"

She smiled, exposing her perfectly white, and presumably very sharp, teeth. "It'd be worth it to taste that man."

I shook my head once. "Nope! Do not want to hear this."

She laughed. "Haven't had human flesh in three decades. Not going to start now." She winked at me. "Probably."

I narrowed my eyes. "Is there a reason you're interrupting my coffee break?"

"You don't take coffee breaks." She stood and smoothed down her perfectly crisp gray suit, then leaned close. "When Jim got the call about the accident, he cried. Known him longer than you've been alive. Never seen him cry."

"Why are you telling me this?"

"Because you're angry. He's worried. Not a good combination. Keep your head down and solve your next case. I'll make sure you get the promotion." She straightened and stared at something over her shoulder. "We never had this conversation."

She smiled, stood, then walked away, pausing only to wave at her sister Eleonora—also a werewolf—who owned the café. The two of them practically ran SHAP, between Sienna working with my dad and Eleonora feeding and caffeinating us, and everyone knew it. They protected their SHAP family—their blood relatives long since dead—with their teeth. Literally.

"That looked ominous." My partner, Jake, sat down across from me with a drink that resembled a Muppet more than coffee. There were sprinkles, chocolate chips, and myriad syrups drizzled across a dome of whipped cream, topped with cookie crumbles, and a bite-sized brownie. He was, unfathomably, in perfect shape despite his preference for future diabetes.

I sipped my coffee with one eyebrow raised, so he knew I was judging him. "She'd love you for saying that."

"She loves me anyway." He loosened his tie, the one he always wore to SHAP trials, then grunted as he stretched out his injured leg. "I got her *Supernatural* on Blu-ray for her birthday."

"Suck up." I gestured to his drink. "You'll kill yourself drinking that shit. Then what am I supposed to do? Find a new partner?"

He glowered. "I've already had to work with a new partner for months after you tried to die."

Ouch. "Jake, come on. You would've done the same thing."

He shrugged. "Yeah, but I wouldn't have crashed." Then the asshole winked at me. *Winked.*

How we were best friends, I'd never know. Though spending long minutes that felt like hours trying to keep someone alive until backup arrived tended to bond people. The cane leaning against his chair and the surgical scars on my back were physical reminders the last decade had been a wild ride.

Despite our injuries, both of us still qualified for active field agent duty. Unlike the human-only agencies, our physical strength and agility were only a small percentage of what made a person fit for duty. Jake may not be able to run a three-hundred-meter sprint, and I couldn't do any pull ups or push-ups, but we had sharpshooter accuracy, could practically build a bomb out of chewing gum and a hair tie, and between his computer abilities and my knack for finding information, we had been one of the top teams for five years.

His blue eyes met mine. "I know you're pissed, and it's one hundred percent unfair. But I'd be lying if I said I wasn't happy the band's back together for one last hurrah."

"We make a great team." Most of me was livid I hadn't gotten the promotion because my father had some messed-up narrative in his head about how I should or shouldn't solve cases, despite my impressive track record. But there was something comforting about joining forces with Jake again.

"How was today?" I asked, changing the subject.

He shrugged. "Straightforward. They confessed. In and out."

"The best kind." Every time we made an arrest, there was an arraignment. Sometimes the person would confess, sometimes we went to trial. Unlike a human trial, there weren't randomly selected juries, but a panel of SHAP representatives, both human and supernatural, who reviewed the details of the case and assigned a punishment.

"You ready for our last case together?" He shoved the entire brownie bite into his mouth, then leaned down and licked the whipped cream. This elicited stares from neighboring tables. To the rest of the world, he was eye candy with his already darkening five o'clock shadow on his white skin, a jaw I could cut my hand on, almost-too-long dark hair, and like six percent body fat—probably seven percent after he drank (ate?) his coffee. To me, he was my weird little brother who could kill someone with a paper clip.

That knowledge didn't stop me from pulling out my phone and putting it in video mode. After all, I could kill him with a spoon. "Do that again. I'm going to make a TikTok and retire on the profits."

"Want me to take off my shirt first?"

"Obviously. Pants, too." He laughed and I smiled at the

sound. I had missed it. Being around a living, breathing human again—one who wasn't afraid of me—made my chest warm. No, had to be the coffee.

He took one more sip of his drink, then pulled a tablet out of his bag and slid it across the table. "I was assigned this case last Friday. Thought I'd need a new partner. Glad it's you."

I rolled my eyes. "Stop flattering me and give me deets."

"What do you know about Thinner?"

"The weight loss company?"

He nodded.

A dozen celebrities had endorsed the program when it'd hit big six-ish months ago, the CEO being a former eighties exercise icon. The company promised any member who joined them for their revolutionary getaway experience would achieve permanent weight loss.

To say I was *extremely* skeptical was putting it lightly. "Overnight fame, likely due to the CEO's platform and the fact she's worth an estimated sixty million dollars. Membership has a ninety-nine percent success rate."

Finishing the whipped cream, he ran his finger along the top of his mug, his tell for when he was thinking about something I would find *very* interesting. "Aren't you curious about how they're achieving that success rate?"

I shrugged. "People will try anything. My guess? It's some surgery, a few facials, killer workouts, and a celebrity chef who creates impossible eating standards. Plus, whatever supplements they're forced to take." The Thinner "getaway experiences" were, on average, a month long—plenty of time to recover from a knife.

Jake bobbed his head. "Could be."

"But you don't think so."

"I don't think so." He leaned back, his chair tipped on two legs, nursing his drink. His eyes held mine for a long moment, and I leaned forward, practically vibrating with excitement. "That vamp from your place? No chip. But he had a work ID on his belt."

"Uh-huh."

Another sip, pausing for dramatic effect, no doubt. "He was a member of Thinner. Got back from a getaway two weeks ago. Left his office for a lunch meeting and never came back."

I pressed my palms on the table, excited. "And the company he worked at?"

"Law firm. No supernaturals registered on their staff."

He settled his chair on the laminate floor and leaned so close I could smell peppermint coffee on his breath. "Thought we'd check in with Thinner. Either they're hiring supernaturals without proper credentials…"

I held my breath, waiting for the juicy part.

"Or…" He tapped the table with his index finger. "There's something way more nefarious going on."

"I love the way you flirt," I teased. "What do we know?"

"Already sent in an agent posing as a reporter to interview the VP Carma Nicks. Agent determined she's likely not a vampire or demon but couldn't determine if she was *only* human."

I tilted my head, running through my mental database of supernatural creatures. "So maybe a shifter? Or werewolf?" Werewolves could register as undetectable most of the month and some older shifters had mastered the human form.

"Why else would they have moved their headquarters to Applechester?"

"Affordable taxes? Access to four major highways?" I countered.

He nodded once. "Fair point. But could also be the fact that Applechester was literally founded by a werewolf."

I rolled my eyes. "Yeah, and Disney was founded by a mouse. It just makes a good story."

"You're such a cynic. And Disney was founded by Walt Disney, not a mouse."

"Whatever." While we did have a high population of werewolves and witches (and way too many ghosts), I was pretty sure the city sprang up here because it was on the railroad. There was still an Amtrak station a mile from my building. "I love a scavenger hunt. Gives me a reason to bother the research and development team."

He raised his eyebrows. "You just think they're pretty."

I rolled my eyes. "Listen. Am I mad they hired a bunch of hot nerds? No. But I have a look-no-touch rule with coworkers." If I was romantically involved with anyone connected to SHAP, it could come back to bite me as I moved up the chain of command.

He held up his hands. "As long as you keep getting me better detection tools, I don't care."

"Piece of cake. No, I hate cake. Piece of pie." I bounced a little in my seat. "What's our cover?"

"You're looking at two future hires for Thinner. You'll be playing Mina Madison, assistant to the CEO."

I pursed my lips. "This name is payback for Jake Jakeson, isn't it?" We got to pick our fake names for our cases—unless we needed specific identities—and tried to use our first names whenever possible for believability.

He shrugged. "Entirely possible."

I play-kicked him under the table. "Fine. What's it this time?"

"Jake Shelley."

"Oh good, so we both have two first names."

"I had like five minutes to pick names. Suck it up, buttercup."

I shook my head. "I've missed your stupid face."

He just rolled his eyes at me and continued drinking his coffee. I unlocked the tablet and swiped through the mission's background information to get to the juicy stuff. *Bingo*. Background on Lucinda Nicks.

I glanced up to find Jake smirking. "How long did it take you to find the Jazzercise clip?"

"An hour. It was worth it."

"You're the weirdest person I know."

He lifted his mug to me in a mock salute. "Right back at you."

I gave him the finger and continued reading. Lucinda had been a pioneer of women's dance exercise videos in the eighties, making a fortune which she then invested in a few lucky companies that made her ridiculously wealthy. She had no need to work, which likely made this a project of her heart. Those were always the most dangerous.

People often didn't see logic when the heart was involved.

Lucinda launched Thinner officially in January with her daughter, Carma, at the helm as VP. I flipped the page and froze as summer-green eyes and long chestnut hair filled the screen. My heart did a weird double beat.

Whoa. I shook my head. She was…stunning.

She was also *interesting*. Her vintage black dress had pink flowers, *wait…skulls?* I zoomed in. *Yep, skulls.* And her winged eyeliner was flawless.

I swallowed hard. This woman was one hundred percent my aesthetic. Heat curled low in my stomach, a feeling I hadn't had in years.

"Mina, what's wrong?"

"Hmmm?" I looked up. "Nothing." *I'm going to have to stay away from this woman.* "Just enjoying the eye candy." *Note to self: charge vibrator.*

He narrowed his eyes. "Uh-huh."

I cleared my throat and turned off the screen. "So, when do we start?"

He smiled. "We 'interview' tomorrow."

Chapter Three

T WO SUCCESSFUL INTERVIEWS later, I walked into the sprawling brick building that housed Thinner's headquarters wearing a fitted black pant suit, my favorite gun (a pistol named Sydney), and a few of my favorite supernatural detecting accessories. Thinner took up half a block of prime real estate in downtown Applechester. I was greeted by the receptionist with shampoo commercial hair, glowing bronze skin, and a smile so fake it gave me ghost bumps. (5'8", slender build, pencil skirt and heels would inhibit running. Risk assessment: unless looks could kill, low threat.)

"Hi again. I'm Mina Madison, Ms. Nicks's new assistant." As I spoke, I pressed a button on my watch, which should tell me in thirty seconds or less if the receptionist was human. The last two times I'd come across her, there had been additional people in the room, potentially interfering with the data.

Her smile stayed in place, but her eyes narrowed. "ID."

I handed her my fake license and waited as she studied it and me. She gave it back and quickly pulled her hand away as if I disgusted her. She could give Sienna a run for her money.

"This way, Ms. Madison." She pressed a button and

walked over to a thick, spotless glass door with large copper handles.

I nodded my thanks as I walked through the door, pausing to glance down at my vibrating watch. *Inconclusive.* I tapped the watch face and tried again, getting the same result. So it *wasn't* the other people last time. It was her. *Hmm.* Maybe werewolf?

Shampoo Commercial led me to the lower level and through a maze of hallways that would require me to leave M&M's to find my way back if I hadn't studied the blueprint. *No thinking about candy before lunch because then you'll be hungry.*

Think about...cucumbers? Ugh. Cucumbers were like not eating at all. Crunchy water.

"So, you on the program?" I asked. "I've heard only great things."

"Yes."

Wow. Talkative. I studied her back, trying to pinpoint what exactly made her seem...different.

She walked like she was dancing, each move fluid and quick. I had to practically run to keep up with her, and she was wearing stilettos. Impressive. When she stopped suddenly, I almost tumbled into her back.

With a flourish of her hand, Shampoo Commercial directed me into an office encased in glass with two desks. My new manager, Maggie, was the complete opposite of the perfectly coiffed receptionist. A middle-aged woman who perpetually wore a headset and looked even more harried than last time I saw her. (5'6", athletic build, A-line skirt and sneakers. Risk assessment: could beat up a mugger with her purse, if she wasn't on the phone.)

She still had a pen cap between her teeth and her cell phone on speaker, all while making handwritten notes on two different note pads. She lifted her eyebrows in greeting as Shampoo Commercial disappeared back through the cave of wonders.

I set down my shoulder bag and grabbed a pad of paper and a pen from my new desk, then gestured to the phone in Maggie's hand. With a relieved look, she handed it to me, and I jotted down what the speaker was saying.

A man gave me the name and cell number of Michigan's governor, then requested a personal call back from Lucinda Nicks. With a quick flick of the earpiece on my fake glasses, which were actually a combination of a top-of-the-line camera and video feed, I took a photo of the note which automatically uploaded it to SHAP's secure network.

Maggie flung off her headset and rushed around her desk, hand extended. Everything she did, she did with speed. Our handshake lasted only two seconds before she was hustling back to her computer.

"Welcome to your first day! Thanks for not sucking." She paused, then gave me a quick once-over. "Please tell me that wasn't a fluke and you actually don't suck."

I smiled. "I work hard, love organization, and I know how Google works." I clicked my watch button and refocused on her.

She nodded while glancing through the file folders already in her inbox. "I like you. You're better than the last one."

"The last one?"

Maggie nodded. "He popped his gum."

I cringed. "I've broken up with people for less." She laughed and gave me a relieved smile. My watch buzzed and I glanced down. *Human.*

"IT will be by to set up your log in, and HR will be by with paperwork when they eventually grace us with their presence. In the meantime…" Maggie dumped a large binder on my desk. "Read this. Memorize it."

I flipped open the cover and skimmed the first page.

Lucinda Nicks's Preferences.

I had yet to meet the owner and CEO of Thinner in person, although we had talked on video chat during my last interview. She was currently in Washington, D.C., having tea with three former first ladies. Several members of the security detail they had hired for the trip were from SHAP.

"You're the sixth hire in six months," Maggie continued. "If you want to last longer than the rest, you do things the way Lucinda wants them when she wants them. Got it?"

I nodded. "She's not my first *Devil Wears Prada.*" I doubted she'd be as bad as working undercover for a veela who was pregnant with twins—nymphs were outright barbarians when they hit forty-seven weeks—but I knew it was stupid, if not deadly, to underestimate any opponent.

Maggie smiled. "Ah, but I bet she'll be the most memorable. This is one hundred percent a 'Yes, I can' or 'I will look into that immediately' work culture. There is no 'I can't.' Understand?"

"Perfectly."

"Then you can have a temporary ID badge until HR makes you an official one. This will get you in and out of the building and onto the executive level." She grabbed a badge from her drawer and tossed it to me. I caught it midair and clipped it to my belt loop. It read *Executive Pass, Lucinda Nicks* above a small chip.

I didn't get a chance to thank her before an old-fashioned ringing emanated from our desk phones. Maggie's entire face rearranged itself into a customer-service smile before she pulled on the headset. "Hello, Ms. Lucinda, this is Maggie speaking." Her fingers flew over the keyboard. "No, I don't think she can sue. It's in the contract she signed. Yes, ma'am."

When she hung up, she jotted on a sticky note and held it out on her finger, the name Natalie Moranis and a date of birth meticulously printed on the square. "Take this to the records department and ask them to forward the digital copy to me but wait for the paper file as well. Take the paper file to the office down the hall and hand it directly to Carma Nicks. Not her assistant. If you screw this up, you're fired. Got it?"

I nodded and took the sticky note. "Records, digital to you, paper into Carma's hand. Check."

She pointed past the door. "Look both ways before you step into a hallway." The phone rang again, and Maggie picked it up without another word.

As instructed, I looked both ways, only to be nearly flattened by a group of five men in suits that probably cost more than a year's rent. Good lord, they walked faster than I jogged. I flipped the glasses to video mode to catch their speed. If someone was rushing, there was usually a good reason.

There weren't any smiles or greetings from the passersby, just snorts or quiet conversations on their AirPods. Either random newbies wandering the halls looking lost was a common enough occurrence to disregard, or people were so busy they didn't care if I was a lamp post or a human. Fine with me. The more invisible I was, the more I could observe.

Jake was right. There was a really weird vibe to this place. Neither my watch nor the EMF reader ring on my pointer finger, which glowed if I came across a strong electromagnetic field of energy, had alerted me to anything suspicious. Still, I couldn't shake the internal vibration in my chest, the one that told me to keep my guard up.

"Excuse me," Jake said as he stepped out of the elevator to my right. With the exception of a brief glance to my wrist, he acted as if I were a complete stranger. "Can you tell me how to get to…" He looked down at his phone. "Mina Madison's office? I'm from IT."

"Hi! I'm Mina," I said, playing along. His eyes met mine, and I shook my head once, indicating I had zero idea what was going on.

I made a show of telling him how to get to my office, using a lot of hand waving. "I'm headed to records, but maybe I'll see you when I get back." He nodded, then squeezed my elbow once—indicating he had also come up blank—before walking away. He was using his gunmetal gray cane today, which had been fitted with surveillance equipment and storage space for a knife and a bottle of holy water. Never knew when either would come in handy.

The records department was at the end of a long hallway that sloped downward, only adding to the suspicion there was something supernatural at work here. Sure, all the executive offices could be on the lower level because of space or to lower heating and cooling costs, but likely it had to do with sunlight or noise. I mean, wasn't having a window office the perk of being an exec? But vampires and sun did not mix well, and werewolves hated noise.

Supernatural creatures all had very real origins. It was an incredibly diverse group, hailing from all over the planet. Every country, every state, every major city. Every skin color, religious background, sexual orientation, and political party had non-humans.

Through both genetic and viral mutations, as well as scientific experimentations—in the days before such things were considered "cruel and unusual"—the line between what we considered normal and fiction blurred. We knew both zombies and vampires were caused by a rare, but often fatal, virus spread through their venom that once blood-borne was difficult to cure.

Werewolves started from a scientific experimentation to cross a wolf and a human. While the practice had been outlawed in the 1970s, new wolves still popped up. The genes sometimes stayed dormant for generations, usually activating during times of physical trauma. Werewolf bites weren't what turned others into wolves—it was the trauma of surviving an animal attack.

My badge unlocked the record room's door, and I was startled by an ultra-clean, ultra-modern space. I had expected rows and rows of manila files along a back wall behind a cluttered desk. Instead, a man with an intense stare raised his dark gaze and studied me from behind a smudge-free glass desk. (5'10" wide shoulders, slender build. Sneakers, no glasses. Risk assessment: scrappy in a bar fight.)

After clicking the button on my watch, I held up my badge. "I'm Ms. Nicks's new assistant. I need the paper file and Maggie needs the digital." I handed him the note, which he glanced at and returned.

My watch buzzed. *Inconclusive.*

He stood and moved into the back with startling speed. With that bird-like stare, I would've expected some kind of avian relation, maybe even the grandson of a harpy. If only I could take a blood sample…

While the detector was an amazing invention, ultimately it was a fancy smart watch with special calibrations. It scanned a body for vital readings, like heart rate, core temperature, and breathing patterns. Vampires would be colder than humans, while werewolves would be warmer. Heart rates and breathing patterns (or lack thereof) had helped us identify dozens of creatures over the decades, but like humans, the supernatural were always evolving.

My watch reading "inconclusive" wasn't scary, just annoying. Likely, it meant whatever made these people different just wasn't an option in the software. As supernaturals procreated, their genes mutated and over time, SHAP needed to recalibrate our watches to track younger generations.

The far less likely but infinitely more concerning option was someone had created a new breed of creature that wasn't in the database. I had only seen it happen once, after a bunch of teens tried to turn themselves into vampire-werewolf hybrids after watching *Twilight*. The six people who survived the transition now all worked for SHAP.

Keeping an eye on the doorway, I pulled my phone out of my pocket and set it on the counter, then *oops*, clumsy me, pushed it off the other side. I made a big show of looking mortified—just in case someone could see me—and ran around the counter to get it, fiddling with my glasses to grab shots of what was on his monitor.

The rustling of a paper warned me I was out of time. I swooped down, snatched my phone, and returned to the other side of the desk as he came around the corner. He hesitated as if he sensed the air shifting but didn't miss a step. Interesting. What a very unhuman-like thing to do.

He handed me the file, staring at me as if tracking every movement. I swiftly tucked the file under my arm.

"Been here long?"

He didn't blink. "Year."

Did the Thinner program remove these people's conversational skills? "They treat you well? Do you like it?"

"Yep."

"What's your favorite part of the program?" There. Try another one-word answer.

"Success."

I should've seen that coming. I had plenty of experience with my dad, after all. I smiled wide and leaned on the counter. "Can you tell me how to get to Carma Nicks's office? It's my first day and I'm all turned around." I knew where her office was, but sometimes the helpless female act broke the most stoic of men.

He didn't bother to use words. He grabbed a pre-printed map and placed it between us. Using a highlighter, he drew a line from the records department to Carma's office. Then he turned back to the computer. Something in my chest eased as soon as his gaze was off me, as if he saw through my facade and was moments away from uncovering my secret.

With a deliberately awkward wave—being the clueless new girl was always a great cover—I backed out of the room and into the hall. The folder burned in my hand. I needed to get a copy of it. As much as people didn't seem to be paying attention to me as they passed, I wasn't naive enough to start scanning through it in the hall.

I made my way to the restrooms, pushing through the women's room door and into a stall. The stale air was heavy with disinfectant and potpourri, but I was blissfully alone. I turned my glasses onto video mode and scanned over each sheet of paper.

Health charts, mental health worksheets, goals…and *bingo*. A membership contract.

Member agrees to enter into an ongoing, lifelong contract with Thinner until the member passes away or until member is unable to tolerate program…

Lifelong? Why? And how the hell could they enforce it? What did "unable to tolerate" mean?

The member agrees to the following stipulations:

1) *Member must abide by the program with no deviation, including only ingesting Thinner-approved food replacement meals and beverages, other than water. No other food is permitted, as it may cause a life-threatening reaction with Thinner supplements.*

2) *While on the Thinner program, member agrees they have completed their intended childbearing, as the*

Thinner food replacement is not safe for pregnant or nursing mothers.

3) *Outside discussion of the Thinner program is prohibited...*

The bathroom door squeaked open. *Dammit.* I paused, hoping they'd walk into a stall but instead, they just stopped at the mirror. Awesome.

I only had a few more pages of the contract left to scan but didn't want them to hear the rustling of the paper. I flushed the toilet, using the noise of rushing water to cover me. When it finished, I unzipped and rezipped my zipper, then shoved the file folder under my shirt.

Before I had the chance to open the stall door, the woman walked out, and I nearly sagged in relief. After washing my hands, I barreled into the hall and straight into something.

No. Someone.

The file tumbled to the floor, causing papers to scatter everywhere. This would never have happened four months ago. I was entirely off my game.

Stifling a curse at the sharp pain that radiated through my shoulder, I darted to the ground and tried to shove the papers back into the folder before this person saw what I was hiding.

"Entirely my fault."

I glanced up at the woman who had crouched down to help me—the one I had face planted into—and froze. Green eyes, the color of sun-drenched summer leaves, locked with mine. My gaze snagged on her bright red lips and all the oxygen in my chest evaporated. Helium filled my heart and I briefly worried it was going to burst through my chest and float away.

(5'10" slender build, perfect breasts and hips, A-line dress and towering heels. Risk assessment: to be determined.)

I cleared my throat and rubbed the heel of my palm across my breastbone, unsettled by my reaction. I opened my mouth to say something, but my voice failed me. She dipped her head, her dark hair falling against her porcelain cheeks. My hand started to lift to brush it back behind her ear, but thankfully my brain and arm reconnected before I did something stupid.

"I'm so sorry," I managed, pulling up my awkward-new-girl persona, which wasn't hard. All coherent thought had vanished as I stared at the intricately carved wooden coffin around her neck. It was small enough to look like a whimsical charm at a distance, but up close…

Summers, stop staring at her chest!

"Are you new here? I would remember seeing you." She handed me the folder.

Was…was I blushing? What was this warmth on my cheeks thing? A fever? An allergic reaction? Maybe I should text the SHAP physician.

My laugh filled the space between us. "Uh, yeah. It's my first day." I held out my hand. "I'm Mina Madison, Lucinda Nicks's new second assistant."

The smile she returned was so stunning, I forgot how to blink for a few seconds. She slipped her cool, smooth hand into mine and shook it, not letting go. "I'm Carma Nicks, Lucinda's daughter." She bobbed her head and laughed again. "And VP."

Neither of us moved for a moment, still staring at each other. *Carma Nicks.* "Oh!" I cried, breaking my grip and shaking my head to clear it. I should've recognized her immediately, but I got distracted by the perfect cupid's bow of her lips...

Focus. I clicked my watch and then held out the folder. "Uh, actually, this is for you. Maggie told me to place it directly into your hands."

She accepted the file. "You were just hanging out with it in the bathroom?" Her words sounded teasing, but there was a real question beneath her melodic voice.

I forced a laugh and waved away the prodding question. "I was on my way back from the records room, and the two cups of coffee I downed earlier today..." I trailed off when my watch buzzed. *Inconclusive.*

She smiled, suspicion seemingly forgotten. "Ah yes. I miss coffee."

"No coffee on the meal plan?" I inquired.

She shook her head. "Don't need the caffeine anyway. It's been forever since I've had a cup, but I still love the smell of freshly ground beans."

"Best smell in the world," I agreed.

She gestured to the other end of the hallway. "If you're headed back to your office, I'll walk with you."

I nodded for her to proceed. After looking both ways, we stepped into the middle of the hallway, and she matched her pace with mine. "Why does everyone walk so fast around here?" I asked. "I didn't realize I'd be sprinting all day."

"You'll get used to the pace. I swear, some days these

people have skates on the bottom of their shoes." She glanced down at my feet and took her time moving back up my body.

That weird cheek-heating thing happened again. I cleared my throat. "Is, uh, are skates allowed? Because I would one hundred percent be in."

Her laugh was like wind chimes on a breeze. "Sadly, I think my mom would veto." We stopped in front of my office. "It was nice meeting you, Mina." She said my name like this was an ending to a dinner date, not an embarrassing hallway meeting.

A shiver ran over my overheated skin. *Did* I have a fever? What the hell was happening to me? It wasn't flu season. Food poisoning? Poor quality HVAC system? Alien abduction?

"You too, Ms. Nicks." My voice came out low and husky, like I had forgotten how to talk normally.

"Carma, please."

"Carma, then."

Her eyes flicked down to my lips then back up. She bit her lip and turned on her heel, then walked quickly down the hall to the office next door. I couldn't remember how to look away.

Maggie called out, startling me. "Mina, come meet Jake from IT!"

Jake. Job. Focus. What had just happened? I'd made a rookie mistake.

When I walked into my office, Jake's dark gaze assessed mine. His brow narrowed. He glanced down at my watch and I shook my head once. *Inconclusive*, I mouthed. He noddod, then started to explain how to log into my desktop, as if it was the first computer I'd ever seen.

My mind, however, was still on the woman with the green eyes and red lipstick.

Chapter Four

"THIS PLACE REALLY needs an elevator," Jake said when he walked into my apartment, favoring his left leg.

"We do have one, but it's broken. I told you I would come to your place!" I grabbed the food from him and set it on the coffee table.

"Yeah, but tradition." He sat down heavily on the couch and leaned his cane against the couch, then straightened his leg. He'd never admit he was aching, but I could see it in the pinch between his brows. "We going to talk about today?"

I grabbed the frozen vegetables from the freezer and dropped them over his lower thigh before I laid out Lebanese takeout. We always ate from one of our favorite places on the first night of a mission, a celebration that we'd made it through the day. The first day was often the hardest as we adjusted to our new surroundings and cover identities.

"She is being quite reticent," Sebastian offered from his preferred spot on my couch.

"Why tell the same story twice?" I defended.

"What, pray tell, happened?"

I handed Jake a fork and his fattoush salad, and he lifted the corner of his mouth in thanks. Sebastian glided to the other end of the couch.

"Someone got___" Jake took a bite, "distracted."

I ignored them and grabbed my chicken shawarma. I knew I should be eating a salad, but today I needed carbs and hummus. Maybe it would dislodge the pit in my stomach whenever I thought about Carma.

"Distracted?" Sebastian's gaze turned to me.

"By one of the marks."

"I wasn't distracted!" I defended through a mouthful of food. Dammit, there went my not getting involved. "I ran into her, got a bit wobbly, and then she introduced herself and walked me across the hall. It's not as if we had high tea together."

"It isn't the length of time that concerns me." Jake pointed his fork at me. "It's the 'wobbly.'"

When I finished licking the hummus from my fingers, I leaned back in my chair and rubbed my stomach. "Hit the spot." The pit had definitely shrunk now that it had to contend with food. Maybe it wasn't a pit at all, just hunger. Yes, that was it.

"You done making us wait now?"

"I'm allowed to think someone is attractive without making it weird. And it was like a five-second meeting, calm down. You've thought plenty of marks were attractive before."

"There's a difference between finding someone attractive and being wobbly," he shot back. "And you had that face."

"What face?"

"The face you get when you're flirting."

"I did not!"

Sebastian looked between us. "This is better than a night

out at the opera, although there's regrettably a notable lack of opera dancers."

"You blushed!" Jake threw out.

Sebastian gasped.

Dammit. "It was eighty-five today! I was just warm."

"It was sixty-seven inside," my partner added.

"Listen, I can think a mark is attractive and…like…flirt information out of her." That was a stretch.

"That's entirely rubbish and you know it," Sebastian chimed in. "I've heard you flirting on the phone and it is always disconcerting." He fake shuddered.

I balled up a napkin and threw it at him. Well, through him.

"Just be careful," Jake advised. "Getting involved with a mark is off-limits."

"She's just an attractive woman. There's nothing to be careful about. I'm not going to take her clothes off with my teeth. I'm just going to get information out of her." My job wasn't *just* a job. It was a vocation, a calling, a way of life. No way would I risk it for a few sweaty nights between the sheets.

I stood and refilled our glasses of water to break the tension. "So, what'd you find out today?" I asked when I had returned to my seat.

He was silent for a long moment before responding. "Next month, there are seven camps launching in Michigan alone, including the first one in Northern Michigan. There's already a waiting list a hundred people deep, despite it being in the middle of literal nowhere."

I frowned. "That's unexpected." My mind raced, trying

to pinpoint why they would host a retreat in a place mostly filled with vacation homes, instead of extravagant cities with top plastic surgeons. Then it snagged on one important detail. "Isn't there a supernatural town up there?"

Jake nodded. "Yep, Hayvenwood. The camp's like ten miles west of them. I talked to one of the former hunters, Loren. He worked for the elite SHAP offshoot—HQ—and he promised to keep an ear to the ground. They have some witches, a few werewolves, and a dragon on their radar."

"That'll be an interesting report." Grabbing my bureau-issued laptop, I sat down next to Jake, then placed my badge in the card reader so I could log into SHAP's secure internet database. "I think there's a ninety percent chance something supernatural is going on here. It would explain what I found in the file. But whatever the supernatural element is, our watches aren't calibrated to it. We should try and get a blood sample."

I opened the photos I took with my glasses and scrolled to the member contract. "The line about pregnancy, and only ingesting Thinner-approved food items. Could be a potion or a curse infused into an edible."

Jake leaned forward, studying the screen. Even Sebastian—he who never touched computers, as they offended his upper crust sensibilities—appeared at my other side. "Is that even possible?" my partner asked.

I shrugged. "Forbidden magic is some freaky shit."

He looked out the window, tapping his thumb against his chin. "We need to get access to a food sample, but they're under lock and key. They require members to show identification and sign for each kit. Every used container is saved and sent back to the company for processing to continue the 'no-cost supply.'"

I shook my head. "How's that not suspicious?"

He turned to me and raised his eyebrow. "Exactly."

Sebastian looked at us. "No one has derailed a parcel? Stolen a sample?"

"Not yet," Jake said. "We're working on it."

"I'll get into the cafeteria," I promised.

"You don't have access unless you're a member."

"I'm the CEO's assistant. Watch me."

"Let's make a bet."

"Those are my four favorite words. What's it gonna be, partner?"

He crossed his arms. "If I get the sample first, you have to let my stepmom redecorate this living room."

I gaped. Sebastian gasped and fell to the floor, doing his best dramatic faint. "Wow. Okay, if that's how we're playing it." I straightened my shoulders. "If I win, you have to adopt a ghost agent."

He stared at me as if I had cursed his first-born child. "Wow. *Wow.* You are going in for the kill."

Reggie appeared. "Sebastian just melted through the ceiling. ¿Qué pasó?"

Sebastian popped back up through the floor. "They've called for a duel at dawn. They're going to name their seconds."

Reggie ran over to the armchair and sat down. "Should I make popcorn?" Sebastian sat on the armrest next to him, giving him a recap.

"You up for this, Summers? Magnolia is gonna make it

look like a Crate and Barrel exploded in here when she's done."

"You mean, you're going to have a new roommate who will dig deep into your life and never leave you alone?"

"I think she's talking about you, mano," Reggie said to Sebastian. Sebastian shushed him.

"Well, Mina. Do you accept the terms?"

I smiled. It was going to be so fun watching a ghost agent torture him, too. "Yes, Jake. I accept the terms."

Sebastian stood and walked over. "Shake hands, and I will pronounce the duel official."

I stuck out my hand and Jake clasped it in his, each of us gripping as hard as we could. "With this handshake, the bet has been set in stone." He hovered his hand on top of ours. "May the best human win."

The sound of a video call ringing on my computer broke the excitement. I let out a string of expletives that made Sebastian blush, or would have if he had blood. He grabbed Reggie's hand and tipped his top hat, before disappearing from sight. Sure, he leaves *now* when he could be useful.

"So. Your dad?" Jake asked.

Holding my breath, I accepted the call. I opened my mouth to say "Hi, Dad" to the bulky, balding man on my screen, but he leapt into his speech before I had a chance.

"Both there. Good. Update."

How my mother—a former jazz singer turned environmentalist—ever got together with this taciturn husk of a man, I'd never know. "We believe there's something telling in the Thinner food and we're debating how to source it."

Dad's face didn't change. "Priority."

44

I did *not* respond with "no shit, Sherlock." Out loud, anyway. "Yes, sir."

Jake motioned with his pointer, shifting attention to him. "Sir, the food is well-regulated, but it is one of our priorities. We have also found out some additional information I will email in a report to you this evening."

My father looked at his limited edition Shinola watch, silently asking why he didn't have the report yet. Jake, who wasn't afraid of my father, just smiled. "It was first-day mission dinner, sir. I'm leaving right now to work on the report."

"Roger."

Jake stood with a long exhale, despite my puppy-dog eyes silently pleading with him to stay. He walked to the other side of the camera and held up his cell, indicating I should text him later. I waved and refocused on the impatient man on the screen. He was only seven miles away, but it felt like seven universes. "What's up, Dad?"

His eyebrow twitched. "Your email." He held up a printed copy of the email I had sent to his assistant two days ago, asking for an update on the current interim RD. I wanted to make sure I knew who I needed to beat. "Focus. On. Your. Mission."

I opened my mouth to argue but snapped it shut. Fighting would be completely draining and useless. "Roger," I responded, through gritted teeth.

With a nod, he ended the video call.

I slammed my computer shut and let out a cry of anger, wishing I could go hit a punching bag. My shoulder wouldn't let me. It had been put back together with screws and staples. Instead, I'd run. I hated running nearly as much as I hated cucumbers, but desperate times.

I changed into my workout clothes and shoved my remaining chopstick in my pocket just in case I got any more vampy visitors, then stretched far too quickly for it to matter. I grabbed my headphones and shoved them into my ears, cranking up the volume on my favorite band's Spotify playlist. I was out the door and down the stairs before the chorus of the Sorry Charlie song hit, my feet slamming into the pavement with each beat.

I leaned into the screaming of my muscles, the sweat, the exhaustion from being active and social all day after sitting at home alone—except for with Sebastian and occasionally Reggie—for sixteen weeks and let the anger fizzing in my chest burn itself out. Fatigue hit me a half mile in, an unsubtle reminder I hadn't been exercising enough, and I pushed another two miles just to prove to myself I could. I wasn't weak; I wasn't incompetent. I would make a damn fine RD, no matter what my dad thought.

When I trudged back in, legs no sturdier than spaghetti and shoulder screaming from being jostled, Sebastian was waiting for me in the armchair. My chest tightened at the small, silent show of friendship. He hated that damn chair.

"Bathe," he ordered. "Then join me for a cinematic adventure."

I snuck a sniff of my armpit and winced. Oh yeah, I needed a shower before climbing into bed. "What're we watching?"

"Doesn't matter, as long as the actress possesses generous bosoms."

I rolled my eyes. "You're gross. Don't follow me into the shower."

He brought his hand to his chest, affronted. "I may be many things, Mina, but I would never betray your trust as such. I only jump into people's bathing chambers when I need to scare them."

I paused before walking down the hall. "Who'd you scare in the shower?" I looked over my shoulder.

A wicked smile engulfed his face. "That miscreant you met at the grocery store. I forgot his name. I caught him talking very rudely to his friend about you. He was showering, and I just happen to pop in and say hi. He tripped, screamed, and ran out naked."

I turned fully to face him, mouth hanging open. "That explains so much about the phone call." Said miscreant had been a short fling last year, an indulgence I rarely allowed myself to have. I had left him at my place to grab breakfast, and he had called me in a panic saying he had to go and to delete his number.

"You're my favorite ghost," I admitted.

He nodded. "My long-suffering father would tell you you're daft but thank you. You're very dear to me as well." He held up his hand. "I'll never reiterate that. Be gone."

With a small smile, I bounced to the bathroom. So what if my besties were my coworker and a dead duke and my life was my job? It still wasn't as weird as whatever was happening at Thinner.

Chapter Five

I DIDN'T MEET Lucinda Nicks in flesh and blood—at least what I assumed was flesh and blood—until Friday afternoon. The moment a security guard spotted her black Mercedes entering the parking lot, Maggie's phone rang with confirmation. In thirty seconds, she transformed from agitated but focused coworker to polished executive assistant.

She kicked off her sneakers and slipped her feet into towering heels under her desk. Reading glasses came off, blazer went on. After smoothing her hair, she refreshed her lipstick perfectly without the aid of a mirror, then grabbed a tablet and a stack of messages. She stood and focused on me. "Straighten your coat. Shoulders back. Don't let her see your fear."

Fear, HA! I hadn't been afraid since the seventh-grade soccer tournament when I had pneumonia and we were two points away from winning state. (We won, of course, right before I collapsed.) And maybe, *just maybe*, for the first few minutes after the car accident. While an impressive woman, Lucinda didn't strike fear into my heart.

Maggie nodded toward the hallway. "When she comes in, we close the outside door. She's a celebrity around here and everyone wants in on her business. We protect her business over everything else."

Glancing out in the hall, I noticed all the hurrying people slowed to a reasonable gait, then slowed even more in front of the office, peering in. "Got it."

A woman holding an open laptop in one hand and a Thinner shake in the other rapped on the office doorjamb with her shoe. "She in?" (5'4", same slender build as other Thinner members, custom pantsuit and professionally blown-out hair. Risk assessment: threat to wallet but not to me.)

I'd known Maggie to be overwhelmed, worried, and super focused, but never annoyed. The twitch of her eyebrow and the flex of her jaw gave her away. She tilted her head and put on a sugar-sweet smile. "She's just now arriving. My priority is to introduce her new assistant, Mina."

The newcomer turned to me, set down her drink on my desk, then reached out. "Rachel, Public Relations and Marketing. I'm Lucinda's right-hand woman." (New risk assessment update: threat to Maggie's sanity.)

My gaze darted to Maggie, whose eyes had narrowed into lethal slits. Honestly, I was more afraid of Maggie's wrath than anyone else's. After all, *she* was Lucinda's real right-hand woman. (Risk assessment update: probably plans Rachel's murder daily.)

I cleared my throat to cover up a chuckle. "Mina. Nice to meet you."

She pulled her hand away and grabbed her shake, taking a slurp. "Your hair is so…unique."

I was currently sporting a fake mohawk, since I had needed to cut my hair after the accident—stitches in the back of the head. It was now close cropped on the sides and wavy on top, walking that line between punk-rock and office chic. "Uh…thanks?"

A bell rang and Maggie's annoyance disappeared, a mask of quiet fierceness in its place. She reached for the side gray wall and pressed a small panel that levered up a handle. My eyes widened. *Whoa.* How had the blueprints missed this?

I shook my head to clear it and activated the camera on my fake glasses.

She pulled sideways and a piece of the wall moved with her, a sliding door which had separated our office from Lucinda's domain. Bright white walls, a perfectly sparkling clean glass desk with small laptop on the center, black stone floors with giant pure-white plush throw rugs, a fireplace, white couches around a small flat screen television, and art. Everywhere art.

Giant paintings, pedestals with sculptures, glass shelving with small artifacts and family pictures, and recessed lighting highlighting all of them. The paintings and sculptures were primarily of half-naked women with a few landscapes dotted in. The office was the size of my entire apartment.

Maggie threw me a smile. "I know. It's something, right?"

Rachel stepped right in front of me, positioned to make her way first into the office, and subsequently blocking my recording efforts. I contemplated poking her with the tip of the pen in my hand. I shifted my stance to peer around her.

A glass door on the other side of the office opened, held by a buff-as-hell man dressed in all black, wearing sunglasses and a newsboy cap. (6'4" extremely fit, blazer over T-shirt to cover his gun. Badass. Risk assessment: moderate if I didn't have my gun.)

Then, a woman in her mid-sixties with an ice blond bob cut so severely it could draw blood walked in. She wore a crisp white pant suit and blood red skyscraper heels. This was my mark, Lucinda Nicks. She moved like a dancer, practically floating into the room. (5'10", old-school model body shape, suit costs more than my car. Risk assessment: threat to managers everywhere when she was disappointed in customer service.)

The moment she took off her white rimmed oversize Dolce & Gabbana sunglasses, I knew without a doubt she was Carma's mother. Lucinda's green eyes were piercing, even at a distance.

She handed her purse and shades to the waiting man, who disappeared through a door at the other end of the office. With ballerina grace, she sat in her plush office chair and nodded. Rachel jerked her head to flip her hair behind her shoulder and sauntered into the room. "Lucinda! Great news about the new ad campaign!"

Lucinda held up her hand and Rachel stopped. "I'd like to meet my new assistant first. Take a seat." She motioned to one of the four chairs on the opposite side of the desk. Rachel, who looked shocked and peeved—*hehe*—perched on an end chair.

Maggie placed her hand on my elbow and gently prodded me forward. "Ms. Lucinda, this is Mina Madison, your new second assistant."

"Come here, please." She gestured to her side of the desk with a perfectly manicured finger. I hit my watch as I folded my arms in front of me, trying to keep Lucinda in range and Rachel out.

Her eyes did a brief once-over, pausing at my feet, then moving back to my hair. She pursed her lips. "I prefer my assistants in heels."

I smirked, remembering the training exercises SHAP put me through while wearing a variety of outfits. One never knew what would happen undercover, like when I needed to relocate an endangered firebird's nest, at night, in a *tree,* while wearing six-inch stilettos. They still told that story at orientation. "Ms. Lucinda, I can do anything in heels, but I can do my job faster in flats."

Maybe it was my looming thirtieth birthday, maybe it was the car accident, but after a day in heels I wanted to cut out my spine. I had a high pain tolerance, but why waste it on footwear?

She fought a smile. "I see. Your hair is acceptable. In fact, it's growing on me." She turned to face Rachel. "I'm thinking about doing the same to mine." She ruffled her shoulder length, perfectly styled bob. "What do you think?"

Rachel's mouth moved like a fish. I nearly snorted. So, Ms. Lucinda had a cutting sense of humor. I liked her immediately, which would make this job more fun. Until I had to arrest her.

She turned to face me with a charismatic smile. "I'm sure you've heard many terrible stories about me." She leaned forward and stage whispered, "They're all true."

I laughed. "Good. I can't wait to work with you." It wasn't a lie. I was a sucker for a good villain. They made life fun.

A knock on the open door made us all swivel as Carma walked in. "Hey, Mom." My helium heart returned at the sight of her in a green dress and heels. Must have been the double shot of espresso I had this morning. Her gaze met mine and she smiled.

Clearing my throat, I bowed my head and backed away as Carma moved past me, her arm brushing mine and her strawberry scent lingering between us. She kissed her mom on the cheek, and then sat on the edge of her desk. Her hem dragged up a few inches and that floaty feeling raced down my arms to my fingertips. I was probably just hungry again.

Maggie sent me a smile and nodded her head back toward our office, our sanctuary. I walked out like I was being chased, then secured our outer office door from passersby. Falling into my computer chair, I grabbed a protein bar and shoved it into my mouth. After washing it down with some water, I refocused on the stack of handwritten correspondence—seriously, who took the time to handwrite cards?—and got to work typing up replies for Lucinda to review. The job wasn't mentally straining, but it was distracting.

My cell vibrated and I scanned the text from my partner.

Jake: *Heard target was in. Reading?*

Me: *Inconclusive. Photos uploaded. Placement should be *thumbs-up emoji**

Jake: *ok*

Jake: *Having a good day?*

Me: *Not bad. Kinda fun. U?*

Jake: *Need some sugar*

Me: *I've got a protein bar in my purse*

He never remembered to pack a snack, so I always made sure I had one for him.

Jake: W/ choc chips?

Me: Duh. I'll text when free. Meet you @ bathrooms?

*Jake: *heart emoji* *drooling emoji**

"Boyfriend?"

I startled and dropped my phone, like a winner. God, I was rusty. I should've heard someone approach at least ten seconds before they reached me. I looked up to find Carma leaning against my desk. I forced my gaze to stay on her face and not wander lower to the shadow just above the V-neck of her dress.

"Don't worry, I don't care if you're playing with your cell," she promised. "I may be VP, but I have zero control over who Mom and Maggie hire or cut loose." She gestured around us. "This is their domain. I just control the Thinner managers and in-house vendors."

"Not a boyfriend!" I came out with, a bit too loud. My cheeks heated and I looked down at my fidgeting hands. "Not a girlfriend, either." I looked up, not sure why I'd said it.

Flirting with men was easy. I just fluttered my eyelashes and pulled my neckline lower. But beautiful women were almost as terrifying as giving bad news to my father. I could take down a pack of cannibal shapeshifters with my feet bound and a fractured wrist, but god forbid I tried to buy a woman a drink. Not that I had much of a dating life anyway. People tended to get pissy about me disappearing without much, if any, contact for weeks at a time.

The cell in her hand rang, and she glanced at the screen then scrunched her face. "I've got to take this." She turned to leave the office but paused at the door. "It's not my now *ex*-girlfriend, either."

Her words simultaneously slammed into my chest and lifted me six feet into the air. I should be very, *very* concerned. Mixing business with pleasure was absolutely forbidden when on a mission.

Yet, I couldn't control the airy, giddy laugh that tumbled out of my mouth.

BY THE TIME Lucinda's 4pm meeting with her team of lawyers rolled around, my head was full of ways to listen in. With Jake's help, we had arranged a flower delivery from a "satisfied member" to Lucinda, who absolutely wanted the flowers on display in her office. When they had arrived, I volunteered to unwrap and arrange them, pasting the small listening device to the center of the bouquet. It had about ten hours of battery and was water resistant. My week's goal was to install more permanent devices in the office when no one was around.

Too bad Maggie never left her desk. When I asked her if she lived here, she just laughed and waved the question away. She was here when I arrived and still working when I left at night, and I honestly wasn't sure if she ever went to the bathroom for more than sixty seconds. While I could place temporary bugs quickly, one minute was nearly impossible. My offers to cover the office while she took a lunch break, or to stay late instead of her, were always denied.

Just before four, Maggie went to greet the lawyers in the lobby and left me to finish arranging a coffee cart, pitchers of water, and freshly made Thinner shakes for those observing the program. I was moving the tray of shakes from the attached kitchen to Lucinda's office when Carma walked in with her arm through her mom's, heads close together as they conversed in low tones. I strained to hear but couldn't catch more than every other word.

Mindful that the bug tucked in the vase would only pick up a limited parameter, I placed the flowers on the side of her immaculate desk, closer to where the lawyers would sit. Outside of her computer, there was nothing else cluttering the surface.

"This, Mina, is why I do this job." Lucinda stopped to finger one of the gorgeous red peonies. "Not flowers, per se, although these are lovely. Even if I prefer white roses. But because I," she looked up at her daughter, "*we* give people hope when they're hopeless. When they need help and don't want to wait years for a result."

She walked to her desk chair and sat down with her ballerina grace. "It isn't just about weight loss, you know. A person can be fat and still healthy. Or maybe they aren't in perfect health but love the way they look. They're not the members for us."

Glancing up, she smiled at me. "I'm here for the ones who are so desperate, for whatever reason, they may try something that would cause serious harm."

"Yes, ma'am." I held her gaze, knowing she was sharing this because she wanted me to understand why she did what she did. This was important for her, which meant it was important for the investigation.

"I almost died, you know, trying one of those desperate ways. I combined diet pills with a juice cleanse after a photographer said no one wanted to see my aging saggy stomach anymore."

"People are garbage," I muttered.

She smiled softly and nodded. "So was my plan." She reached out and took Carma's hand. "Luckily, my daughter found me in time. She saved my life. Now, I want to help people be successful like me."

I nodded. I'd been trained to spot a lie from across a room, and I knew Lucinda believed every single word she said. I looked over to Carma, who used her thumb to carefully dab at a tear in the corner of her eye, without mussing her makeup.

These two clearly believed whatever they were doing was helping others, and maybe they were. But all villains were the heroes in their own stories. I wanted to ask them more questions, to keep them talking, but Maggie appeared in the doorway, followed by three lawyers. With a brief nod, I stepped aside for them to pass, then moved back into my office. Once the lawyers were seated, Maggie rushed out and closed the door behind her, securing it flush with the wall.

The outer office door opened, and Rachel barged in, as if she had a tracking device on Lucinda. "Heard she's here!" Without waiting for an answer, she turned toward the space where the open door should have been and took two steps toward it. "Need to tell her about this new—where's the door?" Her hand hit the wall, exploring. But without either

Maggie or me hitting the button that released the handle from its locked position, she was unsuccessful.

I delighted in her petulant huff. I caught Maggie's eye, and her look had said what I was thinking. *Can you believe this woman?*

In her cool, calm tone, my partner in crime said, "She's in a private meeting right now. She asked not to be disturbed."

"Is it with *Michigan News*? She asked me to be in on that meeting. Why didn't you call me?" Her hand went back out to the wall. "Please hit your button."

"Not the news." Maggie kept her smile light, but her arms tense at her sides. "It's a private concern."

Rachel gave up on the wall and moved to Maggie's desk. "Who's she with?"

Maggie smiled. "She asked me not to share that information."

The other woman rolled her eyes, then turned to me. "Can you believe this? You know Lucinda's gonna tell me as soon as she's done."

This was probably true. Lucinda liked to share everything with her team, even things that were probably better left private. I had learned more about her best friend's bikini wax from hell during a lunch call than I ever wanted to know. Still, I wasn't opening my mouth.

I shrugged. "I'm the *second* assistant. They don't tell me anything."

She frowned, clearly annoyed at being unable to break the newbie. "Fine. I'll just call her myself." She spun on her heel and stomped out of the office.

Maggie chuckled and slid into her chair, then kicked off her shoes. "That woman exhausts me."

I laughed. "Which one?"

She waved her hand in the air with a smirk. "All of them, honestly. But especially her." She pointed out toward the hallway. "I spend half of my job cleaning up hers, like when she schedules interviews and doesn't factor in drive time."

She rolled her shoulders. "Sorry, I shouldn't have said anything. I didn't sleep well last night. Kept thinking I'd come in to find you were just a dream and I had gum-popper back."

My smile wobbled and I schooled my expression. "Don't worry. I'm not going anywhere." *Yet.*

"I'll go to the caf and get us a cup of tea. When she's in with the lawyers, it's practically the only time she won't call me." She stood and I clocked the sneakers on her feet.

This could be my chance to grab a food sample. I stood. "I could go for us. You can rest instead."

Maggie shook her head. "Until Lucinda gives you the in or unless you do the program, cafeteria is off limits. Sorry, kid. You like green tea?"

Dammit. I smiled and nodded. "Green tea sounds perfect." She turned to leave. "Maggie, why work here if you're not on the program?"

She paused. "My sister, Joan, works in Lucinda's residence as the house manager. You'll meet her soon, no doubt. When this job opened up, Joan handed my resume right to her."

"And you like it here?"

She laughed softly. "It's definitely not for the faint of

heart. But yes, I love a challenge. On the bad days, I just remember we're helping people. That's what matters."

I smiled and she tapped on the corner of my desk before walking out. I watched her leave. I really liked Maggie and the thought of having to arrest her made me shift uncomfortably in my seat.

Refocusing, I reached into my purse and palmed the second listening device. In a perfect world, I'd cut open Maggie's external computer speakers, place it inside, then reattach the screen, but no amount of quick dry glue would work in the time it took to make tea. Instead, I slipped it underneath the lip of the half cubical wall between us. It should pick up most of our phone calls and anyone who came to talk to us next to the desks.

Me: 2nd bug planted
Jake: *thumbs-up emoji*

I deleted the text thread from my phone, then sat back in my seat. I'd just opened a spreadsheet when Maggie walked back in carrying two paper to-go mugs. She set one on the desk, along with a creamer, a packet of sugar, and a pouch of honey. "I didn't know if you preferred your tea with sweetener or milk, so I brought you options."

I touched the edge of the creamer as emotion balled in my throat. This was ridiculous. All she had done was bring me tea. Had my hard edges faded during my months on leave? I better hit the gun range this week and make sure I could still shoot a target blindfolded.

It was just…she was taking care of me. No one had done that in such a long time. I cleared my throat and tried again.

She may be a great coworker, but she was still part of Team Enemy. "Thank you."

She smiled and sat down at her desk, nursing the tea. "You're welcome. I'm so happy we hired you." She rested for a few more seconds, then sat up straight, setting her tea on her desk. "Alright, back to work."

I stashed the creamer, sugar, and honey in a drawer, then turned back to my computer screen. I was loading addresses into a spreadsheet for a luncheon at Lucinda's home, and my fake glasses were working overtime to record all the contact information. I only had about an hour of battery life left and had to keep moving quickly.

A mouthful of hot tea did nothing to dissolve the guilty feeling in the pit of my stomach. *This is your job*, I scolded myself. *You're here because they could be very dangerous. They could be killing people. It's just tea.*

I eyed the cup. I had never worked at a job where I had felt so appreciated in only the first week. The last time I was an undercover assistant, I was literally washing dog poop off the bottom of shoes and taking phone calls at 2am from a drunk boss.

I couldn't shake the feeling that the fallout from this sting was going to be different than any of my past assignments.

Chapter Six

I SET BOTH of my grocery baskets—one for me, one for the Andrews—down on the counter and pulled out my wallet, snatching a twenty from the billfold. "Full Moon Madness?"

The cashier, Anthony, flashed me a smile and slipped his hand into his apron pocket, producing his cash. "Definitely." He flipped on his "manager requested" yellow light. "Yo. Krisztina! FMM time!"

Full Moon Madness was the only form of gambling I allowed myself (outside of bets with Jake), the goal being to guess how rowdy the grocery store crowd got during a full moon. Werewolves could be scary, but the one summer I worked here on assignment proved humans were way more terrifying during the end of a lunar cycle. Anthony, who had started the same summer as me—as a bagger, not an agent— was now the assistant manager and my most formidable opponent.

Applechester Grocer's manager, Krisztina, walked over and flipped off Anthony's light. "I have better things to do than be forced into your stupid game every month." Despite her complaining, she pulled out a small notebook from her apron and flipped to the back. "There were six manager complaints. Two from Doris Manalin, three *about* Doris Manalin, and one about the new packaging on a cereal box, as if that's something the store has control over. One fist fight over the last box of Mrs. T's Pierogies, two cars who hit carts, and one cart that hit a car."

Anthony cheered and I let out an expletive. With a grimace, I slapped the bill into his hand. Krisztina rolled her eyes and walked away. "If you're gonna drag me into this, the least you can do is win!" she called back over her shoulder. "His ego'll be impossible now."

"Yeah, yeah," I grumbled. "I didn't see the cereal box coming."

Anthony picked up my grocery basket and started scanning the items. "Pays to have a psychic in the family." His uncle and sister both worked for SHAP, his uncle as a ghost and his sister as a psychic, which not only led to unparalleled insight, but really fun bets.

"I really need to get a better house ghost. Store's only a mile away, well within his tether. He could've done some recon for me."

"Cheat much?"

"Uh, psychic. Tomato, to-mah-to."

He laughed. "Touché." He took his time bagging my produce, which is why I put up with his shit. Not having bruised bananas and peaches was totally worth it. "Hey, you know anything about an unregistered vamp?" His voice was casual, but he was frowning.

"Yep. Following a lead. You know anything?"

He scanned the surroundings before lowering his voice. "Clay Thompson, the dairy farmer?" I nodded, knowing the name. "Wife was in this morning, talking about how Clay had scared off a suit who was hanging out in the barn. They found an open wound on two of the cattle. They died the next day."

I glanced quickly at my total, not even really seeing it, and shoved my credit card into the card reader. Despite my loathing for vampires, even I had to admit the ones who lived in cities were extremely careful. One bad vampire could bring down hell, or worse, Doris Manalin, on the whole community.

"When?"

"Last week."

The blood. When I killed that vampire, it had covered me in goo and blood, which made sense if it had just fed. "Thanks. That particular one will likely no longer be an issue."

With a nod, he handed me my bags. "Good. Also, Amber called to ask if we could order her seven pounds of sage. Won't be in until Wednesday. Promised her I'd drop it off on my way home."

I scrunched my nose. "Ho boy, never a good sign." I grabbed my bags. "Headed there now. Let me know if I need to swing by Wednesday, yeah?" He waved and I headed back out to the parking lot.

A summer storm was brewing; the sky was thick with clouds, the air heavy. A shiver of unease raced down my spine. I tossed the bags into the back of my truck—likely undoing all the precise fruit packing Anthony had done—and scanned my surroundings.

"Get in." Sebastian's voice, although I couldn't see him.

I didn't question. I slammed my hatch, dove into the driver's seat, and started the engine. "Sebastian?"

He materialized in the passenger seat, staring straight out the windshield.

I followed the line of his gaze. "What is it?"

"Something wicked this way comes." Ghosts didn't often get feelings, so when Sebastian did, I listened. Even when he was being uber pretentious and quoting Shakespeare.

"Tree line. Northeast corner," Sebastian warned before disappearing.

I opened my glove box and grabbed binoculars. I swore as I focused on a woman staggering through the trees. (5'1", mid-forties, disoriented. Risk assessment: injured, no risk.) She was clutching her neck, blood spotting her blouse. She was limping, one shoe missing, and she had an Applechester Grocery bag around her arm.

I threw my truck into drive and dialed SHAP headquarters.

"Dispatch," Val, our most veteran dispatcher, answered. Thank God. I didn't have time for any small talk from a newbie.

"Val, it's Agent Summers. Got a woman bleeding from the neck." I ran off the pertinent details. "Ghost Agent Kenworthy is assisting."

"10-4. Support incoming."

I pulled up to the curb, tucked Sydney into my waistband, grabbed a sweatshirt I had in the back seat, then leapt out of the truck. The woman darted back with a cry, and I put my hands up. "I'm not going to hurt you. I'm here to help. My name is Mina. What's yours?"

Sebastian emerged from the woods behind her and gave me the all-clear signal. I refocused on the disoriented woman. I didn't recognize her from town, but that didn't mean much. There were upward of 60,000 people in Applechester and I mostly only knew the ones who caused trouble.

"Kendra?" Her voice shook and she answered like she wasn't even sure who she was. "I was—" she looked down at her grocery bag "—getting dinner?" She swayed on her feet and I rushed to steady her.

"Let's sit." I gestured to the curb. "Kendra, why are you bleeding?"

"Am I bleeding?" She stumbled and all but collapsed into a sitting position. She pulled her hand away from her neck where a pool of blood was smeared on her hand. "Oh."

I clicked my watch, then pressed the sweatshirt against the side of her neck. "Do you know what happened?"

She shook her head slowly, still staring at her hand.

"She's about to swoon," Sebastian warned in my ear.

I got my arm around her shoulders before she landed face first on the cement. "Good call." My watch buzzed and I glanced down. *Human.* For now.

I laid her down on the grass while trying to keep pressure on her wound and felt her pulse. It was slower than I would've liked, especially after an attack. Where was her adrenaline?

A silver car and an ambulance turned into the parking lot and headed straight for us. The moment they parked, we were surrounded by a flurry of activity. Kendra was loaded onto a stretcher and placed in the ambulance. Agent Bonn, who had arrived with the ambulance, used gauze to clean the wound on the victim's neck, exposing two puncture wounds.

"I can't tell for certain without running blood analysis, but I'd say the bite radius is pretty consistent with a vampire's," they said.

"Dammit." I pressed my fist against my forehead. "Three in less than a month."

They pursed their lips. "We haven't had back-to-back vampire attacks in this city in two decades."

"I know." I wondered what Gerard, the retired RD, would've done in this situation. I didn't trust vampires as far as I could throw them—which wasn't far, they were heavy—but they had kept their end of the bargain for nearly twenty years. Any vampire using live feeding could only do so from a registered feeder.

If Kendra had been a registered feeder, she would've been chipped as part of protocol and the watch would've alerted me. Feeders were high-risk, as consuming a single drop of human blood while the vampire venom ran through their system would turn them. We once had to put down a feeder who had innocently kissed her boyfriend's busted lip after a fight and turned into a vamp and attacked him. There was no amount of money in the world that could make me turn into a feeder. To be fair, I was privileged enough to not be desperate for money, either.

Once the on-duty agents were debriefed, I climbed into my truck. "You here?"

"Yes," Sebastian answered. "In the boot."

I glanced in my rear view and saw him hovering over the groceries. "Why?"

"Keeping your goods cold."

I pressed my lips together. I was so used to the chilliness that surrounded Sebastian, I didn't even notice it anymore. "You know, sometimes you're not a huge prick."

"Love you, too."

My car phone rang, and I clicked my steering wheel button to answer it. "Jake, what's up?"

"Another vamp attack?"

"Yeah." I filled him in on my shopping trip as I started driving home. "And I lost FMM."

"Not your night. What did you in?"

"Cereal box rebranding."

He laughed. "Listen, I haven't heard the entire tape yet, but my contact in tech says the meeting was about Natalie Moranis. They want to settle with her out of court, even though they claim no wrongdoing. She signed the contract of her own free will."

"Sure, sure. It's cheaper to settle then to fight it." I pulled into my assigned parking spot and caught a shadow gliding across the roof of my apartment building before disappearing. I was so not in the mood for this. I leaned my head back on the headrest, exhausted. "Listen, Jake, gotta drop off groceries. Catch you later?"

"Yeah, sounds good. Will keep you posted."

"Thanks." I pushed open my door. "Sebastian, let's go. We have company."

Chapter Seven

IT WAS THE demon wearing a crocheted sweater and eating from the dumpster that really topped off my night. He was hard to look at, almost like watching a 3D movie without the colored glasses. He was all gray—as if he stepped out of a pencil drawing—had a nose as big as his two horns, eyebrows that reminded me of racoon tails, and long fingers with even longer talons.

I stormed over and held up the cross on my keychain. Sebastian hovered at my back. "Belphegor, you know Applechester is off limits!" *Fucking demons.*

He snorted and kept on eating, his long, thin tail swatting away flies. "Put that away. You haven't been to church in twenty years. And why are you covered in blood?"

I looked down at my shirt and groaned. Another one for the trash. "Another vampire."

"We need to talk about these vamps."

"You and half the town. How long will you curse us with your presence?"

He pulled at his sweater. "Calm your tits, I'm just visiting." He pointed to the Andrews's window. "Your landlord is a piece of shit. Had to fix a few things before George tried to do it himself. Sink's been leaking for weeks, straight into

Doris's apartment. Last thing we need is for that bitch to start sticking her nose where it doesn't belong. Every time she gets that priest to bless the building, I can't come back for, like, a month."

"Don't call women bitches," I snapped. Sebastian pointedly cleared his throat. "And thank you for helping. I don't know how to do plumbing repairs."

"Never thought I'd hear a thank you from *you*."

"Fuck off. You done here?" Despite my feelings toward Belphegor, I was glad he liked to help out the Andrews. George had tried to change a light fixture a few years back, and it had not gone well. Firetrucks and ambulances were involved.

He held up his food container. "Just grabbing dinner before heading home."

"Don't test me, Belphegor. I've had a long day and I'm not playing."

He jumped out of the dumpster and took a step toward us. Sebastian flashed in front of me. "Refrain from stepping closer."

Belphegor laughed. "Oh, does the pretty princess need a strong protector now?"

"So I don't screw up my shoulder again? Damn right I do. Also, since when are princesses considered weak? They grow up to rule entire countries."

"Fair." He eyed my shoulder. "What's not fair is the bloodsuckers feeding in Applechester. We all live by the rules and we still get shit on. You don't get these vamps under control, I can't promise the rules will still be followed. You got me?"

"Because I can control a bunch of rogue supernaturals?"

"Literally your job, kid."

"Piss off, demon."

He shrugged. "Just giving you fair warning. You know the demons are waiting for any excuse to come visit. Applechester is like a fine wine. The flesh here tastes better— *not* that I've had any in a decade." He finished eating— container and all—then let out a noxious burp.

I stepped back and made a face. "God help me if more than one of you shows up."

"I don't want to share Amber," he warned. "Get this shit under control or we're both gonna be unhappy with the results."

"Yeah, I'm working on it."

He ran his talons up and down his sleeves. "This wool is so soft. Alpaca, you know."

"It's eighty-nine degrees."

"Yeah, cold!" He hugged himself as if he was shivering.

"Listen, tell your buddies no one, and I mean *no one* feeds without authorization in town. And if they do, they will die. Likely at my hands. Got it?"

He looked outright disgruntled but nodded. "Except at Amber's? She makes these mulled wine cookies—"

"Human feeding, Belphegor. Human feeding. Fix shit, eat the damn cookies, then leave. Yeah?" I looked upward to the gray sky, only to have rain fall straight into my eye. Today was so fun.

He bowed mockingly but then ran a talon across the ground and opened up a gaping hole. "You can unwad your panties. I hear you. Hey, you got insight on who's gonna win

The Bachelor?"

"Do I look like I have time to watch reality TV?"

Sebastian motioned with his finger. "My guess is Serena."

The demon winked at me. "Pleasure doing business with you." Then he jumped through the hole in the ground that sealed behind him.

Rain pelted us from every direction, soaking my work clothes. "This is bullshit."

Sebastian nodded then gestured ahead of him. "After you."

I walked back to my truck and grabbed the groceries, then headed up the front walk. "Serena?" I asked as he fell into step with me. "You watch *The Bachelor?*"

He shrugged. "Why not?"

My response was cut off when we walked into the building. The common area to the right of the door—which amounted to a love seat, scattered chairs, an obsolete fireplace, and a half-played game of chess—was littered with ghosts, all six of whom gasped in unison. (The humans preferred to hide in their own apartments like respectful neighbors.)

"We're fine!" I called, making my way to the stairs.

Reggie poofed into being in front of me. "¡Dios mío! Another one?"

"Wasn't after me this time."

Dani peered around Reggie. "I've got a bad feeling about this. Vampires just randomly running around town biting humans isn't the thing."

Me, too. There weren't vampires at Thinner, at least that

I'd met. So what linked the two? Was the vamp who attacked me just a coincidence? Did he get a membership before he died and transformed?

"Wait…" I looked at Dani. "Say that again."

She looked startled but complied. "Uh, vampires running around biting humans—"

I held up my hand to silence her. Frown frozen into place, I reached back into my memory to the night that vampire launched himself at me. *Five foot eight, around one-ninety. Open collared shirt. Dirt and blood on the front. Expensive watch, no wedding ring. No visible tattoos.*

Closing my eyes, I focused in on the memory of his neck as I gripped it to hold him off me. *No visible puncture wounds.*

Holy shit. I set down an armload of groceries and reached for my phone.

> **Me:** *The vamp that attacked me, did he have puncture wounds?*
>
> **Me:** *I didn't see any on his neck*

"Mina?" Sebastian asked.

I held my hand up, not ready to explain.

"She's back!" someone whispered, but they were immediately shushed.

> **Jake:** *Opening autopsy report*

I nearly screamed at the three dots dancing next to his name. *Come on, come on, come on.*

> **Jake:** *photo message*

I clicked on the photo, a screenshot of the report. *Visible puncture wounds: None*

My eyes widened as my stomach turned over. This was so much worse than we thought, but also this was our first major break in the case. Vampires often had puncture wounds because it was the easiest and most effective way to introduce the venom into the bloodstream, or because it was a side effect of feeding.

There were cases where the venom was introduced in alternative ways because fangs scarred. I've seen models, actors, and politicians change without puncture wounds, using several intramuscular injections to start the change. It was expensive and rife with complications, from sourcing venom to maintaining potency between extraction and injection.

Venom was rarely potent enough from being ingested to survive stomach acid. But what if there was a way to make it more digestible? The possibilities were endless. It could be put in capsules, food, and beverages at an affordable price. It could easily create vampires en masse. Full covens overnight.

Me: *What if we're not looking for a few vampires hunting out of turn or a botched transition attempt?*

Jake: *I'm listening*

Me: *What if they found a way to make venom edible?*

Jake: *Not even our labs could do that*

Me: *But what if? Could turn a large group at once*

Jake: *How is Thinner involved?*

Me: *Working on it*

I tucked my phone back into my pocket and stooped to pick up my groceries.

"Lightning strike?" Sebastian asked.

"Major."

Someone cleared their throat and we all looked left, only to find Doris standing outside her apartment door. She stared at me, as I stood in the middle of the foyer, my bloodstained shirt soaking wet, holding a dozen bags of groceries, talking to what she assumed was myself.

She shook her head and pulled her purse closer to her body, as if I was going to drop my load and snatch it from her. "Oh my goodness."

"Hello, Ms. Manalin."

"It's a little early to be drunk, Mina."

Sebastian moved closer to me as if he could protect me. She couldn't see him; what was he going to do?

"Not drunk, just talking on my headset." I didn't actually have a headphone in my ear, but how would she know?

With a nod of my head, I headed for the stairs. No doubt Doris was about to spin a new story about what was wrong with me. There were always "random" pamphlets for alcohol and drug addiction treatment programs in my mailbox, and occasionally people from her church would knock on my door and ask if I had heard of their Lord and Savior. To her, I was the random woman upstairs with a penchant for talking to thin air and "not being able to hold down a job."

Most SHAP employees tried to avoid her. She was a full human and the kind of busybody who would open her mouth to the wrong person and blow someone's cover.

Maybe we should recruit her as a spy.

As soon as I made it to my apartment, I tossed my bags onto the counter, shifting through to pull out the refrigerated items, then changed my clothes. As soon as I was presentable, Sebastian followed me down one floor.

The door swung open and Amber, who was 4'11" on a good day, smiled and pulled off her reading glasses, which hung on a beaded chain. "Hello, dearies," she said. "Come in, come in."

Sebastian removed his top hat and executed a bow. Amber giggled at what she called his boyish charm. We followed her into the kitchen, where I set down her bags and started to unload the items onto the counter. We worked in tandem as she put the perishables away, then wrote me a check for the total.

I would argue with her—I didn't need her money since I hardly spent my own—but it was a fight I knew I wouldn't win. This had been a weekly tradition ever since she stopped driving three years ago. She patted my arm in thanks as I folded the piece of paper and shoved it into my pocket.

Gesturing for me to sit at the table, she followed with a plate of cookies in her hand. "You deserve these."

I looked between her and the plate, then reached out and took a still-warm morsel. I chewed on a corner of the cookie, the chocolate chips still soft and melty. I swallowed quickly, trying not to let her magnificent baking distract me from why I was here.

Amber shook her head. "I can tell by your face that you saw Belphegor. He's been so helpful, and I had a new sweater for him."

"Beautiful yarn, as always," Sebastian complimented. "You knitted this one! I thought you preferred crochet."

"I like both." She winked at him. "I'm bi-stitch-ual!"

I laughed. "Mrs. Andrews, you know I'd be happy to help with house projects, instead of you summoning a demon. Belphegor being here violates several SHAP policies."

She wielded the cookie plate between us as if it were a lifeline. "Another cookie?"

I shook my head. "We talked about how we're not trying to attract supernatural creatures with the tendency to..." *How did I put this delicately?*

"Eat, maim, attack, seduce, kill, or generally cause a ruckus?" Sebastian suggested.

I pointed at him. "Yes." I tapped on the table. "If Belphegor ever came up in a report, things could get messy. For both of you. It's luck he hasn't yet."

"I know, I know." She stood and walked over to the sink, grabbing a cloth. She ran it under hot water, then began wiping down the already spotless counter. This was her favorite distraction when we had to have the hard conversations.

Sebastian gave me a long look, as if silently asking *why* I hadn't filed a recent report about a demon hanging around. I hadn't because I was too busy recovering for the last four months, but now, I had no more excuses. Letting Belphegor slip through the cracks was fine until more demons arrived. Then it would be mayhem.

I studied the wallpaper, which should've been overkill with its giant, bold flowers, but it made the room feel cozy.

Normally our apartment manager didn't allow us to decorate with wallpaper, but the Andrews were one of the first tenants, and therefore were allowed to decorate however they wanted. At least that's how the ghosts told it.

When she had moved to scrubbing the stove, I cleared my throat to get her attention. "Mrs. Andrews, why are you determined to summon these creatures to your home? It's dangerous. They're bad creatures."

She paused, her shoulders sagging. When she turned around to face me, I was astonished by the tears in her eyes. *Oh no.* Not crying. I was terrible with crying. Jake was the one who handled the tears, not me.

She twisted the cloth in her hand. "It's a big world for me and George to be all by ourselves, you know?" She walked over to the sink and laid the material over the side. "I know we always have you and Sebastian, and quite the group of ghosts, but…"

She blew out a watery breath. "Figured if I could help make another lonely creature feel better, maybe it would lift my mood, too."

Sebastian shifted in his seat, blowing out a breath and looking everywhere but at me. He was a big softy sometimes. I watched her for a long moment, rolling her words over in my mind. "You summon demons to make sure they're not lonely?"

She scoffed. "Of course not. They have to earn the sweaters or any of my garments, in fact. They're happy to help for a sweater or a pair of socks, although the socks are harder to fit. You know, with the hooves."

All I could do was blink. "What about the poltergeists?"

She waved my question away. "Accident. I was trying to get my great aunt Mildred's molasses cookie recipe, my copy was irreparably damaged, and I wanted to make them for the church bake sale. I ran out of Oil of Theobroma for the spell and tried to substitute coconut oil. That didn't work."

I opened my mouth and then closed it, not sure even how to respond.

She turned to face Sebastian. "Thank you for your help, by the way."

"Happy to be of service, ma'am."

Her eyes turned back to me and studied me. "Why are you making that face?"

"If you're going to summon magical creatures, why not an Earth magic witch or one of the werewolf puppies?"

She released my hand and picked up the cookie plate, walking over to the counter. "Mina, not all supernatural creatures are inherently bad, even ones from the underworld. Some of them just have bad jobs to do. Belphegor is smack in the middle of eighty-four siblings."

Her head disappeared as she bent down to get a plastic bag from a cabinet, then placed it on the counter. "Torturing humans was just the job he was assigned to do, like it or not. Demons don't have the choices we do. But every two weeks, he makes it a point to stop in and see if I need help—he wanted to be a carpenter you know, but that wasn't where he was needed—so I let him come help in exchange for a sweater. He knows if he bothers anyone in town, our friendship will crumble."

She finished putting the cookies in the bag and sealed it, then walked back to the table.

George, Amber's husband, scuttled in, leaning on his walker. He was barely taller than Amber, his shoulders slumped from years of desk work. He smiled when he spotted Sebastian and me, then went over to Amber and bussed her cheek. "Are you talking about Belphegor? It was so good to see him today. That sink has been leaking for three months, and you know Tony only does repairs when he's sober."

George opened the bag, nabbed a cookie, and sat down next to me. "Yep, Belphegor is a good boy. But his brother Astaroth, he's just not nice and isn't welcome here." He inspected the treat in his hand. "Honey, these are some of your best cookies."

"He always says that."

"That's why I married her. Well, and her ability to see the best in even the worst people."

Her cheeks reddened and she shushed him. She resealed the pack and pushed it toward me. "These will freeze, so don't eat them all at once."

My eyes widened. Jake was going to swoon when I shared them with him tomorrow. "Are you sure?"

"Very sure." She patted her slightly rounded stomach. "Enjoy them. And remember, there's more to a demon, sometimes, than their claws."

"And their penchant for eating people?"

She nodded. "That's why I always make cookies when they visit, dear." She winked.

We said our farewells and I trailed after Sebastian, my mind racing with Amber and George's take on demons. On life, really. I couldn't wrap my head around how they couldn't see the evil in Belphegor. A creature who did bad things, in my book, was inherently bad.

"You will injure yourself if you keep thinking that hard," Sebastian teased.

I gave him the finger, then sighed. "I just can't wrap my head around Amber."

He gave me a half smile. "You're barely out of short pants. Give it time."

My cell rang as soon as I unlocked the door. "It's probably Jake."

Sebastian nodded. "I'm weary. Going to rest." He waited until I closed the door before disappearing.

For a ghost to stay visible, it needed to expend less energy than it pulled from the atmosphere. Today was exhausting for both of us. Sure, he could pull energy from me, but that wasn't the safest or most comfortable situation for a human. If he pulled too much, I could go into a coma fast.

I answered my phone before it went to voicemail. "Yo."

"You home?"

I dumped the bag in the freezer, then fell onto the couch, wishing I could just fizzle away, too. "Just. Had to have a chat with the Andrews again. I'll have cookies for you tomorrow."

"You're my favorite human."

I snorted. "I'm telling Eliza." His sister would never let him live it down.

"And here I was calling to be nice."

"You're lying. What's up?" The shuffling of papers in the background proved my point.

"I had Val pull vampire attacks for the last six months

within the entire country."

I sat up. "And?"

"Ten."

"TEN?!" I ran a hand through my hair. "Jake, we haven't had ten attacks since the 90s."

"I know."

"There's more." It wasn't a question.

"All the attacked were traced to six separate vampires. None of those six vampires had puncture wounds."

"My theory stands." I ran my hand down my face.

"Your theory stands."

We were silent for a long moment as the consequence of this discovery settled in. "But how does Thinner connect? Is Lucinda a cover? Is it bad luck? Is someone using the member database to find victims? How are all these vampires connected to Thinner when there are none at Thinner?"

"What if they don't work for Thinner? They buy memberships so they can get in and out of the building, rent the real estate for after-hours use. It would explain why the entire business is basically underground."

"Like an after-hours vampire breeding orgy?"

"Is that any weirder than the dry cleaners?"

"Ew." I wasn't easily grossed out, but that was a case I never wanted to remember yet couldn't forget. Let's just say they weren't dry cleaning clothes.

"Alright, looks like there's going to be a large-scale electrical problem over the weekend that will require multiple electricians to fix. We'll get cameras in."

"Awesome. Keep me posted."

I laid on the couch for a while after we hung up, too exhausted to roll off and make dinner. This week had kicked my ass, and my neck and shoulder were so tight they throbbed. I hadn't been doing my stretches as much as I needed to, and typing all day wasn't helping.

Opening a browser on my phone, I searched Natalie Moranis. Maybe she had a Facebook profile or a blog post. I clicked on the third link from a local news company.

"WDC News. West Bloomfield, Michigan, resident Natalie Moranis, age thirty-three, filed a lawsuit against the new star-studded weight loss company Thinner saying the mandatory food and supplements have made her sterile. She claims her period stopped when she began the program...

The company responded that all members must sign an extensive membership contract, one which they promise was reviewed and approved by their doctor. They did not have a comment on if their food or supplements may have a negative impact on conceiving..."

It wasn't new information, but I bookmarked the page anyway. Periods stopped for so many reasons, including dramatic weight change. What on earth could both make someone lose weight and make them sterile? And how did it connect to Thinner?

Something very strange—stranger than usual—was going on. It was like someone had taken all the supernatural-human rules SHAP had laid out decades ago and tore them in half. Or maybe they didn't know there were rules to play by. It wasn't, however, my responsibility to teach the rules. It was my job to enforce them, no matter the reasoning.

No matter the consequences.

By Monday morning, news of Natalie Moranis's lawsuit hit national news. Morning talk show hosts blasted both Natalie and Thinner. Natalie, for wanting to lose weight, and Thinner for existing. The next segment was how to "maintain your beach body all year round," followed by two weight loss supplement ads. The people at the station clearly didn't understand irony.

I called Jake when I climbed in my truck. "Yo, see the news?"

"Yeah." I could hear him washing dishes in the background. He couldn't leave a dirty dish in the sink all day, *unlike* me. "Requested permission to view her medical chart and lab work. Damn HIPPA. So far, nothing."

I snorted. "Chances?"

"*Hmmm.* Thirty percent?"

"Well, we've done more with less." I tapped my steering wheel, trying to think of the next move. "But a standard metabolic blood panel isn't going to tell us what we need to know. We need an actual blood sample to run it through SHAP protocol."

SHAP could test for werewolf genes, vampire antibodies, and at least seventeen different types of human hybrid creatures. Unfortunately, we would need a few vials of blood to do so. "Start with the medical chart. I'm going to leave a message for Dad and see if he'll reach out to Natalie's lawyer about a complex blood sample. It's probably an even longer shot, but maybe she's crazy enough to do it without asking too many questions."

When trying to deal with humans who didn't know about the existence of SHAP or supernatural creatures, we used a cover. SHAP became SAFE, a "special FBI task force dedicated to keeping citizens safe from unidentified threats."

The Thinner office was already chaos when I arrived twenty minutes early. Rachel and her entire department were camped out on Lucinda's sofas, brainstorming about what they could do to mitigate the fallout. Maggie had her cell and her landline against an ear, and my desk phone was ringing.

Dropping my purse into my desk drawer and turning on my computer, I grabbed the handset and a pen. "This is Mina." I didn't mention it was Lucinda's office. I'd played games with the media before, and the less information they had, the better.

"I'm a good friend of Lucy; is she in? I just want to check on her." The caller was a woman with a syrupy voice, but she made three mistakes. One, no one ever call Lucinda "Lucy." Two, I literally had a list of her closest friends. Three, I heard the hint of a southern twang.

"And who is calling, please?"

"Tell her it's Sarah."

Sarah was a good choice. It was a popular enough name to appear on Lucinda's friend list twice. But I knew one Sarah had an Israeli accent and the other was a born and bred New Yorker who just adopted a dog named Derek.

"Hi, Sarah." I smiled menacingly. Did these people think I was new? Well, I mean, I was new, but I wasn't an idiot. "How's Derek doing? What'd he think of his new place?"

"Oh, you're so sweet for asking. He's great, loves his new

place. Plenty of natural light and storage space."

This was increasingly amusing. "Oh yes, he did need a *lot* of storage space."

She kept going. "Of course! Now, sweetie, I'm in a hurry. Is Lucy around or should I call her cell?"

Fun fact: Lucinda didn't use her cellphone to "chat." It was only for emergencies, and the number came in as "blocked." She always called from either her bodyguard's phone or a family member's cell. Apparently, there was a disgruntled ex and a really scary stalker incident that was long before my time.

No one but Carma, Maggie, and Lucinda's head bodyguard even had the number. Not me. Not even *Rachel*, who tried to get it at least once a day.

"You better try her on her cell, okay? Give Derek an ear scratch for me."

"What's her numb—"

I hung up with a chuckle. Feeling someone standing next to my desk, I looked up to find Carma staring at me, surprised.

She gestured to the phone. "How'd you know it was fake?"

"Derek is Sarah Sinclair's new dog. I shipped a dog bed to her from Lucinda last week. It may have been top of the line, but in no way did it have 'plenty of natural light and storage.' And, you know, they wanted her cell."

"That's why I hired her," Maggie whisper-yelled before returning to her calls.

Actually, that had been a mix of luck, computer hacking, some fake resumes, and a few bribes—including gum-popper, who didn't even like gum. He was now working another super cushy desk job. But I wasn't going to argue with Maggie. Had I lived another life, and something super concerning wasn't going on, I would've enjoyed being here and working with Maggie.

And...admittedly, Carma. "You are a breath of fresh air," she said. A soft smile pulled my attention to her lips.

My phone rang again and with my best customer service voice, I answered. "No comment." After hanging up, I turned toward Carma. "Assuming I'm no-commenting all the media?"

"Who was it?"

"*Michigan Lakes Gazette.*"

She made a face. "Weren't they the ones who *refused* to cover the dog being elected mayor of Applechester campaign? Who'd even want to read them now?"

I lifted my hands up. "Right?! Madam Barks-A-Lot makes a really great mayor. She's very 'for the people.'" The real Applechester mayor was a werewolf who thought having a dog as the figurehead would be hilarious and good for tourism. She wasn't wrong.

"Yeah. I have her interview in the *Applechester Journal* bookmarked."

Carma smiled and my insides grew all floaty again. Maybe I really did need to cut back on the caffeine. Tomorrow, only two cups of coffee before leaving the house instead of three.

Her cell rang and she let out an annoyed huff then became all business. "Anyway, yes. No comment for everything. Rachel will reach out to who we want, when we want, with what we want. In the meantime, hold down the fort. I need to go have a talk with the front desk."

She spun on her heel and practically skated out, her phone to her ear. I tried not to stare after her. But the way her perfectly tailored pants fit against her hips, the curve of her butt, the strength of her thighs…

My desk phone rang again, interrupting my leering. Rude. "Mina."

The next several hours was a blur of no-comment-calls, damage control in Lucinda's "public email" inbox—Maggie and I had to tag team to keep up—and power walks on the rare bathroom break. I was so busy, I nearly missed the SHAP team, disguised as electricians, loitering in the hallway and climbing up ladders near the office. My guess was they were installing cameras that would cover the entire floor. By the time Lucinda called a meeting in the executive conference room for Rachel's team, Carma, Maggie, and the department managers, I was twitching. I'm pretty sure my body was at least eighty percent caffeine and thirty percent protein bar…which didn't add up to one hundred, but I was too far gone for math.

If I was simply an overworked assistant, I wouldn't be mad I was excused from the festivities, so to speak. My brain was numb from fielding calls from Lucinda's actual friends, distraught members who somehow got routed to my line instead of member services, and reporters. This was Thinner's first major scandal, which was what—I assumed—made it so juicy. My internet search earlier proved all the major weight loss companies had similar lawsuits during their tenure.

As an undercover agent, however, being excluded from the meeting left me scrambling. I had managed to plant two lower quality microphones I kept in my purse on the table legs in hopes they'd pick up the entire room. But someone tapping a pen on the glass top could sufficiently disrupt my listening.

Then, I had *graciously* offered to be in charge of putting together a drink cart for everyone, hoping it would either get me down to the cafeteria or would allow me enough time to grab a sample of a shake.

Apparently, no one trusted the new assistant. I mean, they shouldn't, but still. Maggie ordered the Thinner refreshments and had them delivered to the conference room. Then, with her arms stacked with notepads, spiral calendars, and a precariously balanced cup of tea, she left me alone. I pulled out my wireless headphones and tucked them into one ear, then called Jake's cell.

"Yo, planted devices A56 and A57. Can you patch me in?"

He made an affirmative noise. "Hello, nice to talk to you to. How's my day going? It's really busy but not too bad. How are you?"

I rolled my eyes. "How's your day going, bud?"

"No, no. Too late now." He paused. "Okay, so here's what we're going to do since I'm pretty much done for the day. I'm going to patch you into A56 and me into A57. Then you only have to listen to half the conversation in case you have to grab a call or whatever."

"This is why they pay you the big bucks."

He chuckled. "Medium bucks. Also, Magnolia wants to

know if you're coming to family dinner next Sunday."

I smiled. When Jake's stepmom asked if I was coming for dinner, it was only in question form as a courtesy. "I'll be there at four thirty pm and will bring wine."

"Roger." With a few final keyboard strokes in the background, the sound came through.

The first ten minutes was Lucinda outlining corporate's response to the lawsuit, followed by twenty-two minutes of Rachel yammering on.

"I'm seriously thinking about sticking bamboo shoots under my fingernails for fun," I grumbled.

Jake snorted. "I never knew there was a preferred ratio of good press versus bad press."

"And now you know."

"In excruciating detail."

Maggie started to speak, and I shushed Jake.

"What we need is an event that would highlight Thinner as an asset to the community," she offered, "and quickly."

"Sweetheart," Lucinda said, "are you still hosting that Red Cross fundraiser?"

"Yes, in two weeks," Carma replied. "We are fifty percent full. All the materials are printed and the press releases—"

"Well, you can just reprint them," her mother interjected with a finality I could feel through the speaker. "Thinner's your new biggest sponsor."

Carma sputtered. "We'd need to redesign all the promo, the programs—"

"Whatever it takes."

"I would need two of me, Mom! I can't do it alone with a day job."

Jake interrupted my stream. "Make an excuse to go into the room right now. If you can help Carma with the fundraiser, it's an automatic in."

"On it." I dropped my headphone on my desk and took off toward the conference room. I knocked hesitantly, acting the part of a new assistant unsure of the ropes, and then stuck my head in. Lucinda stared at me, her eyes narrowing, as I gestured to Maggie. "I'm so sorry," I said. "Maggie, I need to ask you a question, please."

Lucinda motioned with her hand. "Just come in and ask her. It's fine."

I walked straight to Maggie and squatted down near her chair. I focused my attention on my manager but said it just loud enough for others to hear. "The cafeteria just called saying they thought they sent up the incorrect beverages. They had a new person fill the order. I assured them I would check for any discrepancies."

Maggie nodded then addressed the room. "Did everyone get the refreshment they requested? It seems there's a new employee in the cafeteria."

Everyone nodded, confirming their order was correct.

I made it a point to stand, look around, and nod. "I'll let them know all is well."

Lucinda sighed. "It's such a shame good help is hard to find. We lucked out with our Mina here." She pointed at me. "Carma, she's the one you need for the fundraiser. Mina's only been here a week, and already my office is running smoother."

I stuck my hands in my pockets so I wouldn't fist pump. *Bingo*. "I would be happy to help in whatever way I'm needed."

Lucinda tilted her head and looked at Maggie. "Can you spare her? I know you're already stretched thin."

Maggie nodded. "We'll make it work."

Lucinda scrunched her nose, as if she was second guessing Maggie. Time to tip the scales. "I don't mind working after hours or on weekends, for the fundraiser."

"I don't pay overtime," Lucinda warned.

"How about two vacation days instead?"

She smiled. "Done." She pointed at me then looked around the room. "If we had a hundred more of her, we could franchise the entire world." She looked back down at her notepad and put a check mark. "Exchange numbers with Carma and you two can start planning."

I looked at Carma, who was smiling at me. That weird helium feeling returned, and I shifted on my feet, trying to dislodge it from my chest. "I'll email you," I told her, then bolted from the room and shut the door behind me. I didn't stop until I made it back to the sanctuary of my office.

Grabbing my headphone, I put it in my ear. "Bingo."

Jake sighed. "You're the best."

"I know." I leaned back in my chair with a smile.

Chapter Eight

DOWNTOWN APPLECHESTER GOT a facelift about once a decade. A mix of franchises and small startups littered Main Street. The Cat Café was snuggled next to the four-dollar movie theater that still served over-salted popcorn. A mom-and-pop burger joint shared a wall with the bakery where Mom and I had ridden our bikes every Saturday until the divorce. Her favorite pizza place still stood next to laser tag, although the video store on the other side was now a hardware chain.

The driver's ed building was still across the street from the Coney Island where Mom and I had lunch whenever she was in town. I had long ago forgiven her for choosing to take her dream job across the state after my folks divorced. Not wanting to switch school districts during high school or quit my internship at SHAP, I had stayed with my dad. I never regretted my decision because it brought me closer to my dreams.

But I really missed not having my mom around. It had been the little things—the cute notes in my lunch box, the afternoon walks where we talked about anything and every-thing, the self-manicures while watching our favorite movies, the affection. When I had a bad day, my dad wasn't the soothing "you'll get through this and be alright" type of guy. I think we had hugged a total of twenty-nine times in my life; one for every birthday.

"Mina," he'd say, "learn how to get through it yourself to be a good agent. Bad days are part of the process. Don't depend on anyone else, except you and your team."

If Jake ever heard my thoughts, he'd probably mumble something about my complete lack of emotional availability, and then Sebastian would inevitably comment on this being the reason I was single. I mean, they weren't wrong. There were things one had to give up to be the best.

But I missed my mom so much. She'd been traveling with her boyfriend halfway around the world for their charity foundation when I had my accident. We had talked on the phone the few times she had service, but I hadn't seen her since Christmas.

I hadn't been upset; I was used to her being gone for long stretches at a time. But as I climbed out of my car, emotion built thick in the back of my throat. I had the strangest urge to...cry? Absolutely ridiculous. I cleared my throat and took a deep breath.

When I opened the diner's door, Mom stood up from the table, her smile lighting up the room as always. She rushed toward me and wrapped her arms around me. I tempered my immediate reaction to being touched—flipping my mother to the floor—and brought my arms up around her waist.

"Hi, baby," she sang, her subtle but familiar floral perfume cocooning us.

She rubbed my back, her bracelets tinkling. "I'm so sorry

I couldn't come home and help you recover."

I shook my head. "It's okay. I'm fine." And I was fine, even if part of me wondered if her being there would've made it more tolerable.

We broke apart, but she held on to my shoulders, giving me a long look. "You look beautiful." She touched the edge of my hair. "I like this." She let out a watery sigh and dropped her arms, then looked over her shoulder. I startled, surprised I'd missed that we had company.

My mom's boyfriend smiled at me. "Hey, Mina. Hope it's cool I crashed your lunch."

"Of course," I said, even though something inside of me twisted at the surprise of seeing him. I thought I'd have her all to myself for a few hours. "It's good to see you, Isaac."

We gave each other a one-armed awkward hug before we all sat down. It wasn't that I didn't like Isaac; he was pretty cool and made Mom happy. Was it weird he was only thirty-eight? A little. But what did I care?

I wish she would've told me he was coming. I hated surprises. I watched my mom as she leaned into him for a moment, a private smile on her face. How could I stay mad?

I tried to soak in all of her. Her blond hair, pulled back in its usual braid, had gone grayer at the temples, and the laugh lines around her blue eyes had deepened, but she looked healthy and happy. That's all I ever wanted for her.

She handed me a menu as if I didn't have it memorized. "I like this new haircut. Makes you look like a badass."

"Very Pink circa 2017," Isaac added.

I ran my fingers through the top. "Thanks. Thought it was better than the cut the hospital gave me." I traced the scar on the back of my head with my pointer finger.

"I'm so glad you've moved to RD. You'll be far less likely to end up like hamburger meat at the hands of some psycho." She reached out and grabbed my hand. "I like you in one piece."

I flinched. This is what happened when I didn't suck it up and call her. "Actually, I didn't get the promotion. Gotta work one more small job first."

Mom's cheery smile morphed into a scowl. She reached into a giant woven purse and pulled out her cell. *Oh no.*

"Mom, don't call him."

Isaac put his arm around Mom's shoulder. "Beth, deep breath."

She pointed her phone at me. "Was your father the reason you didn't get the promotion?"

I shrugged. "Yeah, but—"

"Then I'm calling him. He always thinks he knows what's best for everyone else. Ha!"

I put my hands over hers. "Mom, it's okay. I'm doing an undercover office job. No dangerous high-speed chases involved." Theoretically.

She sighed and dropped her phone onto the table. I gave her hands a long look, making sure they stayed still. My brow pinched at the gold band around her left hand. "That's new."

I looked up to find her exchange a look with Isaac. She was blushing. "I didn't want to tell you over the phone. Isaac and I are getting married!" She grabbed his hand and held tight.

My stomach dropped. I threw a smile on my face before

she noticed my reaction. "I'm so happy for you!" I managed. "When's the wedding?"

I wasn't upset Mom was getting remarried (I had never harbored the illusion she and Dad would get back together) and I absolutely approved of Isaac. Except it suddenly felt like she was going from "my mom" to "Isaac's spouse."

That was the most selfish thing I had ever thought. I looked down at the menu.

"It's okay to feel weird about it. It's a big change," Isaac said.

Shut up, Isaac. I didn't say that.

Mom nodded. "I know Isaac probably isn't the man you envisioned your fifty-five year old mother with, but he makes me so happy." She tugged my menu down and grabbed my hands. "I'll always be your mom, no matter who I marry." She squeezed me and then pulled back. She chewed the bottom of her lip while she focused on the menu.

My shoulders didn't relax until the waiter came over. As per usual, I ordered my regular, not willing to try anything new. Mom and Isaac tried the special, always up for an adventure.

She thumbed her gold band and took a sip of her iced tea. "We haven't picked a date yet, but probably in the next few months. Just a small thing."

"We want to get married before our next trip," he added.

That weird, thick-throat feeling was back, and my chest ached. I didn't want her to leave again but being apart was more normal than being together for us. I just...wanted something. An anchor. It was like I had finally looked up from my map only to realize I was adrift at sea.

I took a sip of water and ignored the feeling. "Where're you headed?"

"The Galápagos Islands," Isaac explained. "We're joining forces with a foundation that's doing amazing animal conservancy work."

While they continued to tell me more about their plan, I silently panicked that my mom was going to be in Ecuador for the foreseeable future. She'd be so far away. We'd talk at first every week, but the time change and her mission would interfere with our conversations, and soon they'd devolve into a few texts or an email with some cool photos.

Mom reached out and grabbed my left hand, cradling it between hers. "I know your life is here, but would you consider coming with us?"

I blinked up at her. "What?"

"Take two weeks off and come reset with us. I know the flight is long, but you'd get to make amazing memories and we'd be able to spend more time together."

Go with them? I opened my mouth to respond but couldn't find anything to say. I couldn't. Not until this job was done and I got the promotion. *But then what?*

Then I'd continue to do my job. And continue not seeing my mom. And continue doing nothing but working and sleeping and occasionally watching television with my house ghost.

Wasn't this what I wanted? Wasn't this everything I had worked toward my entire life?

"I'll think about it." I could tell by their faces they didn't believe me. I didn't believe me, either.

They told me more about the trip until the food came. I

just stared at my plate until my mom picked up my fork and put it in my hand. "Eat."

I did.

"Mina," Mom said, breaking through the silent awkwardness that had settled between us, "I just don't want you to feel like you have no other options."

"Options for what?"

"In case one day you feel too lonely in the life you've created for yourself." She smiled her mom smile, the one meant to cushion the blow of whatever she said.

I frowned. "Being alone doesn't make me lonely, Mom. It makes me a better agent."

She shrugged. "I'm sure you're right."

Isaac, for his part, stayed silent.

When we had finished and she'd paid the check, I walked them to their smart car. It looked like it would crumple if someone sneezed too close to it, but they were determined to leave as small a footprint as possible.

She fussed over me for a moment. "I'll call you when we have a wedding date set. Hopefully you can take the day off?"

I nodded. "Absolutely."

She wrapped me in a tight hug and rocked us back and forth. "It's okay to find new dreams." She pulled back and put her hands on either side of my cheeks. "I love you."

"Love you, too."

With a wave, they slipped into the car and then out of the parking lot, leaving me standing there, reeling. How did she always know what to say to shake up my world like a snow globe? I pulled out my phone.

Me: Mom's engaged

Jake: Are we excited or upset?

Me: *shrug emoji*

Jake: Be there in an hour

✕

JAKE LET HIMSELF into my apartment just under an hour later. I was cocooned on the couch with my favorite blanket, having turned my AC down enough to accommodate the extra layers.

"¡Bendito Dios!" Reggie rushed over to Jake, having veered off his pace-a-thon with Sebastian. "It's freezing in here and I'm dead."

"She won't talk to us," Sebastian explained.

My partner dropped two pizza boxes on my coffee table, set his cane handle on the arm rest, then lifted my feet off the couch and slid in underneath them with a huff. He put a pillow between my foot and his thigh. "So, upset?"

"Excited?" I mumbled through my blanket.

"Then why are we watching, and I quote, 'the worst serial killer documentary of all time?'"

"Because I can have simultaneous emotions?"

He reached forward and snatched the remote and paused the television. "Here's the plan: We're going to turn on something you don't hate and I'm going to turn off your AC because I think it may start snowing in here. Then we're going to eat pizza."

"I hate pizza."

"You love pizza and only tell yourself you hate it so you

don't eat it every day."

Okay, that tracked. "Fine."

Reggie sniffed and we all turned to look at him. "It's just, you two are friendship goals."

I rolled my eyes.

Sebastian elbowed him. "And I'm not these so-called friendship goals?"

Jake turned to me. "I better make sure I get that food sample first. I could not live with a ghost."

I sighed and threw off the blanket. "These two are so emotional for ghosts."

"Hey!" Reggie sniffed again. "Ghosts have feelings, too."

"We can't all be mostly dead inside like you," Sebastian teased. "Well, figuratively speaking."

"I'm not dead inside. I just don't have any desire to express my emotions out loud."

Jake snagged a pizza box and opened it, holding it out to me. "No, you just like to watch the same show five hundred times in a row and shove down all your feelings until they volcanically erupt and burn everyone around you."

I nodded and snapped. "Exactly." I grabbed a slice and shoved half of it into my mouth.

He shook his head. "I thought we liked Isaac."

"We do like Isaac," I argued through a mouthful of food.

"Then why are you mourning like you did when *Supernatural* ended?"

I sighed and stared at my hands. "I don't know how to explain it. It's just...she's going to get married and then they're off to Ecuador and she'll have her new family with him and the animals she's saving and her crew and I'll never get her back."

Jake grabbed some of my blanket and covered his chest, then leaned back on the couch. "I see."

"See what?"

He turned to look at me. "She left a long time ago. She's been to more countries than I can name. Isaac's been in the picture for four years. Only one thing's changed here, and that's you."

I narrowed my eyes. "Meaning?"

Jake ran a hand down his face. "You need a female friend or a girlfriend or something. You'd be less likely to punch them for saying things you need to hear."

I play-kicked him. "The last thing I need is another person who'd be a liability."

Sebastian tutted. "Yet you're curious about why you're single."

"It's on purpose." Mostly.

Reggie heaved an exasperated sigh. "Can't you all see my Mi Minita is just lonely?"

We all turned to stare at him. "I'm what?"

"Lonely?" Jake asked, his brow pinched.

Sebastian gave him a puzzled look before he turned to me, his head tilting as if he was coming to some realization.

"No," I said.

"How am I the most emotionally stable person here? I'm dead." Reggie just shook his head. "¡Ay por favor!" Sebastian opened his mouth, but Reggie just patted him on the shoulder. "No, mano, you have the emotional depth of a puddle."

Jake grabbed a piece of pizza. "So, she's got her coworker

and two ghosts. Huh. I see your point."

I play-kicked him again. He knew he was the younger brother I never had. "Call yourself that again and I'll tell your stepmom about what really happened to her ginger-bread house last Christmas." He pinched my toes and I squeaked. "No touchy."

"You're so annoying. But I love your stupid face."

"Ugh. Same."

Reggie sighed and sat down in the orange chair. "If only I had changed the batteries in my carbon monoxide detector, I might be with sane people right now."

"My sensibilities should be offended, but I'm inclined to agree with you," Sebastian added, sitting on the arm of the chair.

Jake picked up the remote. "That's it. We're watching something not about murder." He spun through my streaming and selected a Taylor Swift concert. "I expect you all to sing along."

Reggie cheered. Sebastian just looked amused.

"I only know, like, three songs," I admitted. "I don't think…" She appeared on stage and my mouth fell open.

"You're welcome," Jake said. "Are you going into a bi-panic now?"

"Shush," I ordered. "There's a beautiful woman on my screen."

"Speaking of beautiful women, has Carma contacted you yet?"

That broke through the bi-panic. "Why was your lead-in 'speaking of beautiful women?'"

"Just checking in on your wobbly feeling."

"The wobbly feeling is gone, thank you," I mean, I wasn't technically having it *right now* so it wasn't a lie. "And no, not yet. I'm sure I'll hear from her soon."

He leaned back on the couch, his hands behind his head. "Keep me posted."

As we watched the performance, I looked over the motley crew gathered in my apartment and couldn't stop my smile. The ache in my chest from my mom's impending wedding announcement had eased back into a dull throb. Sure, I may not have my mom, or a girlfriend, or more than one human friend, but I had these weirdos. That would be enough.

It had to be.

Chapter Nine

A S PER STANDARD Mina protocol, by the time the sun came up the next morning, I had suppressed any unpleasant feelings about my mom's impending marriage. She was an adult who knew what she needed to be happy, as did I. What made me happiest was work.

I was already up and piecing through the reports Jake had sent me about the surveillance results—so far a big, fat nothing—when my phone buzzed.

> **Carma:** Good morning! Hope this text doesn't wake you.
>
> **Carma:** It's Carma Nicks by the way
>
> **Carma:** Text me when you're up and about and we'll start talking details.

My stomach did that weird swooping thing. I dropped my phone and quickly sifted my fingers through my hair, making it less *actual* bedhead and more implied bedhead. There. Now I was cute enough to text back.

> **Me:** Morning! I'm already up, too! Where would you like to start?

I hit send then blanched. TWO exclamation marks? Oh god. Too much excitement. Why didn't I proofread the text?

Carma: We have so much work to do

Carma: I'm starting to freak

Me: I'm here to help

Carma: Were you serious about working weekends? Or were you just trying to appease Lucinda

Me: Serious. I'm free until dinner. Where do you want to meet?

I knew I was being forward, but one-on-one face time with Carma would mean uninterrupted access to information. People always dropped their guard when they got comfortable with me, and when they dropped their guard, they told me things they shouldn't.

Carma: I know you don't know me well, but is my house okay?

I smiled. *Bingo.*

Me: Sounds good. Send me your address. What time?

We hammered out the details, and I forwarded them to Jake.

Carma: Seriously, thank you

Carma: You can be my voice of reason before I do something crazy like add a puppet show

I blinked at my phone.

Me: Puppet show?

Carma: A reprise Ramona & Juliet

Me: Ramona & Juliet...

Carma: *They were lesbians and didn't die at the end*

Carma: *they knew how to communicate*

I barked out a laugh.

Me: *I just laughed so loud I scared the neighbors*

Carma: **winky face* glad to be of service*

Service. I couldn't stop the image of her kneeling in front of me asking to service me. My hands gripping her hair, her strawberry scent wrapped around me while her tongue...

My entire body clenched at the thought. I shook my head and took a deep breath. *What the actual hell?* I could not think about a mark that way.

Me: *As incredible as that sounds, I'm not sure the donors are ready for a puppet show*

Carma: *They rarely are*

"Are you ill?"

I shrieked at Sebastian's intrusion and dropped my phone. "Dude, what the hell?"

"Why are you smiling at your telephone?"

"I like being awkward in my own home without questions, thank you."

He raised an eyebrow. "We all have dreams, Mina." My phone buzzed against the wood laminate floor, and we both looked down. "Ah."

I scooped it up. "You see nothing. It's a work thing. Thinner thing."

"A Carma Nicks thing."

"It's about the fundraiser. I'm doing my job."

He was silent for a beat. "Your cheeks are rosy."

Dammit. Why was I blushing so much?

He pursed his lips. "I see."

"See what?"

"Why Jake's worried."

"What makes you say that?"

"I reside with you. I know you more completely than I knew my mistress. Being attracted to a mark is not a good sign."

I rolled my eyes. "I've worked with plenty of attractive marks before."

"There's a difference between an attractive mark and *being attracted to* a mark, love."

I looked up to the ceiling. "Why do men always think they know better than me? I know how to handle my own sexuality, thanks."

He disappeared, apparently too pissed to even respond. Well fine. Let him stew. I looked down at the unread message on my phone.

Carma: *I'll see you soon*

Chapter Ten

I RECHECKED THE address on my phone, then looked back up at the house. Did Carma seriously live here? I blinked, as if trying to clear fog from my vision. I was used to weird shit. Hell, I built my career on expecting the unexpected.

I was not expecting the VP of a weight loss company to live in a house that looked like a cross between Martha Stewart and *The Addams Family*. I climbed out of my truck, barely remembering to snap a few pictures with my phone. The ornate black iron fence protected a cascading bed of plants and flowers, all deep purple and black, with the exception of light pink roses along the front of the house.

The walkway was pure white stone, which lead to a light pink door that matched the roses. Deep gray siding and stark white gingerbread trim made the entire scene like something out of a dark fairytale. Walking through the gate and into the garden felt like crossing into a different world. Two blue butterflies swirled around me before chasing each other away.

A crow cawed as I reached the front door, and I knocked more hesitantly than I intended. *Summers, it's a house. Get it together.*

"Hi there!"

I swear my soul left my body for a moment at the sight of Carma leaning against the open door. She was dressed down in overall shorts with one strap slipping down her shoulder and a baggy paint-stained T-shirt tied just under her chest, exposing her stomach. Her hair was pulled back into a messy bun and safety glasses were perched artfully on her head.

Swallowing hard, I concentrated on finding words. "Wow, I…" Nope. Had no more words.

She laughed softly. "I was just finishing up something in my workshop. I thought I'd be done with it by now, but my cats were sleeping on me and I didn't have the heart to move them."

As someone who never had a pet, the sentiment confused me. Why not just move the cats? "Ah, understandable," I managed.

"Come on in. You can keep me company while I finish, then we'll work on the fundraiser." She held the door wider and motioned for me to enter.

I adjusted the large purse on my shoulder. When I was off-duty, I never carried anything this large. Any extension from the body was just another thing someone could use as a weapon. It had been necessary tonight, however, if I wanted to plant surveillance. I doubted she'd leave me alone long enough to do a camera, but I was prepared just in case.

I paused in the entryway to look around, my mouth nearly dropping open. The foyer was painted black with white, pink, and gold cherry blossoms covering the walls. A living room spun off to the left, in shades of cream and pink, vintage furniture creating a cozy seating area with a record player positioned near a high-backed couch.

I followed Carma into the kitchen, which looked like a mix of the 1950s and goth-style decorations. "This is really...impressive," I admitted, trying to take in every detail on the cluster of porcelain china creating a focal point along the wall. I stepped closer to stare at the pattern.

"Famous beheadings," she explained. "That's Anne Boleyn. Do you know it's rumored she tried to talk after they..." She made a motion with her hand across her neck.

I stared at her. "You have everyone fooled. You are so sweet and normal at work."

She smiled before breaking out into a laugh. "That's the trick, you see. I'd be really creepy if I wasn't so charming."

I didn't really know how to respond, because she wasn't wrong. I gestured to the plate with an intricately painted guillotine. "Where on earth did you find this?"

"I made it."

My eyes widened. "You made it?!"

She waved me off. "Not the china. I just nabbed a set and did my own designs."

I just shook my head. "What the hell are you doing working at Thinner? You could sell a dozen of these sets and be good for the year."

"How do you think I paid for this house?" She gestured around her. "Come on. I've got to get this order done tonight."

With one last look at the tea set, I followed her through a white door and down wooden stairs to the basement. Like everything else in the house, it was a surprise. It looked like a hardware store threw up on one side and a craft store on the other.

And, of course, in the center of the room was a coffin. "Am I in a fever dream?" I looked around. I pressed my fingers to the pulse point under my chin. Her singsong laugh just added to my fuzzy head. "I'm afraid to ask?"

"My neighbor ordered one for her husband's birthday, and she wants me to deliver it tomorrow before the party. Just need to finish the hand painting along the edge and it'll dry overnight."

I opened my mouth to ask questions but nothing came out. This had literally never happened before. My brain was my best feature, even if Sebastian swore it was my ass. This brain had kept me alive for fifteen years in the field. Apparently, this brain was shocked speechless. "I have...so many questions. Yet, I can't think of a single one."

She licked her lips and my gaze laser focused on her mouth.

"They're going to use it as an oversize coffee table until they need it." She gestured to a frame over her shoulder. "That'll go around it and I'll lay a piece of glass on top." She picked up a paintbrush and leaned close to the wood. Her hand was completely steady as she made small flicking motions.

"What are you painting?" Across the top of the coffin, she was working on a realistic scene depicting what appeared to be a sports game.

"The University of Michigan stadium the moment UM won the 1997 game against Ohio State."

I just stared at her.

"He's a big football fan." She tilted her head to the corner which housed a white desk covered in hand-painted roses. "Grab a seat. This should only take another half hour."

As I moved toward the chair, I fumbled in my bag for a small microphone, managing to stick it to the underside of the desk. I repositioned the chair on the opposite side of the workbench and watched Carma paint, mesmerized. "You're so quick, yet it's perfect."

Another lip bite. I nearly groaned.

"What can I say? I'm fast." She looked up at me and winked, then refocused on her task.

My entire body clenched at her words. I stared at her fingers as they worked, wondering how they would feel... *Summers! You will never know. She is a mark.*

"So...your house is...unexpected."

Her smile was radiant. "Thank you. I did it all myself. Well, not the plumbing and electrical, I'm not there yet. But the floors, the furniture modifications, and the decoration. The walls were the hardest."

"That's not wallpaper?"

"Wallpaper would be cheating."

I tried to wrap my head around how many hours, days, weeks, months it would take to do all the work. "How long have you lived here?"

She shrugged. "Eight months?"

"You did all this in under a year?! I couldn't even decide on a couch in a year."

"I don't sleep much." She licked her bottom lip, leaving it wet.

"Why aren't you doing this—" I gestured around "—professionally?"

She hesitated and looked up at me, her eyes burning into mine. "I love doing these projects, creating something amazing out of nothing. But I don't need to make money on it. I want to do it just because I enjoy it."

I nodded. "Capitalism wants us to make money on everything we love."

She pointed her brush at me. "Exactly. I'll take special orders—" she returned to her work "—but only from people I know. This is a labor of love, outside of what they pay for materials."

"Wow." All this work for *fun*. "What would you do if not for Thinner?"

Her smile was softer this time, as if she was shy. "Do you believe in ghosts, Mina? You're so pragmatic, my guess is no?"

She had no idea. "As a matter of fact, I do."

This time, I'd surprised her. "That's...oddly refreshing." She finished a few more hand flicks then set her paintbrush down before straightening. "Ever since seeing *Casper* as a child, I wanted to own a haunted hotel. It morphed into more of a bed and breakfast as I got older, but the dream remained."

"How would you know if it was haunted?" Did she know ghosts existed?

She held up her paint-stained hands. "Don't laugh. But I swear I saw a ghost when I was a kid. My mom says it was my brain manifesting it because I watched every ghost movie I could get my hands on, but I know what I saw."

"I believe you."

Her eyes narrowed as she studied me. "You do?"

"My apartment building is definitely haunted." *Oh shit.* I nearly slapped my hand over my mouth. Now she'd want to visit and that was too risky.

"Really?!"

I forced a laugh and shrugged. "I mean, so they say. It was a hospital during World War I, so there's bound to be something, right?" *Like a dozen ghosts who are worse gossips than old men.*

"Please let me come over someday!"

"That can be arranged."

She picked up her painting supplies and nodded to a small laundry room beyond. "Let me clean up and we can get to work."

The moment she was out of sight, I stood, my fingers digging for the camera. If I could position it so it recorded the bulk of the workshop, it would be an unexpected win. The track lighting was probably my best bet. Thankfully she'd gone with a black finish.

Standing on the chair, I tucked the camera into the track. Phone in hand, I texted Jake.

Me: *Visual test, unit 1*
Jake: *Roger*
Jake: *testing*

"Would you like some tea or coffee?" Carma called, turning off the water. "I don't drink it, but I keep it on hand."

"You just want to smell the coffee, don't you?" I teased.

"Busted."

A cold sweat broke out on the back of my neck. *Shit.* "Carma, I—" I looked over my shoulder, but she hadn't reappeared. My shoulders loosened in relief.

"I always want coffee, to be fair."

"Oh! Haha." *Oh my God, I was sweating.* I never sweat under pressure. It was bred out of me by sixteen.

Jake: *We've got audio and visual*

I stepped down, dragging the chair back to the desk.

Jake: *Is that a coffin?*
Me: *long story*

Carma was wiping her hands off with a towel as she walked back into the workshop. "I can't really smell the fumes anymore, but let's head upstairs. You can meet Cheddar and Lucifer."

I blinked at her.

"My cats," she clarified.

"I'm not sure I want to meet a cat named Lucifer."

She waved me off. "He's mostly harmless. His claws aren't long enough to do any disemboweling."

I pursed my lips. "That's not as comforting as you think it is."

She winked at me then started up the stairs. "Don't tell me you're afraid of a thirteen-pound ball of fur."

"Nope. I'm afraid of the demon that possesses him."

Her laugh echoed, and I was helpless to do anything but follow her. This woman was like a drug. Everything she did, every word she said drew me in deeper. The more I learned, the more I wanted to know.

I sat down in a kitchen chair and watched her move around the kitchen. The extension of her arms, the tilt of her head, the fluid movement of her shoulders made the entire thing seem like a choreographed dance. It wasn't just her grinding coffee beans or sniffing the coffee before tucking it into a filter. It was the way her eyes closed and her lips parted at the scent, or the gentle touch of her fingers as they stroked the coffee maker to life.

Holy shit, what was happening? I shook my head, trying to find the sense I had completely knocked loose. This was just a woman. She was only flesh and bone, presumably.

Trying to give myself some semblance of normalcy, I pulled another audio device from my bag and fumbled with it. After clicking it on, I felt along the bottom of the dark cherry table, trying to find a small divot or crack to set it in. Pressing it into place, I pulled back only to find two glowing eyes staring directly at me from my feet.

I gasped and pushed my chair back. The all-white cat looked at where I placed the mic and then back at me, as if it knew what I had done. "Lucifer, I presume?"

He just flicked a tail at me, his ears pulling back. Carma looked over and smiled. "Luci, baby! Be nice. We like Mina." Her eyes met mine. "A lot."

That helium feeling was back in my chest. Lucifer hissed, making it clear the cat did not agree with his owner, and killed the vibe. Carma tutted, and he sat down, pretending to look repentant, but kept his eyes on me, as if calculating his next move.

This is why I didn't have pets, besides the working all the time thing. They saw too much. I already had a ghost who was a pain in the ass, and I didn't have to feed him or clean up his poop.

"How do you like your coffee?" Carma asked.

I didn't dare take my eyes off Little Luci. "Black."

"Why am I not surprised?" She set a purple mug with hand-painted roses in front of me and sat in the chair next to mine.

I nodded my thanks and put both hands on the warm ceramic, locking my fingers together so I didn't reach out and touch her. "I know what I like."

She rested her elbow on the table and rested her chin on her hand. "Tell me, Mina, when was the last time you had *fun?*"

Before I flipped my truck, the high-speed chase had been really, *really* fun. "When I have fun, I tend to go a little overboard. Ever go down 696 at one hundred and ten miles an hour?"

Her lips parted on a gasp as her eyes widened. "That's so fast."

Was I crazy or was she leaning closer? "Too fast. Hit a patch of black ice and flipped four times. Got the scars to prove it." Before thinking about it, I fingered the scar at the base of my skull.

Her hand dropped and her mouth hung open. "How are you even alive right now?"

I shrugged. "I'm fucking stubborn."

She reached out to the scar on my head, her fingers hovering just above, waiting for permission. I closed my eyes and tilted ever so slightly in her direction. I sucked in a sharp breath as her fingertips stroked along the puckered skin.

I opened my eyes to find her inches away from my face. I could kiss her so easily, with just a tilt of my head. She was so close, I could feel her breath on my skin. *Lock it down, Mina.* I leaned back, breaking the contact and forcing myself to lift the coffee to my lips to keep them busy.

Carma jolted back and pointed at me. "See that. Right there. It's like you just packed everything away and flipped on work mode."

"Well, we are here to work."

She smiled. "Alright, you win this round." She leaned down and scooped up Lucifer, settling him onto her lap. He went into liquid form, melting into her.

I was absolutely jealous of a cat.

"Ah, I see."

My eyes moved to hers. "See what?"

"You're all wrapped up tight, like a present. But I bet when you're opened up, you go wild."

Heat burned low in my stomach and I ached for her to unwrap me. My hands loosened around my mug, as if daring me to make a move. As always, the universe was looking out for me. Before I could do something stupid, a black and orange cat jumped onto my lap. Without waiting for an invitation, he settled in and began licking his paw.

"Uh, Cheddar?"

Carma laughed. "That would be him. He's my snuggle bug." She reached out and scratched his head. "Aren't you?" she said in a soft voice, clearly to the cat. She straightened. "He loves to be pet, so feel free."

I looked down at him as he started brushing his paw with his ear. I tentatively scratched around his other ear and he stilled.

She studied me for a moment. "You look like you've

never pet a cat."

"I haven't." I mean, I had touched plenty of weird creatures, including a werewolf, but a domesticated cat? Never. My dad never wanted a pet, especially after Mom left, and Jake's stepmom was allergic, so he never had one growing up either. As adults, we both worked too much to keep another living creature alive. And all my other friends were literally ghosts.

"He likes under the chin, too."

I moved to Cheddar's chin and he happily leaned into me, purring. I smiled. "He hasn't clawed my face off, so I'm counting this as a success."

"It's like you're simultaneously the adultiest adult and somehow still a child all at once."

"Product of divorced, workaholic parents."

Her laugh startled Lucifer and he threw a paw over her hand, as if reprimanding her. "I mean, same." She leaned back in her chair. "Well, I suppose we should get to work, or you'll end up staying here all night."

It took everything I had to say, "Better get busy then." I wasn't quite strong enough to keep my eyes from her lips, however.

Chapter Eleven

WHEN I WALKED into work on Monday, something fluttered in my stomach. I pressed my hand to my belly, frowning. I usually only got this feeling when watching a really good serial killer documentary. I couldn't stop myself from looking into Carma's office as I passed, but I didn't see her or her assistant.

With a good morning wave to Maggie, who was already on the phone, I powered up my computer and opened my email. The graphics team at SHAP had been busy, creating proofs for all the promo materials we'd need for the fundraiser. Downloading the images from a dummy email account, I forwarded them to Carma for review.

I was sifting through and organizing the files left from the previous assistants—mostly just half-assed projects with no useful information—when Carma yelled my name and ran into the office.

Maggie looked up startled as I stood, rounding my desk. "What? Are you okay?"

"Am I... Are you serious?" She grabbed my forearms. "You are magic!"

I stilled and something inside me settled. Like her touch was the answer to a question I didn't know I was asking. I struggled to take in a full breath. Her hands tightened briefly as she smiled up at me, those green eyes wide and bright. Even after she let go, I could feel every inch of pressure she left behind.

"The proofs are perfect! How'd you get them done so fast?" She turned to Maggie. "Did you see them? I don't know how Mina's working here and not at some top five ad agency."

Maggie set down her phone and walked over. "I have not, but I'd love to."

"She's being overly generous but thank you." I walked back to my computer, minimizing what I was working on and pulling up the images. Carma and Maggie both leaned close to the screen, Carma's hand resting on my shoulder.

How could I feel the warmth of her hand throughout my entire body?

"These are excellent, Mina," Maggie said, sounding as if she were a proud parent. "You're going to give Rachel a run for her money." She smiled just a little too wide as she walked back to her chair.

Carma's hand slipped off me and she stepped back, looking down at her shoes, then back up at me. "Thanks again. I'll get them to the printers right away."

"You're welcome."

She stepped away, walking out the door, looking back over her shoulder at me one last time before disappearing.

"I can feel you staring," I told Maggie.

"Hmmm."

"What?"

She just shrugged. "Be careful. I like you."

I held my hands up. "Just doing my job."

"Keep it that way."

I nodded and tried to focus on my computer screen. My left hand slipped over my forearm, pressing where Carma had squeezed, as if trying to hold the feeling there. Realizing what I was doing, I ripped my hand away. It was a simple touch. Nothing else.

I HAD JUST walked in the door after work when my phone buzzed with the wind chime text tone I'd assigned Carma.

Carma: Help!

Carma: Mom wants to change the menu from drinks only to drinks and apps

Carma: Want to meet and taste test? I can't exactly eat anything

My heart thudded hard against my ribcage.

Me: I'm in. Just tell me when and where and I'll be there

I rushed to my room to change into jeans and a black top, spritzing with my favorite scent. I usually only wore it on a rare night out, but why shouldn't I wear it anytime?

"You're strangely joyful for a Monday evening."

I jumped at Sebastian's appearance. "Don't do that. And I've got a work thing tonight. Can we reschedule our *Unsolved Mysteries* marathon?"

He nodded. "Does this include Carma?"

I glared. "It's literally my job to get close to her."

"You applied perfume."

"Because I don't have time to shower."

He made a noise.

"What?"

He walked over to the side of my bed and sat down. "When was your last evening out with a potential suitor?"

"Potential suitor?" I mocked, looking at him in the mirror while I fixed my hair. "Uh…I dunno…eight or nine months?"

"Yes, now I recall."

I turned to face him. "Okay?"

"It is strange to me that you're more excited to go to a 'work thing' than you've been in the last two years."

"That's not true." Except it was.

"If Carma wasn't your mark, would there be anything else that would keep you from pursuing her? Disregarding that you have the emotional maturity of a cactus."

The silence was an answer in itself.

"Just so." He patted the spot next to him, and I walked over and sat down. "What will you do?"

I shook my head. "Nothing. I can't have a relationship with a mark. End of story."

"And after?"

"Ha! If I started dating someone from my most recent case, there's no way I'd ever get promoted again."

"Even if, perhaps, they were innocent?"

I scrubbed my face with my hands. "When have any of my marks been cleared of all charges? They don't send Jake and me in unless they're sure." I blew out a breath. "And it's usually bad."

He nodded. "Be careful then."

HARVEST CAFÉ WAS a block away from downtown Applechester, a rustic-but-elegant, farm-to-table joint that had a waiting list every weekend night. Despite the traffic, I glided into a street spot, paid for parking on my app, and breezed inside.

The scent of tart apples and freshly baked bread surrounded me as I pulled off my sunglasses and looked around for Carma. A server, dressed in all black with an ankle length apron, approached. "Ms. Madison?"

I nodded.

"Right this way." He led me through the dining room and deep into the restaurant. I glanced longingly at the patio but followed along.

She stood up from the booth when she saw me, her pink sundress fluttering against her thighs with the movement. My heart skipped a beat. She tucked a piece of her loosely curled hair behind her ear and smoothed her skirt self-consciously. We were acting like we were trying to impress each other.

Like it was a date.

"Hi," she said, motioning to the bench across from her. "Hope this is okay."

"It's perfect." I sat down and she returned to her side.

After placing our drink orders, we both stared at the menu. I couldn't even see the words. All I could think about was the shock of pink against her pale thigh.

I shifted and crossed my legs, willing my body to settle. She was only a pretty woman in a dress. I was a trained assassin. I could do this.

Trying to focus on something else, I turned to look out patio windows that stretched along the entire length of the restaurant. We were too far away to have residual light on the table. It had been a cloudless day, still only in the low eighties with almost no humidity. The sun was crawling its way down the sky, enjoying the long day before a gorgeous sunset.

"Sorry to force you to be inside on a night like this," Carma offered.

"Oh!" I turned back to face her. "No, it's okay. Just admiring the view."

She smiled, then glanced outside. "Skin cancer runs on both sides of the family, and I burn *so* easily." She rubbed her arm with her palm. "So, safer to stay inside."

Even though Michigan only got good sun a few months a year, it was worth it. "That sucks."

She shrugged. "I'm healthy otherwise. I'm lucky. We all have something, you know?"

"Yeah. We do." I smiled. "But I like the way you look at it."

Her French-tipped nail picked at the menu, the corner of her mouth curving up. I stared at her smooth, long fingers, the diamond flower on her right ring finger, her bare left hand.

She twisted the flower with her thumb. "My mom gave it to me when I graduated college. She finished high school with a GED while traveling the world with her parents—

military. Fell into the exercise video business after doing some modeling, and her career just took off. She never went to college and wanted me to have the experience she never got to have."

She toyed with the bottom of her wineglass, then pressed her palm flat against a table. "I went to college for business. I have a weird obsession with spreadsheets, so it seemed like a good fit." We both laughed. "But I turned down a dream opportunity in Dallas to stay here."

"Why?"

She shrugged. "You're going to think it's stupid."

I shook my head, then bobbed it side to side. "To be fair, that's because I know present-day you. I might have thought so back then."

She laughed. "Yeah, all my friends thought I was making a terrible choice." She dipped her head and smiled. "I was struggling with the decision to leave, and then I found my mom unconscious." She picked at the tablecloth.

I placed my hand in front of hers, our fingertips only one irreversible movement apart. I longed to comfort Past Carma, the one who found her mother. A flash of something like desperation prickled across my skin before I shoved it back down deep.

Carma's eyes turned warm. "When she had the idea to start Thinner, it was my turn to give back everything she gave to me. So I stayed."

I could physically feel the love she had for her mom. This is a woman who wore her emotions on her sleeve. Brave, but stupid. The more exposed a heart was, the easier it was to break.

"I would do anything for my mom," I admitted, the words tumbling out before I thought them through.

She smiled, the pads of her fingertips over my nails. "Tell me about her. Does she live nearby?"

I shook my head. "Kalamazoo is home base. But she's headed to Ecuador with her soon-to-be-husband." My eyes widened and I cleared my throat. I absolutely was not supposed to share anything personal with marks. Not this personal, especially. "Anyway…"

"Do you like her fiancé?"

"He's great, even though he's practically my age. But he makes her happy, and they can go off and save the world together."

She smiled but it didn't reach her eyes. "And your dad?"

"He's nearby."

Her head tilted. "Nearby but not close." It wasn't a question.

I glanced down at our hands and slowly lifted my fingers until the tips of mine ran along the tips of hers. We weren't holding hands, nope. This was just a handshake.

She shifted, resting her fingers in between mine. This still wasn't holding hands. She was only down to my second knuckle. It wasn't holding hands; it was holding fingers. Friends could hold fingers. As long as I didn't admit that the touch of her skin settled me. Anchored me.

I shifted my wrist, brushing my fingers on the back of her hand. She squeezed her fingers against mine. Everything inside of me wound tight. *Pull away. You cannot be holding hands with your mark. This is how agents get fired at best or die at worst.*

When our waiter showed up to take our orders, we both yanked our hands away as if we were caught cheating by our teacher. Having not bothered to read the menu, I just pointed. Carma ordered, then handed him the menus.

My gaze darted to her glass of white wine. "I thought you couldn't eat or drink anything not on the Thinner menu?"

She laughed, the sound like windchimes on a soft breeze. "You're right, I can't. But I love this place, and we're going to be taking up table space for a while. I'll get it wrapped up later and drop it off at the corner of Maple and Orchard."

"For Old Joe?" Old Joe—his name for himself—was a veteran who raised money for his family on the weekends. I didn't know all the details, only that the last recession had hit them hard, landing their store and their apartment above in foreclosure, and they were staying with a friend. When I was carrying cash and saw him out and about, I always stopped by with bottles of water and stayed for a chat.

She nodded. "He served our country. The least I can do is serve him some of my untouched dinner."

"That's super cool."

She shrugged. "It's just food. We need to do better for our veterans. I keep hoping he'll call my friend Svetlana who runs a non-profit that may help, which I beg him to do every time I see him. But pride is a powerful thing."

"We'll present a united front."

She laughed. "I like the way you think, Mina."

Her eyes met mine and I gripped the edge of the table. The effect she was having on me was unsettling. Addicting.

While I ate, we talked about her neighbor's birthday party—the coffin was a big hit—and she showed me pictures of the cats. Side-stepping the question about when my birthday was, I asked her about the bed and breakfast she wanted to open.

I couldn't look away from her as she grew more animated. The rest of the room fell away as she dove into her plan for themed rooms and creepy food ideas. When she finished, she looked down at her plate. "I'm sorry. I've been going on and on."

"I enjoyed every minute," I admitted.

Our waiter came over with a box for Carma's food, interrupting the moment. She slid the company credit card to our waiter. "Business dinner," she explained.

"My favorite kind."

She pulled out a spiral notebook and made a few notes. "Glad to hear. I've got three more places on the list to check out, all who have open availability for catering. You in?"

"Absolutely. When's our next taste test?"

My eyes were glued to her mouth when she bit down on her own smile. "What are you doing for dinner tomorrow night?

"Just text me the time and place."

Chapter Twelve

O N SUNDAY, I pulled into Jake's stepmom's driveway, *late*. Magnolia didn't do late. The daughter of a preacher, she thrived on "the three P's": punctuality, politeness, and perseverance. And Jesus. But he didn't start with a P.

After taste-testing with Carma three days this week, she called me this morning wanting to do a second round. I'd eaten my body weight in appetizers and swore Carma's strawberry scent was permanently tattooed in my nose. Fighting my attraction to her was nearly a full-time job in and of itself, and she still hadn't said anything worth reporting about. The microphones and camera footage from her house had produced nothing interesting either, except that she loved singing *Mamma Mia* to her cats.

Now I had indigestion, was late, and had nothing to show for it. It was going to be a long night. I tried to get out of the truck with my seatbelt on and swore. I might be lethal with a shoelace and paperclip, but sometimes I was an idiot.

I held my breath as I walked through the front door, bottle of wine out in front of me as a makeshift shield. I had an excuse on my tongue as I braced myself for the welcome committee, which usually consisted of Jake's niece on his back and his stepmom Magnolia close behind. I was greeted by...no one. I breathed a sigh of relief at the unexpected respite.

Magnolia still struck fear into my heart. While godmother was a meaningless title to most people, Magnolia took her godmother duties over me *very seriously*. Especially now that my mom was always flitting around the world.

"Hello?" I called, inching into the house. A portrait of Jesus hung in the entryway, his gaze silently judging me. "Sorry!" I hissed at it, as if it were sentient and could hear me.

"Out back!" Jake called. "You're late!"

I walked through the living room, the formal dining room, and the new farmhouse-style kitchen, pausing to take in the updated stone counters. Magnolia sauntered in through the screen door, wearing a spotless light-yellow jumpsuit. She looked like a woman on vacation. A shiver ran down my spine.

Any person who can prepare and manage a family dinner with a small grandchild while wearing a spotless pastel jumpsuit was likely as lethal as I was.

"You're a witch, aren't you?" I asked as she pulled me into her arms for a hug.

She clucked her tongue. "You're late and you don't come see me enough." She kissed both my cheeks before letting go.

"You didn't answer my question."

She winked. "I'll never tell." She took the wine from my hands. "And your tardiness is forgiven because you brought my favorite."

"Whew. Sorry, I had to work this weekend for an investigation."

"Never have to apologize for working, as long as you remember to stop and enjoy life once in a while." She pointed outside. "Just put the food out. Grab a chair and make a plate."

As I stepped onto the back deck, I waved. Jake's dad, Morris, was in a good-natured argument with Jake's stepsister, Eliza, over what sounded like a newly formed trade agreement between several countries. I swear, the two of them liked to argue for fun. Daisy, Eliza's daughter, ran at my legs and nearly knocked me over. I bent down and gave her a hug. As soon as I released her, she darted back to Eliza.

Jake pushed out the chair next to him with his hand. "Come eat."

My mouth was watering as I looked over a spread large enough to feed twenty. "God, I've missed your food."

Morris laughed. "We Texans know how to feed people."

Jake took my dinner plate and started piling baked chicken, barbecued tofu, and a spoonful of every side.

"You haven't lived in Texas in twenty years," Eliza teased. While Jake looked like his late mom, Eliza took after Magnolia with red hair, blue eyes, and an attitude to match.

"They kicked your mom out when they found out she liked tofu!" he teased. Magnolia was a vegetarian, a trait not shared by anyone else in her family.

I sucked my lips in so I didn't laugh out loud. When Jake set the plate down in front of me, I pounced, despite still being full from lunch. The Robinson family's cooking made the body ravenous.

"I'm glad you got kicked out of Texas," I said through a

mouthful of food. "This is the only home cooking I get!"

"You're welcome anytime, dear!" Magnolia said, coming through the back door with the uncorked bottle of wine and a tray of glasses. She poured a large glass for herself then sat down in her chair, smelling the red and swirling it around the glass.

"You gonna share?" Jake asked.

"Eventually."

I laughed, realizing how much I had missed being here. I was still recovering from surgery the last time, and the pain killers had made me pretty unforgiving. A bouquet of flowers and an apology card had soothed the sting I'd left behind, but this was the first time I had the guts to face everyone again.

I set my fork down and cleared my throat. "I'm sorry, about—"

My partner reached over and squeezed my knee. "It's forgotten."

Magnolia set down her wine, grabbed the bottle, and poured some into a glass, then handed it to me. "Families fight. It's the showing up when it counts that matters."

I accepted the glass and toasted her. "Thanks." I took a sip, savoring the deep flavor. I wasn't a dry red person, but I made an exception for this wine. My phone vibrated and I eased it out of my pocket.

Carma: *But are we totally sure Harvest Cafe is the right option?*

Me: *It's the best so far*

Carma: **grimace emoji**

Carma: The key phrase there is "so far"

Carma: What if we're missing an option? Let's try a new place

Carma: You free?

I pressed my lips together, trying not to laugh.

Me: Normally I'd be in. But got plans w/ family tonight

Carma: OMG I'm so sorry!

Carma: Will divert panic attack until later

Carma: *winky face*

Eyes on me, Magnolia took another sip then said, "So, Mina. What do you think about your mom and Isaac? Make you want to find your own partner?"

I choked on my wine. Jake, wonderful friend that he was, hit my back. While laughing uncontrollably.

Gasping for a breath, I set the glass down and dabbed at my eyes with a napkin. "What?" I wheezed.

She leveled me with a look. "I want more babies to spoil before I hit sixty. Eliza's already done her job, even if it was out of wedlock."

I rolled my eyes. "Her fiancé died. I think Jesus will forgive her."

Eliza blew me a kiss.

Taking another sip of wine, Magnolia paused for dramatic effect. "Now it's up to one of you. You mean to tell me when you're on missions you don't meet *anyone*? I find that hard to believe."

This was the problem with Magnolia adopting me as one of her own. I got the grandchildren lecture whenever an attractive person walked within ten feet of me. My cheeks heated, and I shoved a forkful of salad into my mouth. I wasn't even sure I wanted kids.

Jake elbowed me, pissed I had the idea first. "Magnolia, most of the people we meet are marks. We'd be fired. And, you know, they're criminals we're trying to put away."

She shrugged. "It's just a little roadblock. When I met your dad, he was engaged."

Her confession was a record scratch. I dropped my fork onto my plate. "Wait, what?" I asked through a mouthful of food. "I don't know this story."

Jake gaped. "Neither do I, apparently!"

Eliza's mouth hung open. "Mom, what the hell? Engaged?!"

Magnolia waved her hand in the air. "Y'all are so dramatic. They hadn't set a date yet. Calm down."

"I can't calm down, I found out my straight-and-narrow mom was a homewrecker." Eliza wheezed, struggling not to laugh.

Magnolia crossed her legs, leaned back in her chair, and sipped her wine. "Morris had proposed to the mayor's daughter before we started dating. She was so dense she didn't know the difference between lima beans and cannellini beans, and I wasn't going to let such a good man with such an adorable son get away from me. So, I tempted him over with my chili and he never left."

Eliza let out a low whistle. "Already wing-manning your dad at four. Nice."

I leaned over to Jake. "Honestly, I don't think I know the difference between lima and cannellini beans either."

He laughed through his nose and elbowed me. "No one expects you to. Your idea of cooking is a number five at Coney."

His stepmom nodded. "You're forgiven though, because you can literally take out a vampire with a chopstick."

I glared at my partner. "You told her."

He held his hands up. "She has spies everywhere. She doesn't need me to tell her anything."

"So dramatic," Magnolia said, shaking her head. "I called Jim."

My head snapped to her. "Wait. You called my dad?" It was no secret that Magnolia Robinson and Jim Summers did *not* get along.

"I wanted to see how he took the news about your mom."

"Wow," I whispered. "Cold-blooded." Seeing as my dad had yet to talk to me about Mom's pending nuptials, I figured I had my answer as to how that call went.

Eliza rolled her eyes. "That's not why she called. Well, not entirely. We have a bit of a surprise."

"Daisy!" Magnolia called to her granddaughter. "Can you come here a moment?"

Daisy was a blur of polka dots as she hopped over to Magnolia's side, her ponytail swinging.

"Show Aunt Mina your trick with the bread rolls," Magnolia encouraged.

Daisy shook her head. "Mom said I wasn't allowed to show anyone but you and Grandpa and Uncle Jake."

Eliza scrunched her nose. "Baby, you can show Aunt Mina, too, okay?"

She nodded. "Okie dokie." She grabbed three rolls, then set them down on the table. She hummed for a few moments. The rolls shifted on the surface, then lifted off, hovering about four inches in the air.

My mouth fell open.

Magnolia clapped. "Such a good job, Daisy. Thank you for showing us."

"Okay!" And with childlike grace, she flounced away from the table and back to Eliza.

I ran my hand over my mouth before looking around. "Whoa. Dude. This is huge."

While neither Magnolia nor Morris had supernatural abilities—honestly, I still wasn't fully convinced Magnolia wasn't a witch, even though she denied it—Jake being able to communicate with ghosts like me and Eliza's ability to write letters to the dead and receive answers proved there was supernatural blood in their lineages. For Daisy to have such substantial power at such a young age meant there must have been supernatural blood on her father's side, too.

He nodded. "I still can't wrap my head around it and I've known for three days."

"And you didn't tell me immediately?"

"Had to get the okay from Eliza."

Eliza smiled apologetically. "I remember Ben telling me a story his great-great...whatever grandma was chased out of Boston during the Salem witch trials. Obviously, both of us needed to have the witch gene for Daisy to manifest powers. Of course Mom's still convinced my gift is psychic ability instead, as she refuses to believe anyone else in the family could be a witch and not tell her."

Jake turned to me. "Obviously, Magnolia and Dad are extremely offended that they didn't have the inside scoop," Jake teased.

Magnolia glared at her stepson. "I'm the only reason you guys know anything about anyone in this family. You're welcome."

Jake put his hands up in surrender. "I didn't say it was a bad thing. I was just explaining."

"Mina's been around long enough to know what's up."

I laughed. "You're not wrong. God forbid anyone tries to keep a secret from you, Magnolia."

"Speaking of secrets, you ever going to share why you keep checking your phone?"

Dammit. My hand, which had been reaching into my pocket, stilled. I cleared my throat, trying to figure out how to respond in a way that wouldn't spark more questions. "I'm helping plan a fundraiser as part of my job on our new case. We're debating caterers. Just trying to get it resolved before it turns into an in-person argument tomorrow morning."

Jake gave me side-eye. Magnolia noticed. She gestured between us with her wine glass. "Why is my son giving you his 'you're in so much trouble when Magnolia leaves the table look?'"

"Am not!" he defended.

I laughed. "That's his 'this makes me very uncomfortable because I don't like to talk work with my family' look."

"Not true. I'm just concerned about this entire mission. It's...tricky." He flinched. The word *tricky* was a mistake. I kicked him.

His stepmom folded her arms in front of her. "Tricky, how?"

He turned to face me with an exaggerated head movement. "Are you fielding this or am I?"

"I hate you," I mumbled. I finished my wine before responding. "He's just concerned because one of our marks is very attractive. He has it in his head I don't know how to work with attractive people." My phone buzzed again and I pressed my palm to my pocket, wishing it would translate the message into Morse code. I'd learned Morse code for fun when I was eleven.

"So...who's this attractive mark?" Magnolia asked.

I leaned my head back on my chair. "You did this," I grumbled to Jake.

He ran his hand over his head. "It's confidential."

Magnolia raised an eyebrow. "You know I'm going to find out when I call Jim tomorrow to check in about Daisy's schedule, right?"

I sighed. She was right. "Carma Nicks, daughter of *the* Lucinda Nicks."

Eliza typed the name into her phone before whistling. "The daughter of the eighties exercise icon? Holy shit."

"Language!" Magnolia warned.

Magnolia held out her hand for Eliza's phone. She studied the screen for a moment, then looked directly at me. "I think you're in trouble, dear."

I waved her off. "I have worked with plenty of attractive people before and was perfectly fine."

"First time for everything," Jake muttered.

I pursed my lips. "I never slept with you and we've

worked together for a decade. I think I can control myself."

Jake looked both horrified and offended. "My family does not need to know about my sex life."

"Or lack thereof," Eliza teased.

Morris laughed and rubbed his hand over his bald head, a gesture Jake had picked up. "While I'd love to have you for a legal daughter, you guys don't have that spark." Jake and I looked at each other and made a pukey face.

"It's nice to have some eye candy while I'm working," I admitted.

Magnolia leaned back in her chair and swirled the wine in her glass. "I see." She motioned to Eliza. "And as for your catering problem, Eliza will help. I'll cook, she'll pose as a caterer. More eyes in the field."

"Uh, Mom, I have my own caseload," Eliza defended.

"I'll call Jim."

"Of course you will," she muttered.

"What did you say?"

"Nothing!" She looked between me and her mom. "Yeah, sure, why not? Doesn't matter if I have to check my schedule or talk to my partner or learn any of the event details."

Magnolia ignored the sarcasm. "See? There you go."

Sighing, Eliza pulled out her phone. "Send me the details. I'll make something work."

I sent her the calendar link from my phone, the four missed text alerts staring at me. Taunting me. "Any chance you can do a tasting on Monday, too?"

She narrowed her eyes at her mother. "No, but there's no way I can't say yes to this. Not this close to my birthday."

Magnolia smiled. "You're welcome."

Quickly, I glanced over Carma's texts and sent one back.

Me: *Have the answer. My fam knows someone in the catering biz. Will set up tasting for Monday @ office if ok*

Carma: *You are magic*

My cheeks heated and I quickly stood, picking up my now empty plate to cover my reaction. "It's my turn for dish duty."

Magnolia opened her mouth, but Eliza stood and started helping. "Let's tag team. You can give me more details."

"Thanks."

She followed me into the kitchen where she made a (slightly frantic) call to her partner and I texted my dad to let him know we were pulling Eliza in, then I relayed all the pertinent information of Monday's tasting and the fundraiser.

When she was finished, I gave her a one-armed hug. "I owe you."

She pursed her lips and nodded. "Big time." She tucked her phone away. "Let's get washing so you and Jake can prep me."

Despite the brand-new dishwasher two feet away—which was only to be used during emergencies and large family holidays—we fell into an easy rhythm of scraping, washing, and rinsing the dishes.

"I can feel your anxiety," I said, looking over my shoulder at her. "What's up?"

"Do you ever think about what life would be like if you didn't work for SHAP? Like, what would you have done?"

Eliza asked it casually, but I knew this had something to do with Daisy's powers. By registering her with SHAP, Daisy would be protected by the agency, but it might also shoehorn her into a life she may not want. Smart, good witches were a commodity, and even though she was only eight, I could nearly guarantee she would end up in a job like mine and Eliza's. Eliza's assignments were more in-office and less dangerous, but it was still an exhausting life.

Were Jake, Eliza, and I shoehorned because of our abilities? No. Right? I mean, just because I could talk to ghosts didn't mean I had to become a field agent. I wanted to, especially because Dad supported the idea.

I shrugged, trying to look casual because I knew that's what she needed, even though my mind was spinning. "Honestly, I haven't ever thought about *not* being at SHAP. It's always been my dream, even as a kid."

She smiled. "I just don't want to take away any opportunities she may have had if I kept things a secret. I know we got lucky. We love what we do."

I bumped her shoulder with mine. "Yes, you are going to take away some opportunities by registering her. She'll likely never be an accountant or actress. But she'll be protected and taught how to manage her powers." As not only the daughter and niece of an agent, but as a personal family friend, Dad would make sure the best agent available would guide and protect Daisy and her family.

"I mean, she hates math," she joked. "So maybe that's a good thing." She looked down at her feet.

"If Daisy only saw ghosts or something, I'd say to wait. But to be eight and telekinetic? She's gonna need the training, and you're going to need the help and protection."

Eliza sighed and tucked her hair behind her ears. "I know you're right."

"You'll also be giving her greater opportunities than you could ever imagine," I added. "She could be the next Territory Director. Of course, she could run away, travel with the Renaissance Festival doing sleight-of-hand shows. I mean, the options to rebel and embarrass you during Christmas dinner are endless."

She laughed. "Thanks." She sucked in a deep breath and let it out slowly. "I know you're right. Parenting sometimes sucks."

"I can imagine being in charge of small humans is about the scariest thing in the world."

"Scarier than helping birth a litter of werewolf pups during a full moon?" Jake asked, walking into the kitchen. He pulled a barstool from the counter to the sink, sat down, then leaned his cane against the cupboard. He picked up a towel and started drying the dishes.

"I didn't have to raise the pups," I defended. "Just had make sure they entered the world without me or the mom dying. Much less scary."

"What about you, Jake? If you didn't work for SHAP, what would you be doing right now?" Eliza asked.

He met my eyes, and I tilted my head slightly, confirming she asked me the same thing. He turned to face his sister, leaning against the counter. "Well, if I didn't work for SHAP, but stayed in Michigan, I'd probably be an engineer."

"Engineers do grow on trees here," Eliza mused.

"If I managed to make it to California however," he added, "I probably would've become Zac Efron."

Eliza and I dissolved into laughter. "With your complete lack of musical talent?" I teased.

"And your inability to memorize lines. Like your fourth-grade play?" Eliza added, a low blow. I had seen that home video and it was *rough*.

"I was nine!" he argued.

"It was three lines!"

I bent double at the waist, laughing too hard to stand up straight. Every time we got ourselves under control, someone would start laughing again. It took twice as long to get the dishes done as it should have, but it was worth it. I couldn't remember the last time I had laughed that hard.

When we finished, Jake opened the drawer where Magnolia hid her chocolate mint candies and gave each of us one. He unwrapped his candy and looked both ways before popping it into his mouth. "Eliza, I know you're freaked. But there's nothing in the world I'd rather do than work at SHAP. And Daisy never needs to go on a mission if she doesn't want to."

"Ha!" Eliza said. "You know she takes after you in the daredevil category."

I put my hands on my hips. "Hey, you know Aunt Mina wouldn't let anything hurt your girl, right? SHAP or no SHAP."

She laughed. "I know. That's why I put up with your bullshit."

Jake leaned against his sister's shoulder in a show of support. "Family. The only people who can insult you and still make it sound like they love you."

Chapter Thirteen

I WAS TRYING to dig into an email Lucinda had received from a member who was gushing about her lupus remission since starting Thinner when my office phone rang. *Dammit.* I wanted to get my hands on this person's file. While reports of members lowering or ceasing some medications, like those for high cholesterol, weren't out of the ordinary, this was something else entirely. A weight loss program couldn't cure an incurable disease.

Not without literally changing science. The only thing powerful enough to do that was supernatural. With a low growl of frustration, I snatched up my desk phone at the last possible moment.

"Good morning, Mina," Carma greeted, her smile clear in her voice. "Is everything ready for the tasting?"

The tension in my shoulders eased. "Yep. Eliza's Eats is on their way. I've already invited a handful of employees not on the program to come sample."

She sighed, content. I ignored the way it warmed my chest. "You are the best thing to walk through those doors."

"Just doing my job."

"Magic. I knew I could count on you."

I pretended to push my hair behind my ear to conceal

my cheeks warming at her compliment. This blushing had to stop. Also, my hair was super short around my ears, so I don't know who I was trying to fool with my bullshit. Maybe I needed to get a long wig, something that would cover my face. Of course, long hair meant people trying to kill me would have something else to grab onto. *Hmmm.*

"See you soon," she promised.

"Yes."

"Bye, Mina."

I hung up the phone and took two deep breaths. Why did a conversation about food throw me off this morning? Maybe cutting back on coffee during a mission was a mistake. I needed to find another cup ASAP.

"You want to talk about it?" Maggie asked.

I startled and swung around in my seat. Oh yes, there was someone else in the office. "Carma was just checking if the tasting was all set."

Maggie nodded. "Smart. I can't remember the last time I ate lunch at lunchtime during the week. So, you two seem to be getting along well."

I shrugged. "I get along with almost everyone." It was my job to get people to trust me and spill their secrets.

She smiled at me. "I know. I'm your boss. And we let Lucinda think she's also your boss." She winked and I laughed.

I nodded. "I know. What you say goes. Is the fundraiser becoming an issue?"

She shook her head. "Quite the opposite. It's nice to see you both so...engaged with planning. But be careful. Lucinda is very...protective about reputation." She held my gaze and I swallowed hard. It didn't take a mind reader to understand what she was saying.

I held her gaze. "I'm a strictly business kind of woman."

She nodded. "Life has a way of surprising us."

In the decades doing this job, I had never felt such a kinship with a civilian during a mission. It was going to suck when I broke this case open if Maggie was caught in the crossfire.

My cell vibrated.

Jake: *Eliza just pulled in. Going out to grab her*

Jake: *Can't believe Carma's putting so much faith in ur taste buds*

Jake: *she know most of ur meals come from a menu?*

Me: **middle finger emoji* I am very skilled in the art of takeout*

The next fifty-two minutes and fifty-six seconds of my life were spent trying to research this member in vain. The database only had her before and after weight, and her name was so common, there were thirty-six within fifty miles. I used my cell to see if any of those thirty-six in the area had a Thinner tag on social media but came up blank.

When Jake texted me everything was ready, I pasted on a smile and turned to Maggie. "It's showtime!"

She forwarded her desk phone to her cell, then practically ran from the office in obvious excitement. I followed at a reasonable pace, stopping at Carma's office. When her assistant saw me, he nodded and gestured to the door next to his desk.

I knocked on the door frame and she looked up and

smiled. We just stared at each other for a few seconds before I remembered why I was standing there. "We're all set up in the conference room."

She stood, closing the laptop on her white desk and standing. The complete opposite of her mother's office, Carma had a vintage-looking desk, a handful of turquoise chairs, and a pastel pink painting of a skull on the wall. It was beautiful, somehow cozy in the minimal decor. "Did you paint that?"

"Yes. Like it?"

"Love it."

There she went, biting her lip again and sending my heart into overtime. How did she keep doing this to me?

"Let's go," she breathed, brushing past me. Her strawberry scent tempting me to follow her to get another whiff. She looked amazing in another flirty dress and sky-high heels, and I couldn't take my eyes off her legs.

Thankfully, my attention was diverted when we entered, and Eliza's studying gaze landed on us. She introduced herself to Carma, and I didn't miss how Eliza's eyes widened when Carma smiled at her. Eliza caught my eyes and mouthed *wow*.

I just nodded in agreement.

Carma waved me over to the seat next to hers as the others wandered—no, more like charged—in. Never stand between coworkers and free food. Carma laughed and shifted, brushing her knee against mine.

When Jake walked in, he greeted Eliza as if she was a stranger, and I bit the inside of my cheeks to keep from laughing. Jake sat down across from me, positioning his gunmetal gray cane so the handle was hanging on the end of the table, the end facing Carma. He was recording this taste test. His eyes held mine for one long moment before he adjusted his fake glasses and smiled. "It's Mina, right? How's your day going?"

"Pretty good for a Monday. Yours?"

He shrugged with perfect nonchalance. "Same."

I turned to Carma. "Carma, have you had the chance to meet Jake? He's in IT. Been down a few times to fix my computer."

Carma turned that devastating smile on Jake who looked shook for a few moments. "I haven't had the pleasure. It's nice to meet you."

"Likewise."

I looked from the meeting room to the attached kitchen, the retractable partition removed to make the space feel more connected. Whenever Carma spoke to me, I could feel Eliza's gaze was hot on the side of my face. In retaliation, I pinched the underside of her arm when she leaned over me to set two serving dishes in the middle of the table.

Carma stood. With the tilt of her head, she commanded the attention of the entire room. "Since no one here—but me—is on the program, you are all free to enjoy the delicious food Eliza's Eats has prepared for us. Let me know your honest opinion. You each have sticky notes and pens next to your plates. Enjoy!"

She placed her hand on my shoulder as if for balance when she sat down. For a moment, the heat of her hand was the only thing I noticed in the entire world. When I blinked back to awareness, Jake was staring at my shoulder.

"So, Jake," Carma asked. "How are you liking Thinner?"

I nearly leapt from the table when a delicate hand squeezed my knee. Holy shit. She was touching my leg. In a room with Jake, Eliza, and Maggie.

Why was it such a turn on? She removed her hand and went back to fiddling with a pen, but my head kept spinning. Sweat pricked the back of my neck. It was a knee touch over my pants. What was wrong with me? I really needed to get new batteries for my vibrator or something.

I shoved a piece of chicken kebab in my mouth, not even tasting it. I chewed over one hundred times to make sure I didn't choke.

"Mina," Jake said, tapping the table to get my attention. "You liking your new job?"

"Um...uh... job? Yes. It's pretty cool." I shifted in my chair, so my leg was resting against Carma's. "How 'bout you?"

He chuckled. "It's cool. Not that I'd say anything differently while eating free food with the VP."

I looked over at Carma, who looked far more composed than I felt. She waved him off. "Listen, I know you're only here for the free food. Speaking of, do you like it?"

I pressed my lips together to keep from laughing at the thought of Jake telling his sister he didn't like her food. He pointedly didn't look at me or Eliza.

"It's great, and I'm picky."

Maggie laughed, leaning into the conversation. "I like you. You aren't afraid to talk straight to the boss lady."

Carma rolled her eyes. "My mom is the boss lady. I'm just her minion." She reached into her pocket for her cell.

"Speak of the devil." She crossed the room and hovered in the corner by the door, talking in a low voice.

Jake leaned across the table and gestured at my plate. "You haven't tried anything."

I glared at him, conveying *I know what it tastes like.*

He raised his eyebrow in response. I picked up my fork, skewered a piece of chicken, and shoved it in my mouth. "Delicious." I paused. "And I like the smoked paprika." I didn't even know what smoked paprika was, but it sounded good.

Jake laughed.

Carma walked back over to her seat. She looked between the three of us. "So, what'd I miss?"

"Food is great," I said. "And we need to book Eliza immediately."

She set her cell phone on the table, clapped her hands, and waited for the rest of the group to settle down. "Hands up if you liked the food?"

Everyone raised their hands. She sat back down and smiled at me, staring directly into my eyes. "Guess we better book Eliza's Eats."

Maggie stood. "Well, I'm off to guard the phones. You know she'll be calling any minute."

Carma laughed. "She's got two more calls to make. You probably have enough time to get a cup of tea and swing by the bathroom."

"You're an angel." She tapped my shoulder. "Take your time finishing up."

Jake gestured at the table. "Want us to take the leftover food down to IT?"

"Yes, please," Carma said. "If any of the Thinner managers find leftovers, they get so pissy. And then I have to deal with their attitudes."

"Thanks for inviting me." He grabbed his cane, twisted a knob at the front that ended recording, and then stood. "Mina, good to see you again." He threw me an indecipherable look, but then joined his IT coworkers as they gathered up the rest of the food and left.

I ran over the entire tasting in my head, making sure I didn't say anything that would imply my attraction to Carma. I hadn't. Right? Why was I freaking out?

The interns, with no more free food, took off running, leaving the table a mess. I jumped up to clean, while Carma motioned for Eliza to sit down. "Let's finalize these details and I'll write you a check right now. I'm happy to get this off my plate."

She pulled out the spiralbound notebook she'd carried with her all weekend. I smiled. "What?"

"You have a computer in your pocket."

"I like how it feels," she defended. "I get a bigger feeling of accomplishment when I finish a written list then I ever have with the computer."

Eliza nodded. "I wish I could still use a paper calendar. I have to sync up with my team, which requires this brick." She pulled out her giant cell. "Let's talk packages."

While they went over details, I studiously avoided making eye contact with Eliza. Without anyone else here as a buffer, I felt exposed. I worked so hard at not looking over at Carma, there was no way it wasn't obvious.

"You do realize I'm just going to call you later, right?"

Eliza murmured as I showed her to the door.

"Maybe I'll block your number just for funsies," I threatened.

"I'll have Magnolia call you."

I shot her a cutting look. She was right though, I'd never block Magnolia. She'd call my dad, then they'd both show up to check on me together and I did *not* want to be on the receiving end of that wellness check. I shuddered just thinking about it. "I hate you just a little bit." She play-hit me with her elbow as she walked by.

After Eliza was gone, it was just Carma and me. Alone. Together. Be careful was probably pretty good advice.

"Eliza's great," Carma said, breaking the silence. "Thanks so much for recommending her."

"You're welcome." I reached across the table for my plate, the last one to clean up, when Carma grabbed my wrist.

"Wait."

My eyes met hers.

"Describe the food to me. Please." She released my hand but didn't look away as I rounded the table and sat down next to her.

I picked up my fork and speared a piece of watermelon from the chargrilled watermelon-pineapple kabob. I swallowed without choking, which was a relief. "Sweet."

"Is that it?"

"Yes?"

"Pretend you're talking to someone who's never had watermelon before. Share the experience."

My entire face heated. I wasn't self-conscious by nature,

but this was pushing a boundary. I wasn't a poet. Still, I couldn't disappoint Carma. For some reason, this was important.

I popped another piece in my mouth and closed my eyes, concentrating. I opened one eye. "I'm not great at this."

"I doubt that." She leaned closer to me. "Try."

I tried to dig deep for descriptions. "Sweet and juicy. Gentle. Refreshing. Muted. Delicate."

Her eyes flicked to my mouth and she licked her lips. My stomach somersaulted. "That was perfect," she whispered.

She closed her eyes and leaned her body closer to mine. The space between us was charged like the moment before a lightning strike. *Strawberries.* "More."

I obliged, swallowing hard and picking a piece of pineapple. "It's vibrant. Dense and sweet but tangy. It's like tasting sunshine."

When I opened my eyes, she was gripping the arm of her chair, her hair falling over her shoulders and brushing my arm. I leaned even closer to her, my forehead resting against hers. "The fruit was soft enough to melt in your mouth, but not soggy." I barely recognized my own voice. "There was cinnamon on the pineapple. It soothed the tang but still made my tongue tingle."

Her lips parted on a sharp intake of breath. I stared at her cherry red mouth. I had never wanted anything more in my life than I wanted to kiss her right now.

"Carma, come to my office, please!"

We jumped out of our seats and leapt apart, sending both chairs spinning. The announcement was like a gun went off. "It's my mom," she said, nearly panicked.

She smoothed down her skirt, blew out a breath, then held out her arms in a silent *everything okay?*

I untangled a piece of her hair then smiled. "You're good."

She opened her mouth as if she wanted to say something else, but the announcement came a second time, and she took off power walking. I quickly cleaned the rest of the table and then stopped by the bathroom. *What was wrong with me? Did I want to lose everything?*

How was this woman so potent? How did she make me forget?

I ran cold water over my wrists trying to slow my pounding heart and cool my heated skin. That had been close. Too close. I needed to finish this case and get away from Carma.

When my cheeks changed back to their normal color, I returned to the office.

"Everything good?" Maggie asked when I walked in.

I nodded, unable to find words. Everything was most definitely not good. If I had any sense right now, I would request a transfer. Whatever had just happened in the conference room was a warning sign. I was absolutely attracted to Carma and we'd nearly crossed a line.

But transferring cases meant either not working with Jake and dealing with an agent who wasn't as skilled or waiting weeks to get back into the field. And my father would certainly deny me the promotion if I couldn't do something as simple as keep my hands off my mark. I was a trained, lethal agent. I would not let some woman in a flirty dress be my downfall.

I checked my cell when I sat down at my computer.

Eliza: *I see why J's worried*
Me: *I'm good*

That may have been the biggest lie I'd ever told.

Chapter Fourteen

As I STRIPPED off my work clothes, the smell of strawberries lingered in the air. I groaned and shoved my outfit deep into my laundry basket. Maybe when I settled into being RD, I'd start dating again. Clearly, I was just lonely and needed to spend some quality naked time with another human.

My promotion would mean less travel, fewer times I'd have to disappear for days or weeks at a time. While this case was practically next door, it was rare I got to sleep in my own bed this much during a mission. Also, I wouldn't have to lie as much, which was exhausting. I had signed my real name on an email today, but thankfully caught it before I hit send.

I rolled my shoulder to loosen it, catching a glimpse of the scars in my closet mirror. I trailed my fingers down the puckered marks, the skin numb. When I was lying in the carcass of my car, with Jake next to me, holding his sweatshirt against my body to try to stop the blood flow, the only thing I was worried about was who was going to clean out my apartment if I didn't make it.

What if it happened today? I would think of strawberries.

I scoffed out loud at myself. I sounded ridiculous, even in my own head. Did I want to have someone in my business all the time? I mean, Sebastian was already, but I never had to check his calendar to see if he had plans. I never needed to tell him when I was going away for the weekend or if I got held up at the office, although I usually did. He worried.

I'd never handled the feeling of being tracked very well. My time was my own. *Ha! Your time hasn't been your own since you were fifteen.*

I frowned at my own inner voice. "Melodramatic much?" I mumbled.

I glanced to the other side of my queen bed, where the duvet cover and pillows were still perfectly smooth from when I had changed the sheets over the weekend. What would it be like to look over and see someone curled up on that side? What if they smiled at me when I walked in the room? Would I like it if they pulled me into their arms after a long day?

This was a ridiculous train of thought. Maybe I was still suffering effects from my head injury. I opened the note app on my phone and put a reminder down to call my doctor if it happened again.

A memory of my mom doing dishes after dinner popped unbidden into my brain. Dad had snuck up behind her and she startled, dropping the pan into the sudsy sink. In retaliation, she scooped up some soap and put it on top of his head. I had run out into the backyard when they started kissing, because seeing your parents kiss was gross. They had been so happy then. Now, Mom was happy again.

Was I happy?

That was a stupid question. Of course I was happy. I shook my head to clear it.

There was no room for attachments in agent life. As much as I loved Jake and his family, he was risking everything by staying so close to them. If something happened to him on a mission, his family would be broken. Worse, if someone wanted to retaliate, they'd have half a dozen options to choose from. It had happened to the previous Territory Director, who had retired after his wife and son were kidnapped.

I wouldn't let that happen to anyone I loved. It was too much responsibility for me to carry. I had enough pressure just trying to be a good agent, one my father could brag to the other directors about. I didn't need more entanglements that would get in the way of my laser focus.

My phone chimed.

Carma: Thank you for today

Carma: I really like not eating food with you

A mixture of excitement and dread filled my stomach. My thumb hovered over the delete button. I needed to walk away. Not respond. Old Mina would throw out some vague reply and ask her leading questions about the investigation.

That was the problem. Old Mina had bailed sometime between trying to crack my skull open on the asphalt and walking through Thinner's front door. It might have been while Jake told me terrible jokes to keep me conscious until the medics arrived. Or maybe it was during the months of physical therapy when I went for days without talking to a living person who wasn't a medical professional.

Almost dying changes people. Sebastian was right.

Because Old Mina wouldn't have ever typed, *I like not*

eating food with you, too. And she definitely wouldn't have hit send. My entire body clenched.

What was I doing? *I'm just texting*, I told myself. *It was only a conversation. She wasn't going to jump out and kiss me.* I was allowed to have friends.

A text message bubble appeared to let me know she was typing something. Then, unexpectedly, she was calling. It had been so long since someone who wasn't Jake called me, I nearly dropped the phone in confusion.

"H-hello?"

"Tell me everything about yourself," Carma said.

I laughed, startled, then sat down on my bed. "Uh, like what?"

"What do you love? Hate? Pineapple on pizza? *Catcher in the Rye?*"

I blinked, trying to remember what I actually liked. "Um… I love hummus? Prefer Toni Morrison to Salinger. I almost exclusively watch serial killer documentaries and *CSI*, but I'll watch *Golden Girls* over either every time. You?"

Carma laughed. "We settled in Michigan because my mom's parents lived here, but we hadn't been back to visit since I was a teen. Root beer from A&W in a chilled mug was my absolute favorite treat as a kid. I love period dramas and all musicals. Tell me more."

I laid back on my bed, pondering how to respond. "I broke my arm when I was fourteen trying to ride my bike down cement stairs, but I told my dad my school's bully pushed me out of the tree and he got sent to boarding school. I regret nothing. My favorite band is Sorry Charlie. I love to be in control, but you wouldn't know it by the state of my kitchen."

"Good to know. Tell me more."

I smirked. "Nope, your turn."

She sighed, pretending to be put out. "I still sleep with a teddy bear. I hate Bruce Springsteen. I once kissed a frog to see if it would turn into a princess. When I told my mom I was a lesbian, she took us to get rainbow manicures. I don't believe you let dirty dishes boss you around."

I shrugged, as if she could see me. "We've all got to relinquish control sometimes. I'm fine with the dishes winning."

She laughed loudly once. "You're a damn liar. You're in complete control at all times."

I gasped. "You're practically a Disney princess. I didn't know you could swear."

This time, her laugh was soft and breathy, and it did something weird to my chest. "That's how you know it was serious. My mom bred a lot of the expletives out of me—a proper lady never swears or some patriarchal bullshit—but sometimes they slip in."

"Oh really? When else do you swear?" I teased. "I saw you slam your elbow into the door yesterday and you didn't make a sound."

"Usually when I come."

I choked on air and dropped the phone. Holy shit, had she just said what I think she said? Scrambling, I picked it back up and held it to my ear. "Carma..." I breathed. I didn't know what else to say. My head was a swirl of imagined images of her screaming out profanity as my hands moved over her.

"Hey, my mom is calling," she sighed. "I've got to take it, or she'll just *keep* calling. Text me later?"

I managed a goodbye before the call ended. I sucked in a deep breath to calm my racing heart. *Usually when I come.* It was like she struck a match and lit a powder keg inside of me.

Sebastian knocked on my door. "Should I be concerned? You arrived home, didn't acknowledge me, and have not quit your room in three quarters of an hour."

Damn house ghost. "Just tired!" *And incredibly turned on.* "I'll be out later."

"But today is true crime evening. Are you indisposed?"

With a growl, I pushed off the bed and grabbed a long T-shirt and shorts from my drawer, pulling them on. "I'm fine." When I opened the door, Sebastian hovered in the hall, arms crossed.

He gave me a once-over. "You're not fine."

I rolled my eyes, trying to appear like my entire body didn't feel like it was on fire. "Just had a long day. How about a Jane Austen movie instead of true crime?"

"I think we should make sure you aren't feverish. Should I ring for a physician?"

I scooted past him, opening the food delivery app on my phone and placing my standard Monday night order. "No biggie if you don't want to watch." I plopped down in the armchair and Sebastian took his place on the couch.

"It's not that I am uninterested. It's that something seems…off."

Ghosts were so dramatic. "I've been off for months."

He laughed, even though it wasn't funny. "I have been

dead for over a hundred and fifty years, Mina, I know more than you think. What happened at work today?"

I shrugged. "I don't know. I'm just...tired."

He studied me, likely correctly guessing it wasn't just a lack of sleep. "You weren't ready to return?"

I picked at the armrest. "Physically, I'm fine. Just sore."

"Not what I was inquiring about."

"I gave up nearly everything to get here. I'm so close."

He nodded in acknowledgement. "You are."

"I want it."

He nodded again.

"But I'm so tired," I whispered. *Of the lies. Of constantly looking over my shoulder. Of always being on alert.*

"Of being alone?"

"I'm not alone. Not really."

He gave me a sad smile. "Mina, I adore you. But you have the emotional availability of wallpaper and that comes with consequences."

"Less baggage."

"Less of a life. You have plenty of time to be a ghost when you die. Don't waste the years that matter."

"Getting attached will get me killed. Or worse, them."

He crossed his arms as my phone vibrated with Carma's text tone. "But aren't you already attached?"

I didn't respond. Just stared at the back of my phone, refusing to pick it up and read the text. "No. I can't be."

"You shouldn't be, but that doesn't mean you're not." He ran a hand through his hair, one of his living gestures he still used when he was frustrated. "I would give every moment of my afterlife to go back and do it right. Find someone I loved and just exist with them for a little while."

"Reggie would be devastated."

"Reggie would say the same thing." My phone buzzed again. Sebastian sighed. "You're going to watch Austen, aren't you?"

I didn't respond. I didn't need to.

"Well. As much as I love calling out historical inaccuracies, I think I'm going to let you enjoy this on your own. Reggie and I will go haunt the cemetery or something." He put his top hat on his head. "Be careful, love. Roses may be beautiful, but they still have thorns."

As soon as he disappeared, I grabbed my phone and read the texts.

Carma: *I'm sorry*

Carma: *So, what are you up to tonight?*

I flipped on my streaming station. Might as well rent *Emma*. Period pieces weren't really my thing, but I knew it would make Carma smile.

Me: *watching the new Emma*

Me: *I already hate her*

Carma: *yes!!! And you're supposed to. That's the beauty of Emma*

Carma: *this movie is exactly my aesthetic*

Me: *Well, maybe if you added some beheadings or skulls*

Carma: *True*

Me: *well was not expecting to see Mr. Knightley's ass*

Carma: *figured I'd surprise you*

Me: *thanks*

Me: *Emma's side butt! This movie is exactly why I'm bi*

I held my breath. I don't know why that felt like coming out all over again. When I came out to my dad at sixteen, he just nodded and then handed me half his newspaper, like he had done every day. My mom had smiled and told me about dental dams.

I still remembered a guy who sat next to me in a bar a decade ago, who had bought me a drink, only to lecture me that bi people didn't really exist. Also couldn't forget how the men I worked with joked about ménages in low tones during meetings, when I couldn't break their femurs without getting caught. Thankfully, Jake usually took care of those situations by slashing tires. He really was the best friend.

Sucking in a breath and blowing it out, I started a new text. I was proud of who I was, but it was still nerve wracking to show myself to someone new.

Me: *Do you have a problem with me being bi?*

I cringed as I hit send. That wasn't exactly what I wanted to ask. Was it? Why would I care if one of my marks had a problem with my sexuality?

My heart raced as her text bubble appeared. *Come on...come on...*

Carma: *Why would I have a problem with it?*

Carma: *You choose a person, not a side. Do you have a problem with me being a lesbian?*

I smiled. Fair point.

Me: *Nope. In fact, I'm glad you dig women*

Carma: *Is that so?*

Carma: *Any particular reason?*

Me: **shrugging emoji* Not really*

Me: *Just thinking about you swearing*

I set my phone down on the coffee table, turning my attention back to the movie. I couldn't shake the feeling I was playing with fire, but it felt so good to be this close to the flame.

Chapter Fifteen

"I AM IMPRESSED you're eating something that did not come in a box with a toy inside," Sebastian said, appearing in the opposite seat at my small kitchen table.

I took another forkful of eggs. "Despite what you think I am not completely helpless."

He sang a few lines of "Helpless" from Hamilton.

"Been watching Disney Plus at Reggie's?"

"Alan loves musicals. Are *you* helpless, Mina?"

I raised my eyebrow. "I believe I just told you I wasn't."

He rolled his eyes. "I was trying to be charming and clever while asking if you had a new crush. Since the song is about—you know what, I'm not explaining this again."

"She should've just throat punched him and walked away. Saved me the second half of the musical."

He pinched the bridge of his nose. "That's not how love works."

I shrugged. "Thanks for the warning."

He sighed, even though he didn't need to breathe, and looked out the window for a long moment. It was the time of year when we had more blue sky than gray, and the leaves on the trees danced on the breeze. It was also so humid it'd be hard to breathe until the sun went down. "So, festival tonight?"

The Applechester Founders Festival always took place mid-July and was basically a cross between an art and Renaissance fair. Costumes, shows, booths, and an absolutely atrocious reenactment of the town's founding.

I nodded. "You and Reggie coming with?"

"Wouldn't miss it. Jake?"

I scrunched my nose. "No, he's going with his family tomorrow night. He's 'powering down' tonight."

"Sounds marvelous."

"What on earth do you have to power down about? You're already dead. You don't have a sympathetic nervous system."

He gave me a penetrating stare. "Living with a woman is a vastly different experience than I anticipated."

I finished my breakfast, then walked to the kitchen to drop my dish into the sink. "This is what you get for being a rake before you died. I'm your retribution."

He made the sign of the cross. "I knew I should've gone to church."

"Would they've let you in?"

"Probably not without a rather large donation."

I leaned against the doorway. "What's on your schedule today?"

"Extra patrol with the vampire outbreak and the demon threats." He stretched and yawned. I reached out and put my finger in his mouth. He just closed it around me and crossed his arms. "You are not charming."

"I am a treasure. You adore me."

He just shook his head. "Go away. I'm exhausted from suffering your presence."

"I'll miss you, too."

As I climbed in my truck, a memory of sitting between my parents on wooden benches watching one of the festival shows crept up on me. The Founders Festival was my mom's favorite. She'd dress up like a wolf, which always annoyed my father, and we'd gorge on food truck snacks until we complained about stomachaches. Once Mom left, Dad took me a few times, but it had lost its magic.

It wasn't until I let Jake drag me a few years ago that I learned to like it from a nostalgic point of view. I would always remember those carefree festival nights with my parents when I was just a kid who wasn't afraid of anything and loved the idea that the town was founded by a werewolf.

Knowing I'd regret the decision, but still hopeful enough to try, I called my dad. As expected, he picked up by the second ring and announced himself by his last name.

"Hey, Dad, it's me." Like he didn't have caller ID.

"Yep."

"Tonight is the start of the Founders Festival..."

He grunted.

"And I was wondering if maybe you wanted to go with me?"

Silence.

Honestly, I wasn't sure what I had expected. "I was just thinking about...going as a family." Why was this so difficult?

"Mina..." He didn't say no out loud, but I could hear it in his long pause.

"Was just an idea. Maybe next year?" I knew he wouldn't come then, either.

It was like the only way he knew how to get over Mom was to just carve her out of his life and physically remove himself from any and all memories of her. Sometimes I wasn't sure why I still lived here, except for the close proximity to work. There was something about being in the place you grew up. New generations of teenagers might sit out on the corner of the ice cream shop with pink hair instead of perms, and miniskirts instead of skorts, but it was still the place where Mom took me after dance class for a scoop of chocolate.

"Don't worry about it," I told him. "Just figured I'd invite you along. I think I may go for a few hours. Spend ten dollars trying to win a two-dollar stuffed animal."

It almost sounded like he chuckled, but that couldn't be it. That would mean we were having an actual conversation. "Dressing up?"

My mouth fell open. He'd just asked me a non-work-related question. "Uh…hm. I may wear wolf ears?" I wasn't really a costume type of person anymore, but it felt wrong to say no to his question.

"Good. Enjoy." He hung up.

I just sat there and shook my head. Looked like I was going to need to find the wolf ears Jake bought me many years ago.

IT WAS A well-known fact work always moved at a glacial pace when one was looking forward to doing something afterward. I swear eleven am dragged on for four hours. I opted to walk down to the Coney Island at the end of the block to grab lunch despite the humidity, just for a change of pace. I didn't often take lunch away from my desk, afraid I would miss something important—or that Maggie's workload would become sentient and swallow her whole—but today I made the exception. Mostly because I was going a little stir crazy.

I was halfway through the best grilled chicken salad I'd had in ages, while looking at the performance schedule for tonight, when someone slid into the booth opposite me. My head snapped up to find Carma smiling at me. How was she so good at being silent?

I set my phone down on the table and smiled. "Hey." My chest warmed thinking about all the texts we had sent back and forth this week. It was one thing when we saw each other in the halls or going in and out of offices. When we were there, I could excuse our contact as "getting to know her so I could dig deeper" and "it's all for the case."

But here, with her sitting across from me on a random Friday? It felt like someone was holding up a mirror and reflecting back everything I ever said to her.

"Up for some company?"

I nodded. "What're you doing here?" I flinched. That sounded a tad accusatory. "Not that I'm not happy to see you," I rushed out.

She just smiled, sending a shock wave through me. God, how'd she do that? She tapped the portfolio on the table in front of her. "Trying to get some Thinner items on the menu. We want our members to be able to eat when they go out with their friends and family."

"That's a great idea."

"Thanks. Rare to see you outside of the office. Did we make your chains too loose?"

I laughed. "Maggie left the key too close to my desk. Snuck out when she was in the bathroom."

Carma tapped the side of her head. "Sneaky, sneaky. Well, your secret's safe with me." She nodded at my phone. "Did I interrupt something?"

I shook my head. "Nah. Just checking out the Applechester Founders Festival schedule for tonight."

She rested her head in her hand. "Ah, yes. My besties informed me they were taking me."

I popped a piece of chicken into my mouth and chewed before I answered. "You ever been?"

"Nope."

"It's wild. Be prepared to realize how weird this place actually is."

She tapped her mouth with a perfectly manicured nail that matched her pink lipstick. I couldn't look away. "Will I see you there?"

"Hmm?" I shook my head and blinked, refocusing on her face. "Uh, I'm going with my roommate later, so maybe?" *Roommate, Mina? How are you going to explain a ghost?*

"Well then. Maybe I'll see you there."

I couldn't tell if it was a promise or a warning, but my stomach did a somersault all the same.

Chapter Sixteen

B Y THE TIME I got home from work, the landscaping in front of our apartment building had been draped with twinkle lights, likely by the ghosts. They lived for the festival, figuratively speaking. A wooden silhouette of a woman slow dancing with a wolf stood on the lawn.

There were children running around in wolf costumes and glittery fairy wings, playing with fake swords and taking pictures. As with any supernatural festival theme, it had evolved into a summer Halloween, with festivalgoers wearing everything from superhero and princess costumes to wolf pelts and historically accurate fashion from 1819, the year Applechester was first established as a township.

When I'd walked into my apartment, I found Sebastian comforting a crying Reggie. With a sigh, I set my bag down. "What's wrong, buddy?"

"I'm going to my first Founders Fest, and this is what I have to wear!" He stood, gesturing to his dark denim jeans, white T-shirt, and cardigan.

"You look like a model for an LL Bean catalog. What's the problem?"

"¡Dios mío, that's the problem, Mina! I'm stuck in these clothes for all eternity, or until I can figure out how to change them! At least Sebastian is wearing clothes from the right era!"

I glanced at Sebastian who was trying to keep a straight face. "I'm not historically accurate by at least half a century."

"It's better than a sweater and jeans in *July*!" he shot back.

Sebastian nodded. "True."

I walked to the linen closet and pulled out an old white top sheet. "I'm willing to sacrifice this sheet if you want to go as a ghost." Reggie just stared at me. "I'll cut out two eye holes and everything. You can scare some of the humans if you can keep it on you long enough."

I tossed the sheet over Reggie's head and Sebastian laughed. The sheet floated over Reggie's body for a moment before sinking to the floor. He muttered something in Spanish that sounded like "Uy tan fastidioso."

"Love you, too." I winked at him. "One day you'll be able to touch and move things for longer. I'm told it takes a while. Unless you're Sebastian, who's just lazy."

He shrugged. "I'm dead. Why do more work than I have to?"

Reggie just shook his head. "I need new friends."

"The only people who'll see you are the supernatural ones, most of whom can't dress up either. You get to be special that way?" I mean it wasn't much, but I was trying.

"Doesn't count. But I know a way you can make it up to me."

I flinched, knowing where this was headed. "You're going to make me dress up, aren't you?"

He smiled, and for the first time in my life, I was actually afraid of a ghost. "Si."

"Dammit."

"YOU OWE ME *so* hard," I whispered to Reggie as the three of us walked into the festival.

"You shouldn't have things in your closet you don't feel comfortable wearing," he shot back.

"I wear it to sleep in!" I tried to tug my gray T-shirt dress lower than, say, my ass.

"You have shorts on. Stop being a prude."

"I am NOT a prude! I just like wearing clothes in public." I was definitely a jeans or long skirt kind of girl. I only had the tiny shorts because of an undercover mission at a bar a few years back. I had forgotten they were buried in the deep recesses of my closet until Reggie and Sebastian had unearthed them. Apparently, my gray shirt, tiny pair of shorts, and wolf ears constituted a costume to Reggie. Well, at least he'd stopped crying.

"Mina," Sebastian said, giving me a once-over. "Stop fidgeting. You're gorgeous. Your legs should be on display at the Tower of London."

I stopped, looked over at him, and burst out laughing. "You're ridiculous."

He tipped his top hat at me.

"¡Hola Reggie! Hey Mina, Seb."

We looked over to see Reggie's brother, Alan, approaching. He wore a flannel shirt and jeans despite the heat, and Reggie looked positively aghast. "I told you to dress up! I left an outfit on your bed!"

Alan shrugged one shoulder. "This is more comfortable."

Reggie spoke in rapid fire Spanish mixed with English, something about how family is supposed to be the most important, and how could Alan just ignore Reggie's wishes since this was the first year Reggie couldn't dress up?

Alan just smiled and crossed his arms, taking it all in stride. Finally, Alan said, "It's my body, Reggie. I'll dress it how I want."

Reggie sighed but acquiesced. "You want to hang for a bit?"

Alan pointed toward the entrance with his thumb. "Lola's meeting me at the gate. Want to join me?"

"I'll wait until she's out of her exorcism stage."

"I promise, I'm telling her our best stories. She'll come around," Alan said, turning away from us. "Have fun tonight!"

"I can't believe my own sobrina wants to exorcise me," Reggie grumbled.

"I can't believe I haven't tried," I teased back.

He rolled his eyes. "Come on, let's go look at stuff you'll never buy."

We walked through the art stalls, pausing to admire paintings and bespoke furniture. Sebastian had not-so-subtly tried to convince me to buy at least four pieces, all of which were several hundred dollars. While I was a huge supporter of paying artists for their work, I would not pay four hundred for a coffee table and then feel good about putting my feet on it. Which, come to think of it, was probably his goal.

A group of ghosts from our building appeared in front of

the vintage photo stand, where people could dress up as wolves or vaguely historical figures and overpay for sepia-colored social media pics. They were hooting and laughing, calling out how historically inaccurate some costumes were, or daring each other to run in and out of frame to see if they showed up on camera. Spoiler alert: they would just look like a lens flash.

I turned to Sebastian and Reggie. "You're about to ditch me before we make it to the haunted walk, aren't you?" It was more like a corny, high school production walk.

"We don't do haunted walks," Reggie said as Sebastian fixed his hair. "They're scary"

"You're ghosts!"

"Yes, but we're not the scary kind," Sebastian added, before gripping Reggie's shoulders. "You don't look a day over dead. Go get your man." He spun him around and pushed him toward the group.

Reggie gave us the briefest wave and took off, sidling up to a man with shoulder length hair and a tight band T-shirt. The man smiled and leaned close to Reggie as they greeted each other. I couldn't help but smile.

"Aw, Reggie's got a ghost crush," I mused.

Sebastian smiled. "He deserves to be happy, and Clint is a pretty cool dude."

I nodded. "Clint has always been cool to me." He wasn't hard on the eyes, especially when he bit his lip and smiled, which he was definitely doing right now. I could practically see Reggie melt.

"You gonna go over there and flirt with a pretty girl? Or boy?"

He gave me a side eye. "I'm perfectly content cohabitating with a beautiful woman. I don't desire any other complications."

"You'll never get to see my tits."

He laughed. "Pity."

"I'm perfectly content, also."

"Hmmm."

As if on cue, someone called my name. I looked up to find Carma walking toward me, dressed as the sexiest wolf I had ever seen. She had on a thin long sleeve shirt, tight dark gray leggings, and a hat with wolf ears. I could only stare as she got closer, her bright red lips burning into my brain.

"Ah. I see why Jake is worried," Sebastian said under his breath.

I couldn't form a response. I just...

And Carma...

"Good evening." He disappeared, a strategic move. If he ever needed to be tapped in for this mission, it'd be better if he wasn't connected with me.

Carma walked up to me and threw her arms around my shoulders in a quick hug, as if we were lifelong friends. My entire body clenched at her unexpected touch. Seeing coworkers outside of the confines of a workday always made people more casual, well people other than me, and I always found it weird.

I didn't find it weird now, as I breathed her in and closed my arms around her waist for a brief moment before stepping back and clearing my throat. "Carma, hey! You look..." *Ugh, what were words?* "Incredible."

She reached up and touched my ears, then smiled. "So

do you." She stepped back and laughed awkwardly, then looked around. "Who was that guy you were talking to? He had an amazing costume."

I sucked in a breath. Carma could see ghosts? Well, that was pertinent. It meant she had supernatural genes. I just didn't know if this was a newfound ability or something she had been born with, and I couldn't very well ask her outright.

I forced myself to relax, look over at where Sebastian had been standing, then wave away her question. "My roommate, who's big into theater. He must've seen something shiny. Or hot."

She laughed. "So, you here by yourself?"

I scrunched my nose. "Looks like I am now. Both my friends took off."

"Mine are running late." She checked her cell. "Ah, later, even."

"So, shall we...?" Why was I so awkward?

"Yes. Please."

We moved toward the "haunted walk," which was really a nearby bike trail draped with twinkle lights and a dozen Applechester community theater actors miming scenes from the town's origin story. I had no idea why it was called a haunted walk. The only thing scary about it was the bad acting. And the garbage bags fashioned to be poor facsimiles of ghosts.

As we stood in line, Carma and I were nearly shoulder to shoulder, so close I could reach out and catch her hand with mine. Which I wouldn't, because if she was here, I was on duty.

Except when her pinky hooked around mine, every thought left my head. Warmth spread up my arm and through my chest. My stomach dropped. I couldn't take a full breath.

We were holding hands.

We couldn't be.

Shouldn't be.

Move your hand, Mina. Ignoring the logic center of my brain, my fingers threaded through hers, our palms pressing together. I swore there was a lightning charge in the infinitesimal space between.

This was exactly the opposite of everything I should be doing, but I couldn't bring myself to let go. Not yet. In a minute.

I nodded toward the entrance. "Are you ready for a history lesson?"

"Absolutely. As long as you're my teacher."

I laughed as we fell in behind a group of high school kids giggling about something on their phones. "Oh, I'd be one hundred percent in trouble if I was a teacher and you were my student."

"I'd never miss a class."

I squeezed her hand and smiled. "This isn't as good as the reenactment, but it's definitely a solid pre-game."

Her eyes widened as she mouthed the word *reenactment.*

I smirked. "This festival is a wild ride." She squealed and tugged on my hand. God, she was adorable.

The trees still had all their leaves, and it wasn't fully dark yet, but everyone just rolled with the campiness of the event. Even with all the people around, there was a calmness in being separated from the main crowd. Carma gasped and laughed at every turn, from the first display of a woman meeting a "scary werewolf" to the last one of them dancing under a full moon next to a sign that read "Welcome to Applechester."

"So, a werewolf founded Applechester?" she asked, staring at the dancing wolf-human couple.

"If you believe in that sort of thing, yeah."

Her gaze shifted to mine. "Do you?"

I didn't look away when I answered. "Not sure if one really founded the town, but I do believe in a lot of things."

"Including werewolves?"

I nodded once. She looked down at our hands, then pulled me off the trail and deeper into the woods. "Hey, watch for poison ivy. It'll jump out at you."

She rounded the trunk of a large tree, did a quick look at the ground, then pushed me against the bark. We weren't completely invisible to passersby, but we were pretty well hidden. An addictive mix of euphoria and hopefulness filled my chest. The kind of feeling I used to get the last night of summer camp, or when I had graduated high school and thought anything was possible, or the moment just before I closed a big case. I had always associated it with an *action*, not a *person*. My subconscious tried to wave a red flag at me, but I staunchly ignored her.

Carma reached up and traced my lip with her fingertips. "It feels like I've known you for years." Her voice was barely above a whisper.

Me, too. Every thought that wasn't kissing her vanished from my head. She cradled my face in her palm, and I pushed my cheek against her smooth skin. I felt…cherished.

"What would you do if I told you I was a werewolf? Would you still let me kiss you?"

I blinked hard, trying to refocus. "What?" I tried to piece together what she was saying. She looked momentarily annoyed. "I'm sorry, it's hard to concentrate when you're touching me."

"I mean, same." She stepped closer to me. "If I was a werewolf, would you still let me kiss you?"

Werewolf, werewolf, werewolf.

"Mina." The distress in her voice yanked me from my whirling thoughts. "You didn't answer."

I shook my head slightly to clear it, and somehow just jostled my brain-to-mouth filter loose. It was the only reasonable explanation for saying, "You're asking me something really important, but all I can think about is how you smell like strawberries and the way you bite your lip and how being around you actually makes me happy, and I can't remember the last time I was happy. I can't risk getting involved with someone I work with, but I swear to God, if I don't kiss you right now, I will die."

Her hands moved across my shoulders, resting against the back of my neck. "Then kiss me."

I couldn't kiss her. I couldn't ever go back once I crossed this line. I imagined pushing her away and walking home, going on with my life as if this moment never existed. Every cell in my body rebelled at the thought, my stomach twisting with regret. I shook my head, my eyes stinging. If I kissed her, I could lose everything. But if I didn't kiss her, I knew I'd regret it for the rest of my life.

I licked my lips then moved my head up, my top lip brushing hers. I hovered there, waiting for my common sense to kick in. Waiting for Jake or Sebastian or even Reggie to come to my rescue. Waiting for lightning to strike me dead so I wouldn't have to make this choice.

Carma's fingers stroked the back of my neck, and the entire world fell away. My heart moved sideways then fell to ground, through the earth, and there was no more choice. I pressed my lips against hers.

We both sucked in breath through our noses, as if we hadn't been able to breathe until we were connected like this. I pulled back and kissed her again, then a third time, sucking her bottom lip between mine. She was so soft, so warm. It was like lying in a strawberry field on a cloudless day.

Her tongue brushed my top lip, and I opened my mouth, deepening the kiss. As our tongues slid together, she moaned and wrapped her arms tighter around my neck. My hands slid from her hips up to the middle of her back, her breasts pressing into mine. This kiss was better than anything I had imagined. It was better than any kiss I'd ever had.

It was as if I was a sparkler and her kiss was a match. I was going to explode into beautiful fire. I nipped at her bottom lip, and my knees nearly gave out when she returned the favor.

I forgot we were in public and was about to move my mouth to her neck when a woman calling her name broke through the haze. I pulled back, looking around for the offending party. These people clearly didn't know I carried a gun. To be fair, it had silver-tipped wooden bullets that were dipped in holy water, which would just mildly injure a human. My targets tended to be supernatural creatures who had lost control.

Carma blinked a few times, disoriented. "What...?"

"You have a visitor."

Chapter Seventeen

S HE LOOKED AROUND me to spot her friends and giggled. I couldn't help myself; I leaned down and kissed her nose, making her laugh louder.

"You're ridiculous."

"You're beautiful." I reached up and smoothed her hair before stepping back and turning to face the newcomers.

Shampoo Commercial was walking toward us from the trail, holding hands with another woman with dark red curls. (5'6" about seven months pregnant, sundress, sneakers. Penetrating gaze behind glasses. Risk assessment: If I hurt Carma, she'd hunt me down.)

Carma stepped around me and leaned in to kiss both women's cheeks. "Mina, these are my best friends. You know Elena already, and this is Hanelore. This is Mina." She gestured to me, putting her hand on my lower back.

I reached out my hand to shake both of theirs. "Elena, nice to see you again. Hanelore, I adore your hair."

"Thank you, yours too!" Hanelore said. She gave me a once-over. "Please tell me you eat real food and not only shakes. This baby needs something fried." She patted her rounded stomach.

"I absolutely eat real food, although not usually fried."

She let go of Elena's hand, linked her arm through mine, and we started walking back to the path. "Thank god. This girl needs to share some fair food with her new friend." She threw her wife a kiss.

I laughed. "When are you due?"

"Nine weeks. Although it might as well be three years. I'm always uncomfortable."

"You are creating an entire being. Doesn't sound like a super comfortable task."

She laughed. "You'd think I'd learn the first time, but no. We wanted two kids. And since Elena's on the program, she got out of carrying this one." She winked at me.

"Is it weird living with someone who doesn't eat normal meals?"

She shrugged. "Thinner gave Elena her life back. Small price to pay."

When we walked back into the main part of the festival, we stopped in front of a brightly painted truck with cartoon elephants, the smell of fried dough and cinnamon wrapping around us. A shocking juxtaposition to the conversation. "Carma's known Elena since they were kids; their moms both did exercise videos for Fat Burn Videos. Elena got really sick, literally withering away in front of me. After her shitass doctor tried to treat her with antacids for a year, she was rushed into surgery for a blockage and was diagnosed with Crohn's."

She waved a hand in front of her watering eyes. "Sorry! Pregnancy hormones. Carma showed up at the hospital and promised she could help. Claimed the program would help."

I shook my head. "Wild."

"Right?" She laughed without humor. "It was the biggest fight Elena and I ever had. I wanted her to start medically proven treatment immediately, but Elena and Carma begged me to wait three weeks. Eventually, I caved. She went to the first official Thinner retreat while I honestly started thinking about how I'd survive without her."

She glanced back at her wife, and I could feel the love pouring out of her. "When she came back, she was in remission. I thought it was bullshit. I dragged her around the country to five of the best specialists, but they all confirmed she was in full remission. The doctors still can't explain it, except to say 'miracle.'"

"Wow." I didn't even know what to say. *How? How was this program curing diseases?* "Did Carma have any explanation?"

She shook her head. "She says it's something to do with the all-organic shakes, but honestly I don't think she even knows. I asked her for the ingredient list, but she said she doesn't have access to it. Her mom's determined to keep it from being stolen and put on the Internet."

I frowned. Carma was the VP and she didn't even know what she was feeding people? And what did this have to do with Carma's werewolf obsession? "Sure," I managed. "If everyone could make the shakes at home, they wouldn't need Thinner."

"Exactly."

I shot a glance back over my shoulder at Carma and Elena, talking with their heads close together. "Is Elena doing okay now?"

"She's healthy and happy, except for some sun sensitivity. She gets bad migraines if we're in the sun too long. But we can live with that."

Sun sensitivity. The more I put together, the less anything made sense. And what did Carma mean about all that werewolf talk? Was she a werewolf? But werewolves didn't have sun sensitivity, and they definitely didn't own cats. Cats did *not* like large wolves.

She gestured to the food truck. "My treat, since I interrupted your make-out session, which Elena is likely grilling Carma about as we speak."

I groaned and covered my face with my hand, then laughed. "I'm not on the program, but I also hate fried food. Makes me groggy. I would consider pizza or a pretzel."

"Fair." She looked over the menu. "Okay, I've got it." She ordered a churro and a pack of cinnamon almonds. She handed me the nuts. "Protein."

I stared down at them then back up at her. My mouth watered as I envisioned popping one into my mouth. "I haven't had these since I was a kid."

"Well then, what are you waiting for?"

I opened the bag and inhaled, the scent of vanilla and cinnamon casting a magical spell on me. Seemed that was happening frequently tonight. I reached in and selected a single almond, then set it on my tongue.

Fireworks exploded inside my brain. Holy shit. It was like the food version of kissing Carma.

"Don't break Mina!" Carma called.

My eyes met hers as I rolled the nut around my mouth, sucking off the sugar-sweet coating. Her lids lowered and her mouth parted. Good to know I was inside her head, too.

"Tell me you're here for the reenactment," Hanelore said, pulling me back into the real world.

I shifted, trying to stop my body from twisting tighter and tighter at the thought of Carma's mouth. "Carma would never forgive me if she missed it."

"As well she shouldn't. Let's go grab a seat. I'm too old and pregnant to be standing up in this heat."

"Hey, Hanelore, do I get my girl back anytime soon?" Carma called.

My girl. My stupid helium heart loved it.

I walked over to Carma and reached for her hand, then started walking toward the makeshift stage area. "Maybe if you're lucky, you can cop a feel during the play."

She giggled and I smiled. What was this woman doing to me? We found an open bench near the back. As soon as we sat down, Carma grasped my hand with both of hers. She was practically bouncing out of her seat. "I am ridiculously excited. I don't even know why."

"Because this is some seriously top-notch theater," I teased.

"You're ridiculous," Elena told her. "Don't you own a Broadway theater?"

She shook her head. "Mom owns an off-Broadway theater, but so what?"

Her dark hair swished as she shook her head. "You'd think you'd be less enthusiastic about community theater."

Carma made an offended sound. "Listen, community theater is vital to every city. It allows people who wouldn't generally be able to access performances to see them, and that's not including—"

I held up my hands to interrupt. "I one hundred percent agree, however this isn't even really community theater. This is Birdie and Jeff Burberry dressed in scratchy costumes reading from the same script they've used since before I was born."

"Even better."

Elena looked annoyed, but Hanelore leaned over and gave her a kiss, mumbling something I couldn't hear. I fiddled with the bag of nuts in my hand, wanting another taste but refusing to pull my other hand away from Carma. Without decorum, I stuck my mouth into the top of the bag and sucked in two nuts.

Hanelore clapped. "Brilliant."

Carma whispered, "Describe it to me?"

Her words fanned the smoldering under my skin into flames. "I can't do that while we're in public." She licked her lips, and I almost laid her back on the bench right there, not caring about our surroundings. "But mybe later." Her pupils dilated and I fell into the promise in her eyes.

Hanelore elbowed Carma. "When you two stop eye-fucking, the show's starting."

We both spun to face the front as a ladder disguised as a castle turret was wheeled out on stage. Birdie climbed up the ladder and poked her head out of the window, flipping her long blond and braided wig over the side.

"Oh, how lonely I am," Birdie called out in an overly enunciated voice. "Will I, Georgina Finkle, ever find true love?"

"Georgina?" Carma narrowed her eyes. "Is she secretly Rapunzel?"

I shrugged. "Honestly, I learned it was best to not ask questions. They used to do Sleeping Beauty as the opener but switched to Rapunzel a few years back. They tried Elsa one year, but it didn't land since Birdie's rendition of 'Let It Go' was...not good."

She laughed softly and leaned into me, her eyes never leaving the stage as Jeff—playing Hutch Collins—proceeded to woo his intended. "Never have I seen a maiden more beautiful than thee!" Carma snorted then slapped her hand over her mouth. I tipped my head against hers to hide my own reaction.

I had been enchanted by the story when I was young, but either it—or I—had gotten more ridiculous with age. It was almost painful to keep from collapsing into peals of laughter. Carma pinched my upper arm when I snorted at Hutch pulling on a wolf pelt as a cardboard full moon was raised via fishing line.

She leaned forward, riveted, as Georgiana rode on Hutch's back, away from the hunters. She gasped as Georgiana bandaged Hutch's bleeding leg, the result of a gunshot wound. She teared up when they built a temporary shelter from a storm beneath a grove of pine trees (which was actually just three artificial Christmas trees on a dolly).

When the play ended, with Hutch and Georgiana welcoming more displaced couples to their new town, Carma shot to her feet and applauded as if she were front row at a world-renowned musical. I shook my head but stood with her, clapping so hard, my hands tingled. She used her finger to wipe away the remnants of a tear.

I stopped clapping and put my arm around her shoulders. "Hey, you okay?"

She laughed and waved me off. "It's just...she didn't care he was a werewolf. She loved him anyway. They created this amazing new life for themselves."

"Ah," I responded, not sure what else to say. Even if she was really a werewolf, that wasn't the problem. It was whatever was happening at Thinner. Anyway, I was fairly certain Applechester was founded by people who wanted to be near the old train station without living on the tracks. "Hey, babe, it's only a story."

Elena and Hanelore stood, and Elena leaned around me to squeeze Carma's arm. "Our girl always did cry over the weirdest stuff." Carma shot her a dirty look.

Hanelore laughed and groaned, stretching her lower back. "Okay, baby says this is our cue to bail, which I feel way less guilty about with you here, Mina."

"I'll keep her company," I promised.

Hanelore gave me a quick hug. "Hope we see you again, soon." Elena nodded a goodbye and wasn't looking at me like she was planning my demise anymore, which was definitely an improvement.

We sat back down after they left and watched a local band setting up on stage. "So," she said, grabbing my hand again. "I know this isn't ideal, since my mom and Maggie would flip, but I'd love to see you again. After tonight. Not at work, I mean, just like..."

I laughed. "I'm glad you're as awkward as I am." I looked down at our hands, hers still cool even in the humid evening. "And I'd like to see you again. But you're right. This is...complicated."

She used her free hand to trace the backs of my fingers and parts of me I didn't know existed ached to be closer to her. *How could she do this with a simple touch?* "Complicated never stopped me."

I met her gaze, and I knew there was only one thing I could say. "Me neither." I would worry about this tomorrow. Tonight, I wasn't going to think too hard. I didn't care about anything else in this moment except for her touching me.

My meanderings were interrupted when a harp made a melodious chord into a staticky mic. We both turned to face the stage. I opened the schedule on my phone and smiled. I held it out for her to read. "Does that say...Mauled by Fawns?"

"Yes. Yes, it does."

Her face was pure glee.

"You are so weird."

She blew me a kiss.

We settled in as a beautiful woman with a wolf hat started playing a popular pop song on the harp. It was the man in a shirt and tie who started screaming the lyrics as if he were part of Slayer that really took the whole experience to a new level.

"This might be my new favorite thing ever," Carma said. "I need a band T-shirt."

I navigated to their website on my phone and texted her the link. "They have them!"

She fist pumped.

I released her hand and pulled her against my side. "God, you're adorable."

After the assault to our ears—despite how talented Mauled by Fawns was, I was not joining their fan club anytime soon—Carma insisted on spending twenty bucks on a ring toss game to win me a stuffed wolf plush. She dragged me onto the Ferris wheel, which I only agreed to after she dared me. I couldn't say no to a dare.

"If I wanted to die tonight," I grumbled, "I could think of better ways to do it than by going on an *incredibly* tall ride made to literally come apart on a regular basis."

She made up for it by letting me kiss her the entire ride. She had perfect lips. Soft, warm, and eager to touch mine.

We closed down the museum tent, going through every single "artifact" the historical society had on display. Then, we walked slowly back to her car, pausing to look at something on our phones or peer into dark window displays.

"There are like five coffee shops on this street," Carma said.

"We love our coffee here." I chuckled and pulled her into my side. "It's one coffee shop, one café, one candy shop, one donut shop, and one deli."

She tilted her head back. "What's the difference between the coffee shop and the café? Aren't they the same thing?"

I covered her mouth with my hand. "*Shush*! If Monty hears you, he'll blacklist both of us from his café and they have the best coffee."

"Lips are sealed," she muttered against my hand.

As we passed the deli, I tugged her down a small alleyway. "I've got something to show you that I think you'll like."

She made an excited noise and then gripped me tighter.

As we emerged, a large Victorian house loomed across the street. It was one of the grandest homes in Applechester, snuggled between an acre of trees on one side and a park on the other. There was a lantern in every window to celebrate the festival. Carma gasped with delight.

"This is Blackburn House, built in 1860 by the then-mayor, who made his money in silver. They usually have tours on festival weekends, but they haven't in the last two years."

She gripped my arm with both hands. "This is amazing. It's everything I'd want in a bed and breakfast."

"Yeah?"

"Some privacy, enough rooms to accommodate things like weddings and family reunions, but not an overwhelming amount. Near downtown. Great history and looks haunted."

"It is haunted." Or, at least, I knew several ghosts who liked to hang out here.

"Think if I cold-called them, they'd accept an offer?"

I laughed. "It has never been for sale, but you can always try."

"Oh well. I couldn't start a new business while wrapped up with Thinner anyway. It's a beast of a job."

"I believe it."

We started walking again, and she told me more about her plans. Everything was someday, when she's done with Thinner. Did I have any someday dreams? I never thought about what I would do when I was done with SHAP. Figured I'd just die on the job in forty years and call it a day.

After another ten minutes of walking, she gestured to her Mini Cooper. "Well, this is me."

"You have a Muppet car. It's even a Muppet color!"

She play-smacked my arm. "It's green."

I pointed to a tree. "That is green. This is…Manic Panic hair dye green."

She giggled. "Yeah, but I like it. It's easy to find."

I exaggerated shaking my head. "If you're going to get a custom color, why get something so ugly?"

"It's not ugly!" She laughed harder. "Okay, it is, but it was already this color when I got it. I bought it used in LA before we moved here."

I pursed my lips. "California is a weird place."

"You're telling me."

We walked around the driver's side and she leaned against the door, making it clear she wasn't ready to depart. To be honest, neither was I.

"This was the most fun I've had in a long time," I admitted, although I shouldn't have said it. Not because it was the wrong thing to say, but because I *wanted* to say it. Because I meant it.

She skated her hands along my hips and pulled me into her. "Me, too." She searched my face for a long moment before she spoke again. "Can I see you tomorrow?"

I looked away for a moment, trying to find some semblance of balance. Instead, I let myself get swept away by the runaway train. "Absolutely. Dinner?"

She shook her head. "Too long to wait. Lunch?"

"Brunch?" I took off her wolf hat and set it on top of the car, then brushed her hair back, kissing her behind the ear. "Or we can have a late-night snack and breakfast."

Her hands fisted my shirt at my waist, and I skated kisses

down her soft neck to the curve I had been dreaming about. She gasped and arched into me. "God, that sounds good. I can't stop thinking about your legs wrapped around me."

I groaned. My arms went around her waist, and I pulled her tighter into me. My entire body throbbed with the beat of my heart.

"Wait," she whispered, and I immediately released her, stepping back. She grabbed my wrists to keep me close. "I wear my heart on my sleeve and spending the night with you is a big step."

I smiled. "Sorry. I just…got a little carried away."

She ran her fingers through a lock of hair that had fallen into my face. I closed my eyes at the sensation. "It's easy to go a little crazy around you." She sighed and leaned her head back against her car. "I should go." It was more of a whine than a declaration. I felt exactly the same way.

"Sounds like a terrible plan," I teased, but took another step back to give her space. To give *me* space. I wanted to dive into her body and not resurface for air for days. Weeks.

She grabbed me by the shoulders and pulled my mouth to hers, kissing me as if it was the most important thing in the world. I stopped thinking. There was no case, no werewolves, no Thinner, no Applechester, no Earth.

Just us.

Her hands cradled my face as she savored my lips and I relinquished control, every touch of her mouth making the years of emptiness slowly disintegrate. How did she have this effect on me? Why was I helpless in her arms?

I didn't want to know the answer. I just wanted more of her.

I took control of the kiss and shoved my hands into her hair. She purred. *Purred.* I would never forget that sound as long as I lived. Her hands stroked the side of my breasts, and I moaned into her mouth.

She pulled back, panting. "I'm sorry, sorry. I just can't control myself." She laughed, but I didn't.

I couldn't. Not when her lips were swollen and wet. I stole one, two, three more kisses before turning away to catch my breath. "Good night, Carma," I whispered, opening her car door for her. "Text me when you get home. Let me know you made it safe." I needed her to go *right now.*

She grabbed her hat and climbed in. I closed the door gently behind her. After starting her car, she opened her window and ran her pointer finger along my bottom lip. "Good night."

I watched her drive away, my heartbeat shaking my body as it tried to climb out through my ribs. I pressed the palm of my hand to my chest and shushed it. "Oh no."

What had I done?

Chapter Eighteen

I SHOULD'VE BEEN sick with guilt by Monday morning. After spending hours stealing kisses from Carma as we worked on fundraiser stuff, the rest of the weekend was filled with daydreams about what it would be like to take off all her clothes. Add in that I purposely disabled the surveillance I had planted (not that we were getting anything useful anyway), I should be walking into my dad's office with a resignation letter in my hand. Instead, I was walking on air, ready to take on anything the day threw at me.

Jake caught up with me in the parking lot. "Hey, missed you this weekend! Thought we'd catch you at the festival Saturday."

"Yeah, sorry I missed you." I shouldered my bag and started walking. "I went on Friday night, then got caught up with doing fundraiser stuff the rest of the weekend."

I wasn't lying. We—and by we, I mean Carma—had been working on bespoke centerpieces that would be raffled off. I had only been there for moral support. She had also convinced the harpist (and only the harpist) from Mauled by Fawns to provide the music.

My job was nearly done, with the exception of sending out about fifty emails to Lucinda's closest friends, inviting them to come. I just had to confirm the valet, follow up on Lucinda's guest list, and get something "black tie" appropriate to wear on Friday.

Jake nodded and shoved his free hand in his pocket, the other holding his cane. "You gonna tell me what's really going on?"

I laughed too casually. "What are you talking about?"

He watched me for a long moment. "Sebastian said you saw Carma at the festival."

"You're getting gossip from him now?"

"Stopped by on my way home from the festival. You weren't there. He was."

"Carma was at the festival with Elena from the front desk and Elena's wife."

Jake grabbed my arm and led me away from the front doors and around the side of the building. "Mina, what the fuck is going on?" He punctuated each word with a tap on the ground from his cane.

"Nothing!"

"Bullshit. You're completely checked out on this case. I know you're doing three jobs right now, and it sucks, but your reports are barely a few sentences long, you haven't uploaded any photos or video to the servers in over a week, and you stopped answering my texts. You saw a mark outside of work over forty-eight hours ago and I found out about it from an agent not even on this case!"

I stepped back, breaking his hold. I readjusted my bag on my shoulder. "I did answer your texts."

Jake threw his hand up and let it slap against his leg. "One word sentences, like your dad."

I gasped. "Harsh," Then my shoulders slumped. He was right. "Okay, actually there is something I wanted to tell you in person." I looked around to make sure no one was watching, then leaned in to whisper. "I think Carma is a werewolf."

Except I didn't. Not fully. But it would distract him.

Jake's brows raised to the sky. "Now that is interesting." He checked his phone. "The full moon is this weekend. I guess we're going to be able to confirm soon."

I nodded. "Yeah. Also, not sure how this correlates yet, but this company really helps people. Elena, the woman at the front desk, had really bad Crohn's Disease that went into full remission when she got on the program."

He studied my face. "Is this in any report?"

"Would it matter?"

He rubbed his palm on his head, his angry tell. "Mina, of course it matters. I get why you didn't put the werewolf thing in yet, but an autoimmune disease going into full remission is a big deal. How can we paint a picture of what's going on if you don't share this kind of info?"

"What do you think I'm doing right now?"

"Yeah, after I manhandled you around the side of a building! Mina, I need you to get fully on board here, because the more I dig, the more suspicious I get."

I crossed my arms. "What's so suspicious?" Why did I sound defensive?

He pointed a finger at me. "See, that. Right there. You haven't read a single report I've copied you on this week, have you?" He held up his hand. "Don't bother to answer. Rhetorical. I just have one question. Why?"

I kept my face blank but couldn't hold his scrutinizing gaze. "I...don't...know," I admitted, then slumped against the wall. "I don't know." *I didn't want to do this mission anymore.* "I think maybe I wasn't ready to come back to work."

His defenses fell like I knew they would. "Do you want out?"

I shook my head. "No. I'll get my head in the game." I needed to finish this mission and let the chips fall where they may. A sharp spike of anxiety slashed through my chest at the idea of not seeing Carma ever again. *Oh no.*

"Hey. You got this. I'm a text away, yeah?" Jake gripped my shoulder then let his arm fall, tugging me from my weird headspace.

I nodded. "Thanks." Taking a deep breath, I pointed to the front doors. "I gotta get in. But how about Indian food tonight?"

He smiled. "Deal."

Before he could say anything else, I spun on my heel and power walked through the lobby. I clenched and unclenched my fists, taking deep breaths in through my nose. What the hell was going on with me? Was I forming an emotional attachment?

No. I couldn't be. Physical was one thing, but emotional? That would not only be unprofessional and idiotic, but deadly. I was smarter than that. I was one of the top agents at SHAP and never, I mean never, screwed up that bad.

Almost dying changes people, Mina. Sebastian's words marched through my head. Was this what he meant? Did almost dying change me?

"Morning, Mina."

I jumped and gasped, my hand flying to my chest. "Oh, morning, Elena. Have a good rest of the weekend?" Seriously, how had she startled me? She was standing right in front of me.

Maybe I needed a nap. Or more coffee. Or less coffee?

She nodded stiffly. "Yes, and you?"

I couldn't stop the smile, even as my stomach twisted at her obvious dislike of me. "Yeah, I did." After the tell-tale buzz, I grabbed the door and held it open. "Catch you later." I don't know why I cared that she wouldn't be my new bestie. I was used to people finding me abrasive and unpleasant. I'd built a career on it.

Jake caught up with me at the top of the stairs, leaning on his right leg. "Hey, have a good day, okay? Text me what you want for dinner and I'll order."

I gave him a thumbs-up. "Will do." I descended two stairs at a time and practically ran to Carma's office, desperate to get a glimpse of her. My heart sank at her closed door. *Blerg.* Mondays.

Rounding the corner into my own office, I mumbled a greeting to Maggie—who was already on the phone—and slumped into my computer chair. I was exhausted, and it wasn't even nine. I turned on my computer and shifted my mouse, noticing a small piece of paper tucked underneath.

My heart was in my throat as I palmed it then opened it under my desk. *Can't wait to see you -C.* I folded it back up then unfolded it again, tracing her curvy letters, trying to hold on to this feeling.

"Have a good weekend?"

I jumped and banged my knee on my desk at Maggie's question. I shoved the paper into my pocket and spun to face her. "Yeah. Went to a fair on Friday and kept things low key. How about you?"

"Saw the grandbabies. Want to see pictures?"

I scoffed. "Duh. Do you need to ask?" Normally, I didn't give two shits about some stranger's grandkids, but working practically back-to-back with Maggie had bonded us in a surprising way. She was like the aunt I never got to meet. Dad was an only child and Mom's sister had passed away the year I was born.

I was bent over Maggie's cell, looking at a video from her granddaughter's T-ball game when the smell of strawberries surrounded me. Carma's hand rested on my lower back, leaning over my shoulder to see the phone. "Maggie, is this Bella? She's gotten so big!"

My manager laughed. "Tell me about it! Every time I see her, she's practically a foot taller."

They exchanged small talk, but I couldn't concentrate on what they were saying as Carma's hand went to my waistband and dipped in, the pads of her fingers tracing circles on my skin. To an outsider, it probably just looked like we were super interested in Maggie's phone, but I swear I was about to burst into flames.

When Maggie's desk phone rang, she sighed. "Always happens."

Carma cleared her throat. "Mind if I steal your girl here for a few moments? I need her opinion on something super-fast."

"Go. Just bring her back before your mom gets here."

Carma removed her hand, and I finally remembered how to breathe. "I got the door prizes finished Sunday night. Come tell me what you think." She turned and walked out, her skirt skimming her thighs and her round butt before flaring out to showcase her long legs. I nearly groaned out loud. I wanted to taste every inch of skin from her ankles to that sweet spot at the apex of her thighs.

As soon as we were inside her office, she closed the door, pushed me against it, and pressed her lips to mine. I wasted no time in fisting her hair and kissing her back. No soft, closed-mouth kisses. These were desperate, starving movements, the need to feed on each other before we faced a day of platonic smiles and averted glances.

"I can't get enough of you," she whispered when we came up for air.

I kissed the edge of her jaw. "The feeling is definitely mutual."

"I really do need your opinion on the door prizes, but I couldn't wait another second to kiss you."

"They're great. The best I've ever seen." I moved back up to her mouth, making it impossible for her to keep talking.

It took us another five minutes to remember we were at work and not in a position to kiss for hours. She laughed and pulled back again. "No, really, I want your opinion."

I pouted. "Fine."

She walked me through the different prizes, but I didn't care. I could only stare at her swollen lips. "They're all great."

"You didn't even look."

I randomly pointed at an item on her desk. "That is a

silk scarf."

"Lucky guess." She gave me one more peck on the lips and then straightened. "Okay, I need to go finalize things with Eliza. And you need to get back before Maggie comes after me."

I shuddered. "She's scary, yeah?"

She nodded. "You never want to see her mad."

I chuckled and followed her out of the office. When I got back to my desk, Maggie studied me for a moment, but she didn't say anything.

"I need to use the fancy printer down the hall, because god forbid the CEO of the entire company has a decent printer in her office," Maggie muttered. "I'll be right back!"

I waved as she left, opening my emails. As I clicked my mouse, I noticed my EMF reader ring started to glow green. I frowned, looking around the room for the intruder.

"Boo!"

I startled and spun around, finding Reggie sitting on the back end of my U-shaped desk. "What are you doing here?" I asked through clenched teeth.

He kicked his legs through the filing cabinet as if he were on a swing set and shrugged. "I've always wanted to say boo."

"Now you have." I looked around, making sure no one noticed him. "You need to get out of here before someone asks why I have a ghost in my office."

"Just tell them I'm interested in the program."

"You're dead."

"Yeah, but I've got this stubborn belly fat..." he padded his slightly rounded middle.

I pinched the bridge of my nose. "You're going to blow my cover."

"No. That's why Sebastian isn't here, since Carma may have made him at the fair. Speaking of, where is she?"

"AH HA! I knew it." I grabbed my cell.

Me: You sent Reggie to check on me?

Jake: ...no?

Me: He's here

Jake: Ok?

Me: Why?

Jake: Have you asked him?

I tossed my phone down on the desk and crossed my arms. "I don't need to be spied on."

Reggie held his hands. "Calmate, jefe. I'm just here because Sebastian was worried. And when he gets worried, he gets anxious, then I get anxious, and it's not a good look. I've got a date tonight."

I momentarily forgot to be angry. "Cute rocker guy?!"

"Clint. And yes." He looked up. "Incoming."

I spun back around and found Maggie walking back in. She looked up, scanned the room, then stared back down at her stack of papers. "Did I miss anything?"

"I'm going on a date tonight!" Reggie told her. She didn't acknowledge his presence, thankfully.

"Not really. Just me fighting with an annoying caller." I shot Reggie a look.

Reggie gasped and pressed his hand to his chest. "Ouch. Words hurt, Mina."

We all turned to the door when Jake knocked. "Got a ticket about Mina's computer not connecting to the Internet?" He gave me a long look.

"Oh! Yes, thanks for coming so fast." I stood, motioning to my chair.

"So, what's going on here?"

"Just can't seem to connect," I said quickly for Maggie's benefit.

"Stopping by for a visit," Reggie explained. "Want to meet the woman who's got Mina in knots."

I choked on air. Slapping my chest, I nabbed my water bottle and tried to quell the reaction.

"You okay?" Maggie asked.

I gave her a thumbs-up. "I think I'll run to the bathroom while Jake works on this."

She waved me away. I glared at Reggie and motioned with my head for him to follow me. "Thanks, Jake. Be right back."

I marched down the hall and into the small alcove underneath the stairs and pointed for him to move into the corner. "Are you crazy? Carma can see you!" I whisper-shouted. "Which means others probably can too! Why are you really here?"

"We were just worried—"

"Reggie, I swear to god, if you feed me that bullshit again—"

"We saw you on Friday!"

I froze, my face and hands turning ice cold. "What do you mean?"

"We saw you and Carma kissing. Sebastian's been a

wreck all weekend because he's worried about the consequences. That's why you haven't seen him."

How had I not realized I hadn't seen Sebastian since Friday morning? Oh yeah, because I either had my tongue
down Carma's throat or was daydreaming about my tongue
being elsewhere. I pressed my thumb against my forehead,
trying to stop the sudden ache.

"Mina…he knows he should tell Jake if you don't."

I sucked in a deep breath then threw my shoulders back.
"This ends now. I'm going to get a food sample today and
the fundraiser is tomorrow. If we don't solve it by then, I'll
transfer." I put my hand over my heart. "I swear. Just tell
him to give me a few more days."

Reggie nodded. "I'll let Seb know."

I turned to leave, but then paused. "Do I get to hear
about Clint later?"

"In excruciating detail."

When I walked back into the office alone, Jake looked
relieved. "All set here. Shoot me a message if it acts up
again."

WITH THE FUNDRAISER scheduled for tomorrow night, it
was all systems go. In fact, I didn't even get pissy when
Rachel stormed in at the exact time Lucinda drove into the
parking lot.

"Friday is completely sold out," she bragged as the boss
walked in.

Lucinda motioned for me. "Have you heard from any of

my friends? If they don't get their asses moving, I will give away their spots."

I nodded and handed her my running list. "Fifteen yeses, thirteen nos. Waiting on twenty-two more responses."

Lucinda glanced at her watch. "Wait until noon, then call those twenty-two. I need answers today."

I nodded once. "Yes, ma'am."

Her security guard walked back to her office and gestured to the parking lot. "Ms. Lucinda, I need to take the Lexus in for service, and I'll bring your Mercedes back. Do you need anything for the next hour?"

She waved him away. "I'm all set, Phil."

With a nod, he left and locked the side door behind him. I turned to leave when Lucinda swore. "I forgot to have him run to the cafeteria for me."

I paused and turned back to face her. This was my chance. "I'd be happy to run to the cafeteria and get you whatever you want."

She pursed her lips and nodded. "You and Maggie are part of my dream team." She pulled off her Thinner ID clipped onto her waist band and handed it to me. "Chocolate shake." She looked at Rachel. "You want anything?"

Rachel handed me her ID. "Each order requires you to swipe an ID card. Passionfruit."

I nodded. "I'm on it." When I walked out, I held up the cards for Maggie to see. "I'm off to the cafeteria. Can I get you anything while I'm there?"

Her eyes widened. "So soon?"

I shrugged. "Lucinda seems to think I can do anything."

"She's not alone in that thought." She pulled the lanyard

with her ID from around her neck "I don't need anything, so grab whatever for yourself. It won't get you a shake though, I know you're sad you can't try one." She winked at me, and I knew she was making a joke.

I fake laughed and took her card. *Dammit.* "Thanks. I'll be back soon."

As I walked along the edge of the hallway, trying to avoid all the people rushing, I pulled out my phone to text Jake.

> **Me:** *got access to cafeteria. Will try to get sample*
>
> **Jake:** *Great job! how?*
>
> **Me:** *because I'm magic*
>
> **Jake:** *fair*
>
> **Jake:** *keep me posted*

I was high on adrenaline when I swiped Maggie's ID at the double wooden doors and entered the cafeteria. The Holy Grail. I held my breath as I walked in, waiting to hear choirs singing. Or at least a security guard to hassle me.

None of those happened. In fact, I was completely underwhelmed. Linoleum tile, tables with fake wood grain tops, and the standard stainless steel food bar.

Thinner cups were shoved into piles of ice, a glass partition separating them from customers. Three women in suits rushed around me, sliding their ID cards at a reader connected to the register. They each ordered a shake and departed as they came, exchanging no money. From what I understood, the food was free with the annual membership.

Double checking no one was behind me, I moved to the cash register and smiled at the sulky teenager. (5'2", average build, baggy Thinner shirt and khakis, clearly here for the paycheck. Risk assessment: Would kick my ass in a TikTok battle...if people battled on TikTok? Was Twitter still a thing? We couldn't have social media as field agents.)

"Hi, I'm Lucinda's new assistant?" I said like a question. "Maggie's busy so Lucinda asked me to come down and get her and Rachel some shakes."

She didn't even bother to fake smile at me. Clearly, she was just a college-age kid earning minimum wage. "Just swipe each of their cards and I'll give you two shakes." Her monotone voice was actually impressive. I think her and my dad could have a monotone-off.

I pretended to look shy and uncertain. To be fair, I was pretty uncertain. "Lucinda asked me to get her and Rachel two shakes each, since Phil had to leave to take the car to the dealership. Apparently, there was some flat tire issue? She just wanted to be all set for her meetings today."

The teenager shrugged. "Doesn't matter what she wants. She made the rules. One shake per ID card every four hours."

Shit. "Bosses, right? But for real, there's no way you can give me an exception? Because she's in a *mood* today. I don't want to go back there with only one shake when she wants two." Her answer was to pop her gum at me. That tracked.

I honestly thought about just jumping over the counter, grabbing the shakes, and dashing out—no way this kid got paid enough to stop me—but then I would probably get fired and lose my shot at my promotion. "Is your manager in by chance?"

"No, Karen. He's busy at the loading dock."

"My name isn't Karen."

"Could've fooled me," she muttered.

Mina, you cannot punch a teenager in the face just because she's being an asshole. I counted to ten and took a deep breath. *Okay, okay.* I'll just text Jake. Maybe he could copy the ID for me, and I could just come back in four hours.

"Just give me the two shakes. Chocolate and passion-fruit."

> **Me:** any chance U can copy ID card v quickly
>
> **Jake:** how quickly?
>
> **Me:** 5 to 8 minutes?
>
> **Jake:** not these. would need computer from SHAP for security chip. Could do it by tomorrow

I shoved my phone back in my pocket, swiped both IDs, and grabbed the shakes from the cashier. I muttered a thank you and studied the cups. They had a plastic top and a safety seal all the way around, meaning there was no way I could open them undetected. A syringe may have worked, but I didn't have any with me.

I could drop one and "accidentally kick it open," and scoop some up, but I doubted they gave replacements. If I didn't come back with both shakes, Lucinda would see it as a strike against trusting me. I needed her to trust me implicit-ly.

As I walked back to the office, I formed a new plan. I'd drop off the food in my hand, then tell Maggie I was going to run back to get something for myself. Her human ID wouldn't get me a shake, but on the way, I'd either swipe someone's ID or...well that was actually the only plan I had.

Most people wore their badges on clip, making them pretty easy targets. I'd just have to hope Sulky Teenager wasn't there when I returned.

When I walked back into the office, Carma was sitting on the edge of her mother's desk. I hesitated in the doorway. She saw me, then looked down at the floor. My heart beat a little faster as I walked in and distributed the shakes and IDs.

"Carma tells me you two have the fundraiser completely under control," Lucinda said.

Carma jumped off the desk and smoothed her skirt. "As soon as I update her on my morning." She grabbed my arm. "I'm stealing her!"

"How'd things with Eliza's Eats go?" I asked, as we navigated to her office.

"All set and ready to go." She closed the door behind her and smiled. Then, she pulled me into her arms and kissed me.

I allowed myself to indulge for a moment, then pulled away. "When do we start setting up?"

She blinked at me for a moment, trying to reorient into work mode. "Any time after seven tomorrow morning."

"I'll be there are seven on the dot."

"You're amazing." She stepped back and I noticed her purse was sitting on her desk, with her ID attached to it.

It couldn't be this easy. I just had to distract her, grab her ID, run to the cafeteria and get a sample, then return the card before she noticed. Before I could think too hard about it, before I had the chance to feel guilty, I grabbed her arm and pulled her back into me.

I kissed her hard, deepening the kiss the moment she

opened her mouth in surprise. Our teeth clicked together as I moved her toward her desk chair, swiping the ID from her purse and slipping it into my back pocket as we passed.

Guilt tried to nudge its way in, but I shut it down. This was my damn job, and I wasn't going to apologize for it.

"I have a feeling you are the kind of person someone spends their whole life looking for," she breathed into my mouth.

I stilled, the words pouring down my throat and warming me from the inside out. No one had ever said anything like that to me before, and I was embarrassed by the way my breath hitched. I didn't recognize my voice when I asked, "Someone like you?"

She kissed her again. "Yeah. Someone like me."

My entire mind went blank and everything came down to this moment. I pressed my forehead against the side of her head and whispered, "Can I touch you?"

She smiled. "Definitely."

I pushed her down into her chair and ran my fingers under her skirt along the inside of her thigh. She scooted forward to the edge of her chair, opening wider. I stopped breathing.

I needed to do this. I shouldn't need anything but the truth from her, but her words did something to me. Made me want to claim her, taste her, make her swear as she came from my touch.

My heart was pounding so hard, it bruised my rib cage. I moved my hand higher, my fingers brushing against the damp lace of her underwear.

She gasped and gripped the arms of her chair. "It's been

so long," she admitted.

"For me, too."

I kissed her again, sucking her tongue into my mouth then retreated. My fingers circled her most sensitive spot before tracing up and down, her body coming alive beneath my touch. "Just so you know, I got a physical last month, all clear."

She pushed her head against mine, the ends of her hair trailing against the skin of my arm. It may as well have been her tongue. Heat boiled under my skin, and visions of her tangled up in my sheets with her hair spread everywhere flooded my brain. I was halfway to coming from the thought alone.

"Tested...everything's negative." She whimpered. "More, please."

"Anything," I promised, no longer thinking. I pressed my breasts against her arm, needing the contact, as I slid my fingers past the flimsy lace barrier and touched the source of her heat. She was so wet, so hot. I swore under my breath as I teased her folds, pressing against them without giving her what she needed.

She gripped my arm and pulled me against her harder, desperation taking over. My breathy laugh made her purr, and I was done for. "You make me crazy," I whispered against the shell of her ear.

I pushed two fingers inside of her and pressed the heel of my hand against her nub, my name a groan on her lips. The silky heat of her body was blocking out anything and everything else. A bomb could've gone off and I wouldn't have stopped.

She ground against my hand, seeking her pleasure. I curled my fingers, finding that spot she needed the most. She wrapped her fingers around my wrist, anchoring me. "I'm close," she breathed. "Don't stop."

Her words sliced me opened and embedded themselves into my skin. "You're so gorgeous when you're about to come."

She stilled, sucked in a breath, then threw her head back, her body tightening and coming apart around my hand. "Fuuuuuck," she whispered.

I gripped the chair handles to hold myself up. Holy hell, her swearing when she came nearly did me in. "Goddamn amazing," I breathed. I was practically shaking with my own need, but I couldn't have her hands touch me. If she grabbed my ass, she'd find the card. She leaned her body into me as she came down, and I tried not to flinch at the weight on my injured shoulder.

Slowly, reverently, I pulled my fingers out of her and kissed her again.

"What was that for?" she asked, almost shy after the encounter.

"Needed you." I kissed her nose and pulled back.

She gazed up at me, her face completely unguarded and relaxed. My entire body thrummed with how much *everything* this woman made me feel. "I should get back to work. I'm desperate to taste you, but if I do, we'll never leave this office."

She grabbed my hand and sucked my fingers into her mouth. My vision went blurry and for a moment I feared I'd pass out.

"Can I see you tonight?" she rasped.

God, I needed to see her tonight or I'd die. *Fuck*. Plans with Jake. "I can't tonight," I forced out.

She hid it fast, but I caught the disappointment in her eyes. It nearly undid me. "But I'm all yours tomorrow, remember?"

"Absolutely." She stood and gave me a quick kiss.

I backed out of the room, soaking up her mussed hair, uneven skirt, and swollen lips. I wanted to remember her like this. With a wink, I escaped from her office and practically ran to the cafeteria.

I was panting, a mixture of guilt, adrenaline, and being wound tighter than I had ever been before.

The universe heard my wishes, and a new teen was stationed at the register. This time, I didn't say a word. Only pointed at what I wanted. In case this was ever traced back to me, I wanted to be as discreet as possible. My hands were shaking as I ran out of the cafeteria and into the closest bathroom.

Me: *Got the sample. Can U meet?*

Jake: *where*

Me: *unisex bathroom, southeast from cafeteria*

Jake: *be there in 5*

Syncopated knocks on the door alerted me Jake was outside. I unlocked it, yanked him in by his shirt, and shut the door.

"Watch the merchandise," Jake teased, shaking me off, then leaning on the sink. "Why're you so wound up?" He took the computer bag off his shoulder and set it on the vanity. He snapped on gloves then extracted a specimen bottle designed to look like a water bottle.

I removed the shake's seal and lid then handed it to Jake, who poured the contents into the bottle. After sealing it, he handed me the plastic cup to return. "Told my boss I had a vet emergency. I'm heading out now to drop this at the lab."

I nodded. "Can we put a rush on?" We needed to find an answer fast. I needed this investigation to be done, for everything to go back to normal. For me not to feel this…this pull back to Carma whenever I walked away.

"Last time I tried to put a rush on, it still took three days. They're backed up since the Madison Heights lab closed for remodeling."

"Try anyway."

He nodded. "I'm gonna motor. See you tonight." He left the bathroom, and I waited a few more minutes before leaving.

Realizing I still hadn't gotten anything for myself at the cafeteria, I made a third trip and got a cup of tea for Maggie. When I got back, her eyes lit up as I set it down on her desk. "I couldn't decide on anything, so I brought you back this."

She cradled the tea in her hands. "Please don't ever leave me."

"Not planning on it."

Carma rushed in frazzled, looking around the floor. "Have either of you seen my ID?"

Shit. "I'll help you look." Palming the card, I dropped it to the floor and kicked it under the edge of the open door. I made a show of looking around the area before half closing the door to expose the card. "Bingo!"

I crouched down to pick it up and held it between two fingers. She grabbed it with both of her hands, squeezing mine before she pulled away. "I don't know what I'd do without you."

"That's exactly what I said," Maggie chimed in.

Neither seemed to notice how forced my smile was.

Chapter Nineteen

"WHAT ARE YOUR plans after you get promoted?" Jake propped his feet on the coffee table, prompting a derisive grunt from Sebastian, who had finally shown back up when I got home. "Buying another new truck? Going on vacation?"

I popped the last bite of naan into my mouth and shrugged. "Just got a new one, just had a four-month vacation."

"Not sure recovering from major surgery is a vacation, but sure." He leaned his head against the back of the couch. "I think…I'm going to go on an extended vacation."

My mouth fell open. "You serious?"

He looked over at me. "Wasn't the same without you, Mina." He sighed. "I mean, Scalzi was cool. We got along fine, but the reason why this job was so good was because I got to work with my best friend."

I elbowed him. "You're a dork. SHAP is your life. You literally just said so two weeks ago."

"Lives can change in a matter of moments." He toyed with his watchband. "Did I tell you Daisy's powers were authenticated?"

I turned my entire body to face him, sitting cross-legged

on the couch. "It's for sure? She's a witch?"

"Not fully developed, but definitely confirmed. Don't know if it will be more than parlor tricks or if she'll be one of the powerful ones. That's what I intend to help with."

"Intend to help…" I blinked hard then laughed, disbelieving. "You're leaving active duty to become a glorified nanny?"

SHAP assigned private duty agents to those who wanted low-risk field assignments. They were matched with a minor or group of people who had recently come into their abilities or supernatural status. Typically, Daisy's private tutor would be another witch, but with Jake's family connection and history with SHAP, he'd likely be approved as her agent.

He shot me a dirty look. "No, I'm leaving active duty to help take care of my family. You were always part of that family, but once you're RD, she'll need me more than you do. She's brand new to this and Eliza is freaked. Anyway, it'll probably be easier on my old bones."

Jake's bones were technically only six months older than mine. But doing the physical jobs that we did, surviving the falls and the crashes, made our bodies feel a hundred. My shoulder twinged as a reminder that I hadn't been stretching it like I should.

My chest hurt at the thought of him leaving life as a field agent. I should open my mouth and say *thank you. You're my family, too. In fact, you're probably the best part of my family. I support you. I think what you're doing for Daisy is the bravest, most kind thing an uncle can do. You need to take care of you, which includes your body.*

Instead, I panicked. Change was scary, even though I was

the one who was implementing it. I opened my mouth wide and stuck my foot inside. "You don't need to worry about taking care of me. I've been on my own for a long time."

His face went cold. "I don't know what the hell your problem has been recently, but, babe, you haven't been on your own for a long time. Yeah, you got the short end of the stick when it came to your dad. But I have always been by your side. So has Eliza. So has our family."

"I see I'm also chopped liver," Sebastian added.

Just apologize, Mina. Pull foot out, close mouth. "That's not what I meant, and you know it." Wow, I was actually making it worse. "I'm not saying you're not my family. I just don't want you to feel obligated to be somewhere you don't want to be because we used to be inseparable."

My former therapist would probably say this was me projecting my feelings onto Jake. That I was totally freaked out about why I felt so off balance with this case and couldn't be vulnerable enough to admit it. Especially after the accident left me physically vulnerable for months. She would also probably tell me to be an adult and discuss what was really going on. Apparently, I wasn't going to do any of that, just stand back and self-destruct.

I stood and cleaned up dinner, dropping the dishes into the sink. Jake followed me into the kitchen and brushed me out of the way, rinsing the dishes and putting them in the dishwasher. Every movement vibrated with controlled fury. Sebastian clucked his tongue and disappeared. He hated confrontation. I left Jake in the kitchen and sat down in the armchair, giving us both space—me to reflect on my stupid choices, and him to cool down.

He limped back into the living room, clearly hurting and still pissed. "You need to figure out whatever the hell is going on with you. I can't believe..."

He just stared at me like I was a stranger. "My entire family sat in the hospital waiting room for days, waiting for you to wake up. My mother had to bully your father into giving us permission to see you in intensive care."

Heat washed over me, anger and embarrassment. "I never asked for any of you to be there! To sit there while they patched me up. I don't owe you for being where I didn't want you!"

I gasped and slapped my hand over my mouth. That was the cruelest thing I had ever said. "I didn't mean any of that," I whispered, but it was too late.

He held up his hand. "I'm going to give you some space before we both say anything else we can't take back." He leaned over, kissed the side of my head, and grabbed his keys from his pocket. "I'll see you tomorrow."

I stood there for a long moment, staring at the closed door. Maybe I really should find a new therapist. Mine had decided to move across the country to someplace where there wasn't seven months of winter, and it had to be someone who believed in supernatural beings but had no connection to my father. My terms.

Sebastian popped in. "Do you want to speak or run?"

"Run."

Chapter Twenty

I THREW ON a tank top and shorts, put on headphones, and took off without bothering to stretch. I had to either run or scream for hours, and I was guessing my neighbors preferred running. Two miles in, and I kept going.

Three miles.

Four.

Consciously, I didn't pay attention to where I was. I only cared about the burning in my legs and the music blaring in my ears. *What if I just walked away? What happened then?* I pushed myself to go faster, trying desperately to quiet my thoughts.

I would lose Dad, Jake, and Sebastian. What if I gave it all up and lost Carma, too?

I stopped on the corner and leaned against the street sign, gasping for breath and trying to ease a cramp in my side. It shouldn't be possible to have a panic attack after running six miles in ninety-degree heat, but apparently it was.

I needed to order a Lyft home. I needed to keep running. I needed to drink my body weight in tequila. I surveyed the area trying to figure out where the hell I was. It looked familiar... I was a block away from Carma's house.

I knew I should call and see if she was even home, but if she said no, I'd crumble right here on the sidewalk. With my heart on my sleeve for the first time in my life, I power-walked to the bungalow at the end of the street. My heart sank when I saw a car that wasn't hers in the driveway.

I couldn't bring myself to interrupt, but I also couldn't find the will to walk away. So I just stood there, hands on her gate, staring at the little pink door.

I didn't notice the three heads staring at me from the large picture window until Hanelore knocked. Startled, I jumped back and looked up to see Carma, Hanelore, and Elena waving. Well, Carma and Hanelore were waving. Elena was standing there with her arms crossed.

Carma stepped out of view and opened the front door but stayed back from the sunlight. "Hey! Come in. I'm surprised to see you."

I rubbed the back of my neck and look down at my tattered sneakers. "Honestly, I didn't intentionally come by. I was on a run and found myself here."

She placed her hands on her hips. "Mina, if you don't come in right now, I will be forced to come out there. Even if the sun is still up. You don't get to bail without a kiss."

"I'm super sweaty and gross," I warned, but still walked toward her. How could I not?

The moment I walked in, she caught me by the chin and planted a kiss firmly on my lips. "Hanelore and Elena came by for dinner."

As much as I wanted to stay and curl up against her body, I definitely didn't want to interrupt her girl time. "Awesome." My stomach ached at the thought of going home to my empty place and back to a life where my only friends weren't talking to me. I leaned in to give her one more kiss, enjoying the way her nearness quieted my mind.

Reluctantly, I pulled back and pointed at the front door. "I was just passing by."

"I'm like six miles from downtown Applechester. You ran that far in this heat?"

I laughed awkwardly and shrugged. "Accident. I wasn't paying attention to where I was going."

"What happened?" She stepped in closer, trailing her fingers down my arm.

"Don't pay any attention to us over here," Elena called.

Carma and I both turned in time to see Hanelore elbow Elena. "I'm sorry about her," Hanelore said in a stage whisper, "she's a middle child."

Carma laughed, but I shifted back-and-forth uncomfortably on my feet. Elena made it very clear she was not a "Car-Min" fan. *Ma-Mi? Min-Car?* "Sorry, again, for interrupting girls night."

Hanelore waved off my apology. "We would've invited you, but Carma said you had other plans. Why don't you grab some water and come join us?"

I hadn't been to anything that resembled girls night for years, and that'd been for a mission. I didn't know what one typically wore but sweat-stained clothes didn't seem like the first choice. "Ah, I really want to say yes, but I'm literally dripping sweat. Why don't I just call a Lyft, and we'll reschedule for a different day."

"I've got a better idea," Carma said. "How about you take a quick shower and I'll loan you some of my clothes.

Then you'd feel better about joining us."

"Yippee," Elena mumbled. Hanelore shot her a look.

"We are not the same size," I mused.

She grabbed my arm and navigated us down the hall. "I wasn't always this size. I kept some of my old clothes, which might actually be too big on you."

We entered her bedroom and I stopped. This was the first time I had gotten a look at her sanctuary. Lavender walls, floral floor-to-ceiling curtains, a cream-colored vintage headboard with skull rivets along the edge, and a vintage royal purple loveseat with a dragon scroll on top in front of a gas fireplace. Everything was soft, silky, and a little creepy. Just like Carma liked it.

"I want to stay here," I breathed, running my hand along the curving cream and gold dresser nearest the door. Realizing what I said, I looked at her with a sheepish smile.

"Thank you." She smiled. "I didn't think floral was really your thing. You are way more rock 'n roll than I am."

"Floral isn't my thing. You're my thing."

She flushed. "And you're welcome to stay here anytime."

I wanted to push her up against the wall and kiss her, but I refrained. "Thanks. I think...I'd like that very much."

"Me, too." She pointed to her bathroom. "You better get in the shower so you can join us. We're assembling the door prizes for tomorrow."

"I thought we finished those over the weekend?"

She lifted a shoulder and looked down at her hands. "I just wanted to add a few more things. These donors deserve to be thanked."

I just shook my head and smiled. "Yeah, alright."

She walked me through where to find everything I'd need, then promised to leave a clean outfit on the bed.

I was drowning in her scent as I stepped into her perfectly spotless shower. She had strawberry shampoo and conditioner, as well as a strawberry bodywash. Imagining her in the shower, smoothing the bodywash over her soft skin, made me ache. My skin would leave burns if someone touched me.

I turned the shower cold. I finished quickly and toweled off, slathering some of her lotion on my skin. I loved when women had amazing body products.

When I left the bathroom, there was a black tank and drawstring shorts laid out on the bed, a stick of travel deodorant next to it, and a water bottle on the nightstand. I smiled at her thoughtfulness. I chugged half the bottle, then put the cap on before I made myself sick. The softness of her blanket brushed the back of my fingers as I scooped the clothes off her perfectly made bed. It shouldn't have been an aphrodisiac, but the thought of Carma naked, fisting the blanket while she moaned out a curse, was enough to make my breathing shallow.

Deep breath in, deep breath out. Why was I suddenly as horny as a teenager around this woman? Not even around her, around her *stuff*.

I shook my head and started reciting the people I had arrested, first to most recent. When I had gotten to four years back, the fire in my stomach had settled to a low smolder. I applied deodorant and slipped on the clothes, then paused to look in her full-length mirror. I wasn't going to win any fashion awards, especially with no bra, but it was a vast improvement from soaked running clothes.

I walked out of the bedroom on the balls of my feet, nerves flooding my stomach. Why was I nervous? It was only Carma and her two friends.

Because I'm too close to the case. I shook my head. I could still do my job.

Maybe it was just because I didn't really have any close human friends, except Jake and his family. Being an active agent meant weeks or months out of contact with others, and often I couldn't share where or why I was going. I knew a few other agents in passing, but we were always on the move, or they were cautious with me because my dad held their careers in their hands.

When I walked into the living room, I felt Carma's gaze slide up my body from my feet to my damp hair. She studied my lips for long enough, I nearly melted into a puddle. I forced myself to look at Hanelore, who was balancing a gift bag on her stomach. Elena handed her a teacup, which Hanelore carefully nestled into a rainbow of tissue paper. Carma took the bag from her and put it onto a plastic container full of identical bags. Cheddar and Lucifer eyed the bags as if they were the Holy Grail.

"There, done." Hanelore said, handing the last bag to Carma. "You're not allowed to add anything else." She shifted and winced, her fist against her lower back.

"Are you okay?" I asked.

"Yep, just super pregnant. My back's been killing me all day."

"I'm calling Dr. Grady," Elena grumbled, reaching for her phone.

Hanelore took the phone out of her hand. "I'm literally growing an entire human. It's not a comfortable process. I'm fine."

Carma pursed her lips. "What if it's back labor?"

"Too early for back labor."

"Yeah, because babies stick to calendars," her wife muttered. She brushed Hanelore's hands away and replaced them, kneading her wife's lower back.

It was such a simple gesture, yet strangely intimate. I looked away, spying the love seat opposite the couch and sinking down. "Is there anything I can help with?"

"Don't let her add anything else to those bags!" Hanelore ordered.

I put my hands up in defense. "Don't touch the bags. Got it."

Carma rolled her eyes but tucked the last bag in the bin and walked over to the couch, sitting down next to me. She leaned in close, then inhaled. "*Mmm*, strawberries."

I laughed softly. "That's literally what I think about every time I'm around you."

Elena made a gagging noise. Hanelore laughed. "Remember when we used to be like that?" Hanelore asked.

"We were never that bad," Elena defended.

"So," I offered, trying to break the tension. "What does one do at girls night? Haven't been to one in like a long time."

"Help Carma out with some wild idea, then watch baking shows," Hanelore explained.

"Baking shows?" I turned to the television mounted on the wall to see it paused on some new Netflix competition show I hadn't watched.

"Just because I can't eat things doesn't mean I don't like to watch other people eat them," Carma explained.

I looked over at her. "You are so weird."

She winked. "I'm told the more you get to know me, the weirder I get."

"She's not lying," Hanelore added.

She restarted the episode, and I savored the rest of my water while Carma curled her legs under her, her knees pressed against my leg. She was adorable as she watched, getting super invested. She gasped when a contestant messed up, cheered when they succeeded, and teared up when the judges were harsh. I could watch her watch TV all day.

"Oh, come on!" Hanelore yelled as her favorite contestant was eliminated. "I call BS!"

Elena mumbled something in Spanish which sounded ominous. So it wasn't just me she didn't like—HA!

When the credits rolled, Hanelore yawned. "Well, we need to go relieve Elena's folks from babysitting. Paulo is too good at weaseling his way out of a bath."

"He's only four. It's gonna be hell when he's a teenager," Elena added. She reached down and helped Hanelore off the couch, then hovered near her as she stretched.

Carma walked them to the door, giving each of them a kiss on the cheek with a promise we'd all get together again soon. Then she locked the door behind her and turned to me with a crooked smile. We were all alone. In a house. And I had no place to be.

I knew if I kissed her right now, I wouldn't stop. Not for a long time. Yet, it felt right. I knew theoretically I should wait until the lab results came back and we closed the case, but how could I when the woman of my dreams was walking over to me, barefoot, eyes locked on mine?

Chapter Twenty-One

S HE SAT DOWN next to me and leaned her head on my shoulder. "Did you have fun?"

I nodded. "Yeah. Thanks for letting me crash your party. I should've called first."

"You never need to call. I always want to see you."

"Thanks." I looked at the front window, trying to hide my blush. "I'm not on Elena's Christmas card list."

She leaned over and kissed my shoulder. "She worries. She's seen all my heartbreaks and it takes her awhile to warm up to people." She trailed fingertips down the still pink surgery scars. "These from the accident?"

I had forgotten they were on display. While the raised curves were numb, the skin around them was extra sensitive. At least, when Carma touched them.

Stand up. Walk out of this house. You're going to lose everything.

"Yeah. Surgery."

She leaned closer, her breath caressing my skin. Then, like a butterfly, her lips fluttered against my shoulder. I stilled, my breath disappearing. My heartbeat was the loudest thing in the room.

I needed her.

A second flutter. My stomach flipped, twisted, fell to the center of the earth. I closed my eyes, all of my attention focused on two square inches of my body.

A third flutter. This time her lips parted, leaving the dampness from a kiss behind. I was melting.

A fourth. Her tongue touched my skin and I gasped. Her hand came to my hip and she scooted closer, her breasts pressing through her tank and against my back.

"Carma," I whispered, the sound nearly inaudible.

Her response wasn't a flutter, but a gentle nip, soothed with the press of her tongue. Her hand moved from my hip to my stomach, the shape of her palm burning me. Branding me.

My head bowed, and I leaned against her.

She sucked on the skin between my neck and shoulder, and a tremor shot through me. Oh god, I needed her to touch me. I needed to touch her.

I reached up and placed my hand at the back of her neck, my fingers tangling in her hair. She shifted so her legs were on either side of my hips and nipped my earlobe. I tugged teasingly at her hair and she purred.

I almost came from the sound alone. I ached with arousal. She was the sexiest woman—human—I'd ever met, and she wanted me.

Her kisses grew hotter, wetter as she brushed the straps of the tank down my shoulders and down my arms, exposing my breasts to the setting sun leaving shadows on the wall. Her fingers trailed down my spine, her lips following. I was shaking by the time she returned to the nape of my neck.

I needed her like I needed oxygen. Maybe more.

"Mina." Her whisper sank straight through my skin, wrapping around my heart. I leaned my head back against her collarbone. Her lips were bright pink, parted with desire.

Her blazing green eyes searched mine as she ran her fingertips over my jawline, my cheekbone, my eyebrows. My eyes closed when her head rested against mine, her hot breath gliding over my skin. I was hyperaware of every inch where our bodies touched.

Her hands smoothed over my shoulders and just under my collarbone. My diaphragm tensed at the sensation and I inhaled sharply. She was so close to setting me on fire, smoke was filling the air around us.

I turned to face her, needing her lips on mine. The tip of her nose touched the side of mine. I dug both of my hands into the back of her hair, the scent of strawberries surrounding us like a protective bubble. The weight of her hair, the smoothness of her skin, the heat of her body. Her tongue darted out to lick her bottom lip, and this time I did groan.

My hands came to her cheeks, thumbs on either side of her mouth. I ran the pad of my thumb over her bottom lip and smiled when her breath hitched. "This is where I remind you that you wanted to go slow," I whispered, hating myself. If I didn't have her right now, I would literally die. I'd become a ghost and haunt her out of desperation.

"This is where I tell you I don't care," she retorted.

"Are you sure?"

"Mina, do you know what you do to me?" She shifted so our bodies were more entwined, her legs unfolding and moving over mine. She reached up and cupped my breast and I arched into her. "I *need* to taste you more than I need to breathe."

I couldn't wait another second. Lifting my head, I brought my lips to hers. How did every kiss feel like the first one?

My world splintered from the pressure of her mouth. This kiss was somehow both delicate and fierce. I shifted away then captured her bottom lip between mine.

She let out a soft cry before her free hand moved to the back of my head and pressed me deeper into her. Her mouth covered mine, her tongue gently prodding me to open wider. Every muscle in my body coiled tighter as we desperately sought friction.

"We need to move away from the window," she breathed as she broke away and kissed down my body. She licked my nipple before pulling it into her mouth and gently nipping.

I gasped and arched toward her as electric shock shot straight through my body. "Literally don't care." I let her pull me down to the thick rug on the floor. She moved to my other breast, sucking the globe into her mouth and tonguing my nipple. I arched into her mouth, holding my breath as sparks lit a fuse to the center of my body.

And then my cell rang. "Ignore it."

She didn't let up. Her hand moved beneath my shorts. Fireworks went off behind my eyes.

The sound came again, the annoying ring of a cell. I growled.

"Do you need to get that?" she panted.

"Let the earth explode. It's fine." Then it rang a third time, then a fourth.

When it started the fifth time, Carma lifted her head

away from my body and I nearly cried. "Answer it. It sounds like an emergency."

I was going to murder whoever was on the other end of the line. "What?" I barked, not bothering with caller ID.

"Where the hell are you?" Jake bit out.

"Out."

"No shit. I'm three minutes out from your place."

I sat up. "Why? What happened?"

"The Andrews have company. Sebastian sent Reggie to find us."

The expletive I groaned was five syllables long. "I don't have my car."

"I'll drive you," Carma whispered.

By Jake's pause, I knew he heard it. "Do you have Sydney?"

"No."

"I'll get her. Get here." He hung up.

I turned to Carma, who was pulling on her clothes. "I'm so sorry. There's an emergency with my neighbors, and I'm the one who looks after them."

She tossed me the tank, then darted into the hallway to swipe her keys out of the bowl. "Let's motor."

We were out the door before I had a chance to panic about her potentially seeing something I couldn't cover up.

Chapter Twenty-Two

T HE CLOSER WE got to my place, the more space I put between us emotionally. I needed to be ready for battle, despite still being able to feel Carma's fingerprints all over my body.

She glanced over at me then reached over and squeezed my thigh. "What do you need? Me to come with you or to just drop you off?"

I pressed my lips together, resisting the urge to pick up her hand. "If I say drop off—"

"Then I'll drop you off." She stopped in front of the building. "Call me later?"

"Promise." I leapt out of the car and took off running, shoving down the guilt of not giving her a proper goodbye.

When I ripped open the front door, Reggie and his crush, Clint, were pacing in front of the staircase. "Jake's here, getting Sydney."

I looked up at the sound of work boots and a cane hitting the stairs. Jake. Our gazes met, and I knew our fight was over for now. He slipped me my piece as he reached the landing, then we moved simultaneously to the Andrews's door. A group of ghosts had gathered, and we walked through them.

Sebastian materialized as I used my key to let us in. "Hurry."

"Amber? George?" Jake called.

"Patio!" Sebastian directed.

The apartments on the main floor had patios that led to a common lawn area, which was surrounded by a four-foot fence, or at least it used to be. A section of the wooden planks had been smashed to the ground. My steps faltered at the sight of Belphegor launching a vampire into an intact section of the fence, before he rushed and scooped up another one racing toward us and did the same thing.

"Took you long enough!" he grunted.

Jake and I leveled our guns at the attackers. "Try to keep them alive for questioning!" Jake ordered.

"Don't think you'll get far. These motherfuckers are feral!"

My partner shot me a look. *Feral?* Feral vampires were rare, since vampires were usually made with intent, but it would explain several of the most recent attacks. Sometimes, if a vampire changed without a guide to help them through the transition, their animal urges took over. It took serious work to tame a feral creature.

"Shoot if one gets too close," I told Jake as I side-stepped toward Amber and George, who were hunched in wicker chairs. Amber pressed a half-finished sweater with knitting needles still attached against George's neck. The yarn was covered in blood.

With a roar, Belphegor threw the female vampire down and put her in a chokehold. "How's George?" he called. The vampire tried to push him off, but he tightened his grip.

I gently brushed Amber aside and inspected George's neck. Two puncture wounds. "Seb?"

"Here!" He appeared next to me.

"Go see if you can find puncture wounds on the new vamps."

He disappeared. I replaced the ruined pillowcase against George's neck and held it firmly trying to slow the bleeding, ignoring his grumbling. "Got a single bite, right side of neck," I called. "Still bleeding, which is a good sign." If it was still bleeding, it meant we might be able to counteract the venom in time.

The male vampire charged us again and Jake didn't hesitate to shoot his leg. He didn't slow down. "Don't make me kill you!" Jake warned.

The vamp didn't care. In the light of the patio string lights and nearly full moon, I could see his crazed stare and dried blood on his lips. The vamp didn't slow. Jake hit him hard with his cane, trying to redirect him as I palmed my cell in one hand and my gun in the other.

As soon as dispatch picked up, I rattled off the info. "Agent Summers. I need medics for vampire attack. We have multiple ferals…"

I tucked the phone between my ear and shoulder and watched the vamp launch himself at my partner, grabbing his waist and taking him to the ground. Not on my watch. With two precise shots in the head from my gun, the vampire slumped to the ground.

Jake stood with a groan and wiped blood and goo from his face with this shirt then looked back at me, face unreadable. The second vamp screamed at the sight of her partner, then tried to fight her way out of Belphegor's arms.

"Jake! Get out of there." If she broke Belphegor's grip, there was no doubt she'd try to rip my partner's throat out.

Sebastian appeared at my side. "Neither have puncture wounds."

"Of course they don't. Because why would this be easy?"

Realizing she was losing the fight, the vamp opened her mouth and bit the demon's arm. He roared loud enough to cover my shout. Demon blood was poisonous to vampires.

I threw my hands up in the air. "Who made you?" I cried, running over and grabbing the vamp by the shoulders. Her mouth dripped with black blood, her eyes already rolling into the back of her head. "Who made you?" I asked again, shaking her.

It was too late. She went limp and slumped to the side.

I shook my head and stood, my brain trying to piece it all together. Belphegor laid her down gently on the grass, then hoisted himself up and moved toward George. "Prognosis?"

Jake stared at us for a beat before answering, his face blank. "We'll take him to headquarters and do a blood transfusion. They'll probably keep him for a few days to monitor, but the sooner the transfusion happens after a bite, the more successful we are at eradicating vampire venom."

The demon nodded and, strangely, looked relieved. "Good, good. When Amber summoned me, I thought she was playing a prank." Red eyes stared into mine. "You told you me you had it under control."

"I told you we're working on it," I snapped.

"Work faster." He shook his arm, which had healed on

its own. "Or we'll come work on it for you."

"Quiet!" Jake ordered. "Stressing a body out just makes the virus in the venom work faster."

Belphegor went to sit with George and Amber, taking over care of George. Jake and I laid out the vampires, taking pictures of them and the scene. As soon as the SHAP medics arrived, Belphegor departed before he "was attacked by another crazy townie."

I helped Amber pack an overnight bag for her and George while the SHAP agents loaded the dead vampires into a van. We watched them drive away, then locked up their apartment. How strange that nothing except the bloody sweater, which Amber took with her, was out of place.

We pushed through concerned neighbors, headed by Doris of course, and ghosts crowded into the hallway. "A stray dog got into the apartment," Jake explained, "and it bit George."

"He's staying at the hospital overnight as a precaution, but he and Amber are in good spirits," I added.

The regular humans filed off in a cloud of murmurs, while the SHAP set heard the real story from Sebastian. My phone vibrated before I even hit the first stair.

"Hi, Dad."

"Vamps had IDs. Thinner members."

I looked at Jake and mouthed *vamps from Thinner*. His eyes went wide.

"Demon?"

Shit. I purposefully didn't put my interactions with Belphegor in reports for this exact reason. "Hold on."

Jake moved around me, jaw tight, and opened my door.

We went through, and I kicked it closed before putting my phone on speaker. "Okay. Yes, a demon. He wasn't a threat."

"Demons go against—"

"Ordinance 37B, I'm aware. But we were dealing with two feral vamps, and he was on our side."

"He wasn't apprehended."

"Because he's not a threat." I shot Jake a frustrated glance. "We were concentrating on the vamps." *Demon?* I mouthed at him. I certainly hadn't mentioned it. Had George or Amber?

"International is going to ask questions about why there was a demon attacking humans alongside two feral vampires."

"He wasn't attacking the humans; he was attacking the vampires." My god, was I *actually* defending Belphegor?

Jake held my gaze for a long moment. "If we report that the vampires trace back to Thinner *and* that there was a demon fighting *with* them, then we'd have enough to issue a cease-and-desist order until we get answers. Then we can work to clear Belphegor's name."

He was right, of course. Demons were considered "heavy weights" in a supernatural case because of their power and temperament. Ultimately, this would probably be no more than a blip on Belphegor's radar. With his help, we'd be able to shut down all Thinner operations until we found the answers we needed.

So then why did I feel like my chest was caving in at the thought of this all ending?

Cease and desist orders were hard to get, since they exposed SHAP legally and literally. When humans were involved, the orders had to be supported by the human police, too. They were only used in circumstances where unexplained supernatural events escalated at an uncontrollable rate.

"Forty-eight hours, tops," Dad promised.

"Roger," Jake replied.

I stared at my phone as the screen went black. *Forty-eight hours, tops.* Why wasn't I happy this was almost over? Why was the looming deadline pressing on my chest and making it hard to breathe?

"What's wrong?" he asked.

I shook my head. "Nothing. Just, a lot happened today."

He looked me over, finally taking in the clothes that were clearly not mine. I crossed my arms in return, afraid he could see right through me to where Carma's lip prints lingered under my skin. "Where were you?"

"Helping Carma and her friends finish the gift bags for tomorrow night."

He didn't respond for a long moment. I held my breath so I didn't fidget under his gaze. "Do I need to be worried?"

"It'll all be over in forty-eight hours."

His eyes narrowed. "I'm going home. I'll see you tomorrow." He opened the door and then paused. "You'd tell me, if there was something I needed to know?"

I dropped my arms. "You're my partner." It wasn't really a yes.

He closed the door behind him, and I stared after him, guilt pulsing through me. I was in over my head and I wasn't sure how I was going to keep it all together. I just needed to get through tomorrow, then I'd figure it out.

Chapter Twenty-Three

AFTER SO MANY years on the job, I could go from a dead sleep to alert in less than a minute. I went from a dream about Carma and me lying on a beach to sitting up in bed with my phone in my hand, answering her call in one simple motion. "What's wrong?"

"Hanelore's in labor."

"Okay, that's good, right?"

"It's too early." She blew out a shaky breath. "I'm freaking."

"Deep breath, babe. What can I do?" I glanced at the clock. Four in the morning.

"I'm headed to the hospital."

I turned on the lamp on my nightstand and swallowed hard. "Are you okay to drive? Do you need me to come with you?" *Please say no.* I wasn't good at being the person people leaned on for emotional support.

"Yes, I can drive." She paused. "I want to stay with them at the hospital until the baby's born, but I need to set up for the fundraiser."

I breathed a sigh of relief and threw the covers back. Taking control was something I could do. I threw open my bedroom door and hurried to the living room, snagging a pad of paper and pen and sitting on the floor so I could write on the coffee table. "I've got it. Hit me with the list."

The panic in her voice ebbed as she concentrated on dictating what needed to be finished, should be double-checked, and what to avoid. "I already gave the front desk your name. They'll let you in."

"I'll get it done."

"I dropped my trailer off last night, but it needs to be unloaded. I had planned to finish setting up this morning. There's still so much—"

"Carma, I've got it." I was going to need to call in reinforcements, but we'd get it done.

"Are you sure?"

"Absolutely. And I'll be dressed and waiting for you at seven tonight."

She laughed, but it sounded like a sob. "Where did you even come from?"

I breathed out a laugh through my nose. "Well, after my parents got married…"

This time, her laugh was real. "Okay, I'm here. Thank you so much."

"Anytime." I leaned back against the bottom of the couch, wiping sleep from my eyes. There would be no going back to bed. I was going to have to call Maggie and tell her I wouldn't be in the office at all today.

Carma's breath hitched, but she didn't speak.

"Babe, what's wrong?"

"It's too early. She wasn't due for seven weeks. What if…what if something's wrong?"

I drew a spiral on the notepad, trying to think of something comforting to say. Comfort wasn't my natural state. The baby might be a preemie or might have serious complications. It could also be perfectly healthy.

Hanelore could have life-threatening complications or be completely fine. Telling Carma there was nothing to worry about wasn't the right thing to do but sitting inside her spinning head wasn't good, either.

"I know I'm being silly," she continued. "But I'm scared to go in."

"I'm not...good at feelings talk..." I wished I was there. I could open her car door and pull her into my arms, make her shoulders lower down from her ears and kiss her until her jaw wasn't clenched anymore.

"It's fine. I'm sorry. I—"

"Listen to me," I interrupted, trying to figure out the words I wanted in the pre-dawn hours. "I know you're worried and I'm not going to tell you not to be..."

Sebastian appeared in the armchair, shaking his head. I gave him the finger. "Tell her she'll be there no matter what happens," he whispered.

I nodded. "But you're going to be there for Hanelore and Elena no matter what happens." I shot a look at Sebastian.

He nodded. "You'll get through it together," he added.

I repeated his words and added, "And I'll be on the other end of this phone whenever you need me."

My roommate clapped his hands, then sat back in the chair like he was a proud parent.

"You know," Carma said, her voice soft, "you're not nearly as bad at the 'feelings' thing as you claim."

I laughed softly. "I won't let it go to my head. You okay

now?"

"Yeah. I'm okay. Thank you." Her car door slammed. "I'll text you soon."

"Can't wait." I set the phone down on the table and rested the back of my head on the couch cushion. There was something about this call that felt different. I couldn't remember the last time someone trusted me enough to be the person they called when everything was going wrong.

It made sense it would be me, of course. The fundraiser needed to go on whether or not Hanelore was in the hospital. I was the obvious choice because I was her second in command.

"Your meanderings are rather deep for this early in the day, darling," Sebastian admitted.

"Why'd she call me? Not her mom? Not another friend?" I looked over at him. "I'm never the person someone calls. At least, not about something non-SHAP related."

He studied me for a long moment. "I'm not sure if I'm more worried you're asking me that question or that you're asking it about *her*."

I frowned. "What's that supposed to mean?"

"I wasn't great at cultivating relationships when I was alive. When I died, all I wanted to do—besides apologize to my mother for being a horse's arse—was to say goodbye to my siblings. Reassure my brother he'd be a great duke and tell my sister how much I adored her."

I sat quiet, waiting for him to continue.

"When we're afraid, we long to talk to the people we hold in the highest esteem." He studied me for a long moment. "The people we love."

My eyes nearly bulged out of my head. "I-I don't...she doesn't. It's not like..."

He shook his head and rubbed his palm on his jaw. "You need more human friends."

"They're so much more work."

"Yes. But one day you will perish like me, and no matter how much you want to be with humans, it will never come to fruition."

I frown. "You're with me like...all the time."

He smiled sadly. "No, love. And you just proved my point." He walked over and sat down next to me. "There's a clarity that comes with being dead and aware for so long. One that I could never hope to explain. But I do know you need to confide in Jake about your feelings for Carma."

My breathing grew shallow and my stomach dropped, a wave of nausea greeting me at the thought. I shook my head. "I can't." I didn't even try to deny the feelings. I hugged my knees to my chest. "I don't know how to do this," I whispered. "If I tell him, I could lose everything."

Sebastian shrugged. "Just so."

"What do you mean 'just so'? Everything includes you, jackass." Ghosts could only stay with an active agent. If Jake reported my feelings for Carma, and I was fired, Sebastian would be transferred to a new, undisclosed resident. I'd lose my job and everyone I loved in one fell swoop. "If you want out, just say so."

"You're ridiculous. But if me vacating your apartment means you'd get to be with the woman you love..."

I glared. "Stop it. You know it's phantoms before madams."

"You should get that embroidered on a pillow."

I crossed my arms, trying not to laugh. "I'm not giving you up for someone else."

He sat down on the coffee table—something he had never done before, as it offended his ducal sensibilities—and waited until I looked up at him. "Mina, if I was ever relocated, I'd never rest until I found a way to see you again. You'll never lose me."

I swallowed hard, my throat growing thick. "Aw, you're such a softy," I teased.

He ignored my comment. "As someone who has had centuries to ruminate on his mistakes, people always regret the same thing."

"Texting while driving?"

"No, dimwit. Losing someone they love." He ran a hand through his hair and let it fall to his lap. "Sometimes you just have to close your eyes and jump."

I raised my eyebrow. "Have you been reading greeting cards again?"

He ignored me. "When the time comes, I hope you make the correct choice. Even if it's the most difficult."

"This is too many feelings for pre-dawn."

He grunted and disappeared, apparently done with this conversation. I had no energy to waste on worrying what he said. Today, it was all about the fundraiser. I unlocked my cell and called into SHAP. "Hey, Val, it's Agent Summers. I need a team. We've got a party to pull off."

IT HAD TAKEN all day to set up the room—honestly, the amount of twinkle lights rivaled Applechester's annual Christmas parade—but it was even better than I could've imagined. Two hours before the doors opened, I rushed home to shower and eat for the first time that day. Jake showed up in a black tux, red tie, and matching red cane, causing Reggie to scream and cover his face because of "the *audacity* of looking so good."

I laughed so hard, I snorted. Sebastian had dragged Reggie out of the apartment, threatening to find him a fainting couch and smelling salts.

Jake just shook his head, shoved a garment bag into my hand, and turned back toward the door. "Gotta go help Eliza and Magnolia set up."

I eyed the garment bag as if it were a baby werewolf about to bite me. "I was gonna wear my black suit."

"Yeah, well, Maggie ambushed me when I said I was helping out and that I'd see you. You'll wear it and you'll like it."

"Got it." Sebastian's words from this morning rang in my head. *Tell him.* I opened my mouth, knowing if I didn't do it right now, I'd chicken out. "Jake, I—"

Jake's cell rang, interrupting the confession. "It's Eliza." He answered. "Yeah." He pinched the bridge of his nose. "The longer it takes for this call to end, the longer it takes for me to get there."

I bit the inside of my cheeks so I didn't laugh out loud.

He hung up with a sigh. "Just...wear that. I already have two melodramatic family members to contend with tonight. I do not need three."

"I'm so telling them you said that."

"I could kill you with lip balm."

I blew him a kiss. With a salute, he left, leaving me staring after him. I should've told him. Should I chase after him? My phone buzzed and I pulled it out of my pocket.

Carma: Healthy baby boy and healthy mom! *Heart emoji*

Me: Tell them congrats for me

Carma: Leaving the hospital now. Be there soon

I unzipped the garment bag and gasped at the rich red velvet tuxedo jacket with black lace top. My fingers caressed the soft fabric, stunned. A sheet of paper stuck out of the pocket. I laid the outfit across my bed and pulled out the note.

Mina

This was Carma's idea and I went along with it. I can't wait to see it on.

Maggie

I changed then stood in front of my mirror for a solid five minutes, wondering how I was going to get the courage to leave the house. Sebastian knocked on my door and walked in when I didn't answer. His hand flew to his chest. "Forswear it, sight, for I ne'er saw true beauty till this night."

"Wow, Shakespeare. You pulled out the big guns."

"You are breathtaking, love."

I fidgeted with the high collar, then pulled at the gathered sleeves. "I feel ridiculous. It's too much." I straightened the jacket, which covered the see-through shirt. While I'm sure it was meant to be worn without anything underneath, I'd slipped on a black cami. This was work, after all.

He shook his head. "If you wear that tonight, Carma will absolutely fall in love with you."

I rolled my eyes. "Stop being ridiculous."

He walked over and hovered his hands above mine. "Stop fidgeting. You look perfect."

"What am I doing?" I whispered.

He smiled. "You're finally learning to live, child." He took a step back. "Go get your girl."

"We both know I can't."

"We both know you can't lie to me."

My phone alarm went off, warning me that I had five minutes to get to the car. "Maybe I should change—"

"I dare you to wear that."

I gave him the finger. I couldn't back down now. "You're such a pain in my ass."

"Love you, too."

CARMA WAS STANDING on the front stairs when I arrived, greeting guests. My breath caught in my chest when she turned toward me, her perfect leg peeking out from the high slit on the front of her ruby red dress. Her plunging neckline exposed the curve of her breasts and the entire world narrowed down to this moment. The dress wrapped around her upper arms, reverently staying in place as she descended the stairs like we were in some goddamn fairytale.

I swallowed hard, trying to remember how to use words. She smiled, her eyes scanning me head to toe, and then stumbled. Instinctually, I rushed toward her and grabbed her arms to steady her.

She looked at me, resting her hands on my forearms and squeezed. "My heroine."

My cheeks heated. "You're ridiculous."

"I'm lucky."

The space between us grew smaller as I tried to take in every detail of her face. Tomorrow, all of this would be over. Would we be over, too?

Her lips turned up at the corners. "What?"

"Just looking." I took a step back and slid my hands away from her arms. The moment we broke contact, my chest hollowed out. "We better get inside. You have fund-raising to do."

She linked her arm through mine, and we started moving up the stairs. "You did an incredible job. How'd you get everything finished?"

"Called in a few friends to help. How are Hanelore, Elena, and the baby?"

"Noah. He's perfect." Her smile was so big, it made me smile. "Noah will need to be in the hospital a few more days, and Hanelore is exhausted, but it's good."

"I'm so glad."

"I don't know what I would've done without you today." We paused when we got to the top of the stairs. "Thank you."

"That's what I'm here for."

Her green eyes held mine, and I was halfway to falling

into them forever when someone called her name. She squeezed my arm then released me, walking over to a group of donors. I wanted to follow her, hold her close, kiss her in the corners of the room, meet the people who were vying for her attention.

"Ah."

I startled and looked to my left to find Maggie in an A-line burgundy gown with a silk shawl. "You look stunning."

She smiled and nodded her thanks. "As do you. Carma has impeccable taste."

I tugged at the coat and looked down at my feet. "It was…unexpected." I looked up at her. "But very appreciated."

She took a sip from her champagne glass then winked at me. "It's ginger ale. Can't drink when I'm on the job, and if Lucinda is within a three-mile radius, I'm on the job. But it makes me feel like I'm joining in."

"Great idea."

"Hmm." She turned back to watch Carma for a moment. "The poet Samuel Rogers once said, 'to know her is to love her.' I mean, the Beatles took that idea and ran with it, but…"

I raised an eyebrow in response.

"My husband was an English professor, so I know more about dead white writers than I care to." She gestured to Carma. "I think she'd agree with me."

"You think everyone who knows Carma loves her?"

She turned to face me. "I think to know you, Mina, is to love you."

I blinked at her, then laughed, shaking my head. "Are

you sure that's ginger ale?"

"Positive." She looked around the room. "Everything you do, you do with all of you." She leaned in close. "And I've never seen Carma smile like that before. You're one of a kind, kid."

"My favorite ladies!" Lucinda cried, walking up to us. She was in a floor-length red gown that sparkled with every movement. "Oh my god!" She grabbed my arm. "Who is this? This isn't my assistant, is it?" She leaned in and kissed my cheek. "You look incredible."

"Doesn't she?" Maggie added.

Carma appeared at the other side of her mom. "Didn't she do a great job decorating, too?"

I waved off the compliment. "I had a group of friends help. I can't take all the credit."

Lucinda put her arm around her daughter's waist. "Monday, I'm giving her a raise!" She leaned in and stage whispered, "As long as Carma doesn't chase her away with her little crush." She gave me a long look in warning.

It's more than a crush and there won't be a Monday.

Carma gasped. "Mom, completely inappropriate! How I feel about someone is no one's business but my own."

"Of course, sweetie. You can love anyone you want, as long as it's not my assistant."

Looking at my shoes, I cleared my throat and took a step away from the group. "Excuse me, there's something I need to check on." I took off before they could respond, weaving my way through glittery dresses and heavily applied cologne until I pushed through the kitchen doors. Magnolia was doing a final check of a half a dozen trays when her eyes caught mine. She clapped her hands. "Good to go!"

The servers took off toward the ballroom. She pointed at me. "You look gorgeous! Why do you have the same face Eliza gets on a rollercoaster before she gets sick?"

I smiled weakly.

She stuck her hand in her apron pocket and pulled out a hard peppermint candy, then handed it to me. "I suck on these when I'm stressed."

I unwrapped it and stuck it into my mouth. "Thanks."

"Hmm." She rearranged a set of plates on a tray, then motioned for another server to take it out before turning to me with a hand on her hip. "The leg slit?"

I laughed, surprising myself. "Yeah...didn't help."

"I bet it didn't."

"Hey, Mom!" Eliza called, "You start plating the fruit while I talk some sense into our girl. Lord knows you're better at managing this than I am."

Thank god for Eliza. She knew how to get Magnolia refocused on food and not on me.

Describe it to me. The memory of leaning close to Carma, explaining what pineapple tasted like, nearly did me in. My face heated and I groaned, rubbing my hand over my forehead.

"Ooookay," Eliza said to me. "Mom, fruit!" Without waiting for a response, she grabbed my arm and pulled me out the service door. With the exception of a critter in the nearby dumpster, we were blessedly alone.

She released me and pulled out a peppermint, popping it into her mouth. "How bad?" she asked around the candy.

I laughed without humor.

"That had." She looked at me for a long moment. "I had a feeling, after the taste test."

"Yep."

"Jake know?"

I shook my head. "It hasn't gone...too far. Not yet." But hadn't it? Hadn't it gone too far the moment I looked into her eyes? The moment we kissed? The moment I felt the heat at the core of her body?

"Can you walk away?"

I looked down at my feet, digging the back of my heel into the concrete ramp. "I could." It would kill me, but I would find the strength because I had to. It was the life I had chosen.

"Are you sure?"

"I have to be," I whispered.

"Not necessarily."

I pressed my lips together but didn't look at her. I couldn't let her read my face. That was the problem when people knew you as well as you knew yourself.

"Jake tells me it's a done deal as of tomorrow night."

I nodded.

"Then the end is already in motion. Either everything's going to be fine or it's not. Either she's guilty, or she's not. Either you stick to the life plan you made for yourself at fifteen, or you don't."

I looked up at her, her blue eyes searching mine. "I can't...I couldn't..."

"Why not? Weren't you the one who told me Daisy could do anything?"

"Yeah, but her father isn't literally the person in charge

of US operations."

"So what?"

My eyes widened. "What do you mean, so what? This has been my dream since I was a child!"

"If you recall, I had a volleyball scholarship in college. Turned those Olympic dreams into a job working for SHAP." She glanced at her watch. "Which I need to go do." She turned toward the door. "All I'm saying is, dreams change. You're allowed to follow a new path."

She opened the door and walked in, leaving me alone with whatever was picking at the trash. What the hell would I do if I didn't do this? Would Dad still even talk to me if I left? He'd barely called me while I was recovering. What would happen if I severed this last tie between us? And what about Jake?

I startled when the door opened. I turned to find Jake stepping out. "Didn't realize we were playing hide and seek."

"Just getting some air."

"If you're out here getting air, you're not in there doing your job."

"Nope. Guess not."

He leaned against the wall. "We gonna finally talk about it?"

My eyes stung and I blinked rapidly, then tried to swallow the tennis ball stuck in my throat. "Sometimes this job gets to me." The words were barely above a whisper.

"The job? That's what you're going with?"

I shrugged.

He shook his head. "You must think I'm an idiot."

"Never."

"Well, it's that or you don't trust me."

"That's not—"

"I have eyes, Mina!" He rubbed his palm over his head. "I've never seen you look at someone the way you look at her."

I deflated and leaned my head against the brick exterior. "Doesn't matter."

"How bad?"

I looked over at him. "I haven't crossed the line." The lie slipped easier off my tongue the second time.

He blew out a breath. "Here's what we're going to do. We're going to go in there and small talk these people to death. We're going to dance. We're going to go home and when tonight's report is done, you're going to drink some wine and go to bed. I'll call you when the C&D order is finalized."

I read the command between the lines. *You're going to stay away from Carma.* I sucked in air, trying to get enough oxygen into my lungs. How could I walk back into that room and not look at her? Not dance with her? Not tell her I was falling in love with her?

"Unless you can't. Then I'm sending you home right now."

I met his eyes.

"I'll make your excuses." He held his hand out. "Give me your phone."

"No way. You know we can't be without our phones."

"You have an entire team of support ghosts. I'll handle it."

I palmed my phone. "You don't trust me."

"I trust you with my life."

I raised my eyebrows, silently challenging him.

"My best friend's heart is breaking in front of me. I'm asking for her phone so she doesn't do something she'll regret tomorrow."

The tennis ball worked its way back into my throat. I handed him my phone and dropped my hand fast, trying to not fight to get it back. He was right. I would text Carma, then she'd call, then one of us would go to the other's place, and I might not survive.

He put the phone into the inside pocket of his tux, then walked to the door before pausing. Without saying anything, he turned back and wrapped me in a hug.

"Jake?" I whispered. We didn't hug. Why didn't we hug? Because I'd had a fortress around my heart until Carma broke through it.

Cautiously, I lifted my arms to his waist and hugged him back. When he stepped back, he cleared his throat and squeezed my shoulder. "Summers, you got this, okay?"

"Okay."

With a final squeeze, he turned around and went back inside. I forced my feet to move around the noisy dumpster and to the parking lot, not daring to look back at the glittering fairy lights.

Chapter Twenty-Four

SEBASTIAN, WHO CLEARLY had a better social life than I did, was out when I got home. The velvet suit was shoved to the back of the closet and the rest of the bottle of wine from my fridge was now empty. I laid on the couch, staring at the television, but seeing nothing.

I lifted my head only enough to check the clock on the stove and groaned. Midnight. Only midnight. How was I going to make it through the night?

I really should keep sleeping pills on hand. Or melatonin. Or cookies. What I wouldn't give for cookies right now.

I sat up. *Wait.* I had put Amber's cookies in the freezer until I could give them to Jake. Did I forget? I tripped over my own feet navigating to the kitchen. Nearly taking the freezer door off, I confirmed my suspicion: I had cookies.

Dropping the bag on the counter, I opened it and took out a perfect frozen disk. I plopped it on a napkin then shoved it into the microwave for a few seconds. The moment it beeped, I yanked it out, then closed my eyes and shoved the entire thing into my mouth. The edges were burning hot and the middle was still cold, but it didn't matter after I began to chew. The taste of chocolate and sensation of warm caramel on my tongue made me moan.

I immediately popped another cookie into the microwave then slowly nibbled it from the outside to the inside, each bite more decadent, more thrilling, than the last. This was what life was about. Cookies at midnight. And women in red dresses.

I reached for my phone before remembering Jake had it. Smart man. His intuition and attention to detail made him the best partner. I would one hundred percent be texting Carma right now.

Sinking down to the kitchen floor, I stared at my distorted reflection in the oven's glass. When this was over, I was going after Carma. As long as she was cleared of all charges. It probably meant I wouldn't get the RD promotion—dating a former mark was considered poor conduct—but I could adjust. Maybe Jake would still do a few cases with me a year.

Once Carma and I got married, and things settled down, I was sure people would see I could be trusted and I'd get another chance at RD. "I have a plan!" I announced to the empty room. I pushed myself to my feet, feeling lighter than I had for days. I had a plan.

Except like all perfect plans, it dissolved when I walked to the window and saw Carma looking up from the sidewalk, trying to figure out which window was mine. She caught my movement and stared up at me.

I was sunk. Cue Celine Dion.

What if there's a vampire lurking? The image of Amber covered in blood as she pressed her embroidery against George's neck flashed before me and my adrenaline spiked. I had to protect her.

I shoved my feet into sneakers and tucked Sydney in my back waistband. I leapt down the stairs and pushed outside. I looked around but didn't see anyone or *anything* in the shadows. "Carma, get in the car."

"Not until you tell me what's going on."

I gripped her arms and started to move us backward toward her door.

She brushed me off. "What's wrong with you?!"

"My neighbor was attacked yesterday. It's not safe to be out here at night!"

She crossed her arms. "I'll get in if you get in."

My heart was pounding so hard, my hands shook. "Please, Carma."

"You get in, I get in."

The hoot of an owl made me jump. God, I was being ridiculous. With a deep sigh, I walked over to the passenger side and opened the door. Eyeing each other, we both slowly sat down, closing the doors.

"Buckle up," she warned before hitting the gas and launching us forward.

"CARMA! What the hell?"

"We are figuring this out!"

"What about your mom?" It was my Hail Mary, my last chance.

She shrugged. "You're more important to me than this job."

You're more important. Three simple words that broke down my remaining willpower. "Carma…"

"You left before we could dance. And you didn't return my calls or texts. I thought something bad had happened!"

"I'm sorry. And I let Jake use my cell and forgot to get it back before I went home."

She shot me a weird look. "Okay?"

I heard all the questions she wanted to ask in the lingering silence, but thankfully she didn't. I didn't want to lie anymore tonight. Not to her. "Carma, this isn't a good idea. We should stop this before it's too late."

Her grip tightened on the steering wheel. "I can't." Her voice was barely above a whisper. She glanced over at me and I saw the truth on her face as we passed under a streetlight.

My organs rearranged themselves in my body, my lungs shrinking down to the size of my heart, my heart growing three times as large. I couldn't do more than grip the edge of the seat.

"I'm falling in love with you."

I closed my eyes, letting her confession wash over me. There was a twisted symmetry that the words that cut the deepest were a barely audible whisper. "I'm not a good choice."

Her response was silence. She pulled over to the side of the road, the darkened coffee shop looming in the background the only landmark. "Get out."

I swallowed hard, my shaking hand unbuckling the seatbelt. "I'm so sorry." I opened the door and stepped out, turning toward her when she followed.

"You owe me a dance."

I blinked at her. "What?"

"I didn't wear this dress to not dance, Mina Madison." She leaned in and clicked on the stereo. One of my favorite songs by Sorry Charlie emanated from the speakers.

She smiled as she walked around the car and stood in the headlights. "May I have this dance?"

My body responded before my mind was able to shut it down. I walked toward her, extending my hand. She slipped hers into mine and wrapped her other arm around my shoulder. Mine fit perfectly around her waist, pulling her against me. Her head rested against mine as we swayed in the stillness of the evening, the crickets and cicadas adding harmony to the chorus.

I lifted my arm and spun her around. She looked up at me and laughed and I stilled, a wave of cold-hot realization washing over me. Some invisible string between us knotted, then knotted again, tying my heart to hers. *I loved her.*

"What?" Her eyes sparkled as she leaned against me, wrapping both arms over my shoulders.

I lifted my hands to her face. Closing the space between us, I lowered my mouth to hers. The moment her lips touched mine, my entire body quieted. Every worry, every ache, every doubt vanished. This kiss was different; it was a declaration.

When we broke apart, she took my hand and led me back to the car. I didn't hesitate. We separated only to climb in. She held my hand as we started driving, silent until we pulled into her driveway.

She led me inside, and I kicked off my shoes, slipping Sydney and my keys inside them. I watched her walk down the hall toward the bedroom, nearly tripping over myself running after her. She stood in the center of the room, a splash of decadent red in her pastel palace.

She snapped her fingers at Cheddar and Lucifer, then

pointed to the hall. With disgruntled kitty yawns, they jumped off the end of the bed and sauntered out of the room. I closed the door behind them, the soft click as loud as a gunshot.

She turned her back to me, brushing her long hair to one side. It felt like I was walking underwater as I moved to her, like it was a cross between a dream and a hallucination. I smoothed the back of the dress and pinched the head of the zipper between my fingers, lowering it until it stopped just above her ass. My palms smoothed around her bottom then gripped and kneaded as I pressed my lips to the nape of her neck, smiling against her skin as she gasped.

When she started to writhe, I spread her dress wider as I tasted her over and over again, a trail of kissing down her spine. I dipped my tongue below the edge of her dress and she full body shivered. Kissing my way back up, I moved my lips to one shoulder, then the other, gliding the straps down her arms and letting the dress fold at her waist. Cradling her head with one hand, I kissed her neck, suckling, nipping, tasting every inch.

Open mouthed, desperate kisses against her skin. I fisted her hair with one hand, and wrapped my arm around her waist, pulled her back against me. She moaned, gripping my arm as if it was her lifeline. Her body melted into mine.

"God, if that's what you can do with my neck..." she breathed.

I spun her around, her green eyes blazing. I paused to look at her amazing breasts before my mouth descended on hers in a deep kiss before pulling back. "I'm going to make you scream 'fuck' until you lose your voice," I promised.

She grabbed me by the front of my shirt. "Challenge accepted."

Our mouths fused together, our tongues tangling. I kissed her as if I'd die without her, as if her lungs gave me oxygen, as if her heartbeat was mine. We broke apart only to pull off my T-shirt. The moment our bodies touched skin to skin, we cried out at the sensation.

"How do you feel like this?" I breathed against her lips.

She just kissed me deeper.

We stumbled to the bed and I laid her down, then pulled her legs to the edge. I couldn't hold myself up with my shoulder, but I could kneel. Worship her body, like she deserved. I spread her legs, kissing her from her ankle to her thigh. She breathed my name as I moved to the other leg, my fingers gently drawing swirls on her skin.

Her hands fisted in my hair. "Please, please."

I smiled as I dropped one more kiss on her hip, then moved to her center. First, a brush of my lips. Then a lick. Then a swirl.

She arched off the bed as my arms went around her legs and I worshipped her. Her cries were music, her ragged breath my badge of honor, her body my new religion.

"Mina, don't stop. Don't stop. I'm so close…"

As if I would. As if I could. My body was on fire. I was so turned on, it hurt. Good thing I had a high pain tolerance.

With a scream, she broke apart, a string of expletives on her lips. She tried to pull away, but I held down her hips and kept going until she moved past the too-sensitive point and back into the flames. I slipped a finger inside of her, then two, and *god* had anything ever felt this amazing? No. Because no one had ever been her.

When she crested the second time, she nearly shattered her windows. Her entire body shuddered around me, clenching my fingers in pulsing heat. When she came down, I moved my hand and she immediately sat up, pulling me down next to her.

"My turn." She kissed me hard, her body pressing into mine.

We moved against each other, beautiful friction, smoldering heat, whispered pleas and profanity. When her mouth nestled between my legs, it was as if she lit a fuse. Sparks cascaded out from her mouth, curling and flaming beneath my skin.

Nothing mattered except the way she touched me, the way her green eyes met mine as she licked and sucked and brought me to the edge before pulling back. Catch and release. Building and building until I was sobbing, begging. She lifted her mouth off my skin, smiled, then sucked me into her mouth once more.

My vision went hazy as I fell apart at the seams, her soft purrs and words of encouragement piecing me back together in a way I didn't recognize. How did she have this much power over me? Why couldn't I walk away from her?

What was going to happen in the morning?

I pushed the thought out of my head as her mouth found mine and I sank back into her arms. Tomorrow I would deal with the fallout. Tonight, I was hers.

Chapter Twenty-Five

S HE WOKE ME up with her mouth on my skin, somehow building a fire that I thought had finally petered out. My limbs were still heavy, my muscles sore from hours of tightening and releasing. "How do you have the energy?" I croaked, as she lavished attention on my breast, shooting pleasure straight to my center.

"I don't need much sleep. Few hours a night, max."

I shook my head in disbelief as she moved to my other breast. Fatigue fell away as she wound me tighter. I pulled her down next to me as we used our hands on each other. We held on as we came apart in the dampened light coming in from the bottom of the curtain.

"Let's not leave bed today," she said, wrapping her limbs around me. She was a full-contact sleeper.

It was strange, having someone touch me without hesitation. I burrowed into her embrace, marveling at how safe I felt, at how much she felt like home. Her skin was cool, but she made me warm. Fulfilled. Happy.

"I love you," I whispered against her neck. I was Carma's. She was like a song, decadent chocolate, sunshine. Now that I knew how she felt in my arms, I could never walk away.

She stilled, then wrapped herself even tighter around me. This time, we made love in slow strokes and gasps, our gazes locked as we both came apart. I buried my head in the crook of her neck to hide the sting in my eyes.

I had to tell her.

I had to come clean.

This could destroy us.

Her fingers ran over the skin of my arms, ghost bumps chasing her touch. Our breathing slowed and I laid my head on her shoulder. "I need to tell you something."

"You can tell me anything."

I swallowed hard. "I'm…" *Afraid? Scared?* "Terrified."

She tightened her arms around me. "I've got you."

"I—"

A door closed.

"Princess?" Lucinda called. "You up?"

"Oh shit!" Carma breathed, rolling out of my arms and scrambling off the bed. "Hold on, Mom!" she called, then quickly slid to the door and clicked the lock.

I pulled on my leggings and tossed my T-shirt over my head. "I can go out the window. Just come back with my shoes."

Carma straightened. "No." She walked over and kissed me hard. "I'm all in if you are, which means telling my mom."

"Are you sure?" I wanted her to say yes. I needed her to say no.

"Hell yes." She gave me one more kiss. "You ready?"

"Let me wash you off my face first?"

She giggled. "Good point." She looked toward the door.

"Mom, we'll be out in a minute!"

I scrunched my nose and poked her in the side. "You said we. She's going to freak out."

"So what?"

I rolled my eyes as we moved to the bathroom. I used her face wash and mouthwash but gave up on my hair. Bedhead was popular these days anyway. When we were as presentable as we were going to get, she took my hand and unlocked the door.

Lucinda was sitting at the kitchen table with two Thinner shakes in front of her. She gave us a long look. "Ah, I figured."

"Mom, Mina and are I in a relationship now."

I squeezed her hand. Carma didn't beat around the bush and I was so proud of her. But, if I wasn't lethal and hadn't had years of Magnolia's stares, I would've been terrified at Lucinda's face.

Her driver opened the front door, saw the standoff, then cleared his throat. "Uh, I'm going to go put gas in the car," he muttered then backed out of the house.

She just studied me for a long moment before picking up a shake. "I see." She picked at the plastic lid. "This is the new extra-strength version I requested. If it's any good, they'll go to market next month. It would cut weight loss time in half. We could be international by next year."

She tried to pull the tab to open the lid, but the tab came off in her hand. "Once we get better packaging." She looked up at Carma. "I was hoping you'd be at my side."

Carma walked over and grabbed the second shake and tried to open it. That tab broke off in her hand, too. She walked over to the kitchen and took out scissors, cutting the lid open. I tensed at her hiss as she shook her hand. "Clumsy me. Cut myself with the scissors."

She handed the opened shake to her mom. "I'll be by your side only if you're okay with Mina being by my side."

"How will it look if my daughter, the VP of the company, is having an affair with my assistant?"

Walking back to the kitchen sink, Carma washed her hand and pressed paper towel to her palm. "Then consider this my resignation, Mom."

Everything happened in slow motion. Lucinda looked to her daughter as she raised the shake to her mouth, a bright red drop on the rim of the cup disappearing under her pink lipstick. Lucinda's eyes narrowed before rolling back into her head, and she collapsed onto the table.

"MOM!" Carma ran over, lifting her mom off the table.

I rushed over and pressed my fingers to Lucinda's pulse point. The low thrum of her heartbeat was slowing. *Oh no.* "Babe, get your phone. Call for an ambulance."

She ran to the bedroom to get her phone as I kept my finger on her mom's wrist, counting her pulse. Forty beats per minute. Thirty. Twenty.

None.

I didn't react, just waited as Carma gave the emergency operator her address. Something in my gut told me Lucinda didn't just casually die in front of us. My suspicion was confirmed when she stirred awake.

Shit.

"Carma, go to your room and lock the door," I ordered. "Please don't ask me why, just go."

"What's wrong?!" She rushed over to us and I knew we were out of time.

Lucinda raised her head as Carma touched her shoulder. I ran for my shoes, grabbing Sydney and sliding back into the kitchen. Carma screamed as Lucinda stood and grabbed her. Lucinda's fangs protruded from her mouth, inching closer to her daughter's neck.

I attacked from behind, knocking Lucinda's arms away. I shoved her back and grabbed Carma, shoving her behind me.

"WHAT IS GOING ON? MOM!"

"Babe, she's not your mom right now."

"Where'd you get that gun?!"

"Don't have time for small talk right now. I need you to go lock yourself in the bedroom." Lucinda took a step toward us and I took a step back, forcing Carma to move with me. "Your mom seems to be changing into a vampire." *Please don't be feral like the last two.*

"W-what?" Her voice shook and I wished I could turn around and hold her, kiss her, tell her everything was going to be okay. But I couldn't and it wasn't.

My gun was trained on Lucinda as she snarled, her eyes locked on me, but she didn't attack. Her understanding the gun was dangerous was a good sign that she wasn't feral. At least, not yet.

"Carma? Dial this number and put it on speaker." I listed off SHAP's main line.

Lucinda tried to round the table and I repositioned us. "Don't move, Lucinda. I will shoot and it's going to hurt."

Carma made a terrified squeak but held the phone out as it rang.

"Dispatch, Val speaking."

"This is Agent Summers. Requesting immediate back up." I gave Carma's address. "I've got a new vampire, Lucinda Marks. Need extraction. Civilian involved. Contact Agent Robinson."

Val had been doing this job long enough to not show surprise, but the extra beat of silence told me she knew this was trouble.

"Contacting Agent Robinson immediately. Extraction team in route. Be careful." The line went dead.

I moved us back as Lucinda skated around the kitchen table. "Take the phone, go lock yourself in your car. I'm going to try to get your mom help."

"What the hell is going on?"

I shook my head. "Not really a good time for explanations."

"Then you better talk fast."

I glanced at her furious face. "I love you. Nothing about that is fake, you got me?"

"I got you."

"I work for Supernatural-Human Accountability Partnership. I was assigned to investigate your mom because some unexplained vampires connected to Thinner kept attacking humans."

"And me?"

I nodded. "And you." Lucinda ran and I shot a warning into the kitchen floor. She startled and cowered back. I maneuvered Carma and me into the living room and near the window. I ripped the curtains open, letting in the morning light. Lucinda flinched and hissed again.

"Mom! Just stay there. Please!" Carma was crying.

I wanted to turn around and kiss her and tell her everything was going to be okay. But I wasn't going to lie to her either. "Carma, your mom is turning into a vampire. I think it had something to do with whatever is in the shake and that drop of blood from your palm. Do you know what's in the shake?"

Lucinda took a step into the living room. A ray of sunshine hit her arm and her exposed skin started smoking. She snarled and took a step back, cradling her arm to her chest.

"Carma, do you know what's in the shake? Is there something that could cause someone to become a vampire?" It sounded ridiculous to me, but there wasn't anything about this situation that wasn't.

She sucked in a sharp breath, her throat clogged with emotion. "Not completely," she whispered.

"Not completely? Not completely sure what's in the shake or not completely a vampire? This isn't the time to be vague. We've got maybe a minute, possibly two before agents flood this house and we're separated. I need to know what you know. You can be pissed at me later, but I need to protect you."

Lucinda moved again, pacing to the hallway and back again.

"Mom said it wasn't permanent!"

Lucinda lunged and I threw Carma behind her couch. I pulled a blanket off the back and covered her as best I could. "You okay?"

"Fine! Help my mom."

I really didn't want to put a wooden bullet into my girlfriend's mom's chest, but if she attacked Carma, I wouldn't have a choice. I nearly cried in relief when Sebastian appeared.

"Jake's forty-five seconds out!" Sebastian confirmed, walking toward Lucinda with no fear. Ghosts could distract vampires without the risk of being a meal. He put his hands in the air, showing he was unarmed. "We're going to get you help."

Her red eyes tracked him as he paced in front of her, talking in a soothing tone about how she'd be better soon. It was a lie, of course. Once someone became a vampire, there wasn't any going back. The virus in the venom made the body its permanent host. The heart slowed and stopped and the lungs ceased needing oxygen. Reversing the virus couldn't bring back a heartbeat.

Taking advantage of Sebastian's distraction, I lifted Carma from the floor and ran into her hall closet, setting her inside and closing the door. I grabbed her side table and yanked it across the floor, relieved when it fit perfectly under the doorknob to keep her from escaping.

She banged against the wood, but I didn't flinch. I just kept my eyes on the dance between Lucinda and Sebastian. "I'm protecting you!"

"I don't understand!"

A crash emanated from the kitchen, and I nearly cried at the sound of porcelain teacups hitting the ground. God, what if I had spoken faster this morning, could this moment have been avoided? What if I hadn't looked out my window last night? What if I had skipped this assignment?

This was exactly what I didn't want to happen. "What

did you mean earlier? When you said it wasn't permanent?"

There was a long pause, but she stopped hitting the wood. "She said as long as we drank the shakes and followed the guidelines, we'd be fine."

"Carma, how does it work? How do members lose weight?" I shifted, making sure Lucinda didn't get near the back door. The worst thing that could happen was her running out into the world. "Carma, babe? Can you answer me?"

"It doesn't make any sense."

"My roommate is a century-old ghost. Try me."

"Uh…she said it was some combination that would slow digestion. She promised it was reversible. But I started to have weird cravings, and I hardly ever sleep, I got more sensitive to the sun…and so I decided to investigate. There's something in the shake."

"Do you know what it is? Were you involved?"

"No."

"Was Maggie? Rachel? Who knew?"

"No! No. Only Mom knew. And I guess the inventor of the shakes. Whenever Mom spoke about whatever the special ingredient is, it was a number."

I made a mental note to hunt down the inventor. If the ingredient was in code, the factory mixing the shakes likely didn't know what it was either, but a secret needed two people. I'd find Lucinda's accomplice.

"AGENT SUMMERS!" Jake burst through the back door, closing it quickly. He took in the scene and leveled his gun at Lucinda. "SHAP is two minutes out."

I tilted my head to the closet. "Carma's safe."

"Who's here?" she asked.

"My partner," I admitted.

"Partner?"

I ignored the question for the moment. "Carma, I need to know right now. Did you know what was going on?"

"No. No, I didn't. I swear."

I nodded. "Okay."

The slam of car doors announced the rest of SHAP had arrived. Presumably the ambulance had too, which they would deal with. Jake and I held our positions as the SHAP team, led by two vampires, entered the house and safely apprehended Lucinda. I talked to Carma through the door to let her know what was happening and where they would take her. She didn't respond, but the soft sobs I heard broke my heart.

When it was just Jake and I left in the house, I pulled the table back and opened the door. Carma walked out but avoided getting close to me, her tear-stained face making me nauseated. How had this all gone so wrong?

"Carma, please pack an overnight bag. I will be escorting you to headquarters for questioning," Jake said.

Carma, startled, looked between Jake and me. I could see her piece together that Jake wasn't just the new IT employee, but my partner. "I'm so sorry we had to lie to you," I whispered. I stepped between Carma and Jake. "She's innocent."

"Mina, don't get involved." He stepped toward me with his civilian black cane. He wasn't recording us, thank God. I wasn't ready.

"I have to," I admitted.

His eyes met mine. "Lab results came in an hour ago. There's vampire venom in the shakes. Venom and animal blood. Just enough to start the change but keep it in constant transition. Members are safe, unless they ingest human blood."

"They made hybrids." It wasn't a question.

He nodded, his eyes never leaving mine. "Charges include making unauthorized vampires, violating the human-supernatural consent agreements, three attempted homicides due to unlicensed feeding, and at least three vampire deaths."

My blood ran cold. Just the first charge alone was a life sentence. The others meant everyone involved would face a grueling trial and likely also face life in prison. "Jake..." My voice shook.

"I need you to pick a side right now, because this is about to get ugly."

Carma stepped closer. "What are you saying? That my mother knowingly endangered her members? Impossible."

My partner closed his eyes for a moment, then reopened them, focused on Carma. "Carma Nicks, you are under arrest for aiding and abetting the creation of a vampire clan—"

"She's not involved," I spoke over him, shaking my head.

"I didn't know!" she added. "I would never, you have to believe me!"

He ignored us. "You will be brought to SHAP headquarters and brought up on charges. You have the right to representation from an attorney of your choice—"

"I'll vouch for her." My words were quiet, but they rang out like a gunshot, silencing the room. I closed my eyes, knowing this was it. Vouching meant an agent had a personal relationship—usually familial—with a mark. It was a line in the sand. To vouch meant I would have to admit, on record, my relationship with Carma.

It meant my career was over with those four words.

Jake didn't look at me when he said, "She's the vice president," through clenched teeth. "Think about this, Mina."

"I know." I blew out a long breath. "But she told me she didn't know."

"And you believe her?"

I nodded once, and it felt like an act of war. "I love her."

He flinched. It took him two swallows before he managed to ask, "Will you go on record?"

"Yes."

He looked at me as he put his weapon back into its holder then leaned heavily on his cane, as if the weight of my words were too much. Pain sliced through his stoic expression. "You know what that means."

I nodded once. "I know." The nature of the relationship would be documented, and everyone, including my father, would know about our affair by the end of the hour.

I would absolutely lose my job and be a blacklisted agent.

He closed his eyes and took a step back, as if I had punched him in the stomach. He looked back at Carma. "You better be worth it."

"Jake…"

"I'm going to make the call." He gave me one more look, and my heart broke at the concern on his face.

I'm sorry, I mouthed.

He paused with his hand on the doorknob and I rushed

after him, grabbing his arm. "Jake . . ."

He pulled me into his arms. "I love you and want you to be happy."

My arms went around his shoulders. "I know."

"This is gonna suck hard." He breathed out a sharp breath. "I won't be able to protect you from the shitstorm."

"I know," I said again.

He released me, his free hand holding my shoulder for a long moment, his eyes glassy. I gave him a firm nod, unable to find my voice in the emotions that clogged my throat. Then he straightened, nodded to Carma, and walked out.

Chapter Twenty-Six

"*BREAKING NEWS TODAY from Applechester, Michigan. Mega-popular weight loss company Thinner has been shut down after federal agencies discovered one of the ingredients in their popular shakes was poisonous in high doses. So far, the death toll is at three and climbing. If you are a Thinner member and have not received medical instructions, please contact SAFE immediately at—*"

I slammed my hand against the radio, turning off the announcement. I didn't need to relive what I already knew. I leaned my forehead against the steering wheel, wringing my hands around it as if were a wet towel.

I needed to get out of this truck, walk to the front door, scan my keycard, walk to my dad's office. I needed to tell him everything. Needed to face his disappointment while we figured out how to keep Carma from getting a life sentence.

Then I needed to do the far scarier thing: See Carma. Beg for forgiveness.

I raised my head and looked out over the parking lot and past the SHAP building, to the large tent being erected for emergency medical care. As early as tomorrow, Thinner members in the area would show up en masse to be examined and hopefully receive a blood transfusion that would eliminate the venom from their bodies.

A knock on my window made me scream. I never screamed. I jerked upright to find Jake. With a resigned sigh, I turned off my engine. He stepped back when I opened my door only the necessary amount to slide out.

I stood there in silence, fidgeting with my keys. He put his free hand in his pocket and turned to face the tent, leaning back against my truck. "Lucinda is secure. The SHAP physicians and the research team are with Carma now."

I nodded, leaning next to him. "Is—" I cleared my throat. "Is she okay?"

He glanced at me. "She's strong. But you already knew that. She wants to be the one to make the calls to the members. She asked to be in the tent as they started treatment."

"Of course." I shook my head. "She'll do all the transfusions herself if you let her."

He bumped his shoulder with mine. "I don't know her well yet, but I can see why you love her."

My breath caught and I had to clear the emotion out of my throat a second time. "Loving her isn't going to save her from this hell."

"No. It won't." The side of his head leaned against the top of mine. "But babe, loving her is going to help her recover. She lost her mom and her company today. We're going to do what we can to make sure she doesn't lose her freedom, too."

I stepped back and turned to face him, wide-eyed. "You believe she had nothing to do with it?"

His gaze held mine. "I believe you, and you believe her. I

trust you with my life. No reason to start doubting you now."

"Even though I kept my feelings from you?" My voice was barely above a whisper.

"What is it Sebastian always says? You have the emotional maturity of wet toilet paper?"

I gave him the finger.

His eyes crinkled, but his smile didn't reach his mouth. "Yeah. Even though you didn't tell me." He nodded toward the looming brick building. "You ready to face your dad?"

"Never." I bit down hard on my lip. "Jake...it'll be the end of everything."

He put his forehead on my shoulder. "I know." After a deep sigh, he continued. "But ends are okay. They allow for new beginnings."

"You sound like Magnolia."

"Good."

We stayed like that for a long moment, our friendship the only thing keeping me upright. "I'm ready," I whispered.

He lifted his head and nodded, then fell into step beside me. He didn't need to tell me he was going to stand by me, and I didn't need to ask.

IT WAS FIFTY-SEVEN steps from the front door to the elevator. Four floors to the executive level. Eighty-two steps to my dad's office door. Three knocks. Two heart beats.

I frowned at the man who sat behind my dad's desk; the opposite of the man I expected. His reading glasses were tossed haphazardly on his desktop, his tie loosened at the neck, his hair in disarray as if his hands had sifted through it unconsciously.

He looked up as we walked in but didn't stand. Didn't hold out his hand to Jake. Didn't acknowledge me with a curt nod. Instead, his eyes studied me, watched me, searched my face for answers.

As Sienna closed his office door behind us, Dad gestured to the two chairs in front of his desk. We sat. I put my hands between my knees to hide the shaking.

No one said anything. The silence tore at my stomach. I tried to suck in a deep breath through my nose, and on the third try I succeeded.

Dad put his elbows on his desk, then clasped his hands together, leaning his chin against them. "Carma will have to face a judge, but she has agreed to fully cooperate with the investigation. With you vouching for her, I doubt she'll face any jail time."

"Good," I breathed. "Then it was worth it."

He nodded once. "However, if Lucinda goes to trial, you're likely going to have to testify and defend your relationship with Carma."

The mask I wore when my dad was around slipped and I covered my face with my hands, then leaned forward over my legs trying to remember how to breathe in and out. I hated testifying for regular cases, but this was going to be a special kind of torture. Being forced to explain how I had an affair with a mark in what will likely be one of the highest profile cases of the decade was going to be hell.

Jake leaned back in his chair and pinched the bridge of

his nose. "Jim, they'll tear her apart. Both of them apart."

"I know," Dad confirmed. I heard him stand and walk. I raised my head when he touched my shoulder, then leaned against his desk just to my left. He'd never sat on his desk before, at least not in my presence.

He looked over at Jake. "Get an update on Carma."

Jake turned to me, silently making it clear he was here to support me first. I tilted my head, letting him know he should go check. "I'll be back."

I blinked hard, but my dad was still here, across from me, trying to comfort me. His hand squeezed my shoulder once and then he let it fall. He crossed his legs at the ankles and gripped the edge of the desk. "We need Lucinda's confession."

I searched his face. "You need me to get it?"

He nodded. "She won't speak."

"I'll do it."

He nodded again. "I know."

I stared at the stapler behind him, willing myself to wake up, back in Carma's arms. Except this wasn't a nightmare. "Dad, I'm sorry," I whispered.

"She the one?"

I looked up at him. "Yeah. She is."

"You gonna be okay?"

I nodded, then shook my head. "What do I do now?" I whispered.

He crossed his arms and sighed, leaning back. "I don't know, kid. We'll figure it out."

"We?"

He pushed away from his desk and crossed back over to

his chair. "Always got your back." He picked up his glasses and perched them on his nose, then looked over the top. "Even when you don't think I do."

I swallowed hard, wishing he'd told me this months ago. Wishing I had come to him in the first place. Wishing I had just stayed in bed. "What now?"

He turned to his computer. "I'm going to fill out your termination report." He met my eyes. "Confession."

We both knew if my employment was over with SHAP, I didn't have to follow the code of ethics. I wouldn't be on anymore SHAP cases. It was time to get a confession any way I could.

"If you'll excuse me, I'm just going to…stretch my legs."

He nodded. "Tell Sienna the cameras are out in cellblock C." His fingers moved swiftly over his keyboard.

I tilted my head. "What a shame. Should get that looked at."

He grunted.

I paused at the door, then turned back to face him. "Thank you, Dad."

He looked up at me and his eye crinkled. "Be careful." It wasn't an "I love you," but it was close enough.

I walked out of his office, shutting the door behind me. I rested my hand on the handle, likely for the last time. This would never be my office and I would never be allowed in here again. Or at least, not for a very long time. There were too many secrets in these walls.

Sienna stood and walked over. "Well, Miss Mina, I had hoped I'd get to be your assistant someday." Werewolves lived for a *very* long time.

I bit the insides of my cheeks until I regained my composure. "The feeling was mutual."

She surprised me by pulling me into a hug. Sienna didn't hug.

"Uh, is this some weird distraction so I drop my guard and you can bite me?"

She laughed softly. "You were always the bravest. I'm glad to see that hasn't changed." She released me and stepped back.

"I don't think having an affair with my mark is 'brave.'"

She just shook her head. "Well, I didn't say you were intuitive." She walked back to her desk chair and sat. "It'd be a shame if, on your walk, you went by C23. A real big shame."

"I definitely better avoid C23." With one final look around the neutrally gray office, I sucked in a shaky breath and nodded. "Keep an eye on him, please."

Her eyes held mine. "Always."

Chapter Twenty-Seven

M Y CHEST HOLLOWED as I walked down the hall, my head held high despite the whispers coming from open doors. I took the stairs to floor C, using my keycard to pass through the security doors. The guard who stood at the desk looked over at me, then promptly turned around so he faced away from cell twenty-three.

Sienna must have called ahead. I jogged to the door, swiping my card and holding my breath until I heard the lock click. I stepped inside and peered through the thick, clear, bulletproof safety window.

Lucinda didn't look up, but her shoulders tensed. There was no way in hell I wouldn't get a confession out of her, new vampire or not. I didn't give up everything for Carma to have her own mother throw her under the bus. This ended here and now. Even if Carma walked away and never looked back, I'd know that I was the reason she was free, and it would be enough.

It'd have to be enough.

I swiped my card at the second door, opening the cell. I pulled Sydney out of my holster, holding her in my right hand. "If you so much as blink at me wrong, I will put a bullet in you. Are we clear?"

She didn't respond. I took her silence as a yes.

"I'm not sorry for lying to you as part of an investigation. But your daughter saved *your* life. Now it's time to save hers. Confess. Protect her."

Her eye twitched.

"You lied to her. You used her. And now you're trying to get her to shoulder part of the blame for you. I will not let that happen." I narrowed my eyes. "You made money off of lying to people while feeding them something you *knew* would harm them!"

"I was helping people!" she raged, her eyes burning brilliant red.

"Yeah, by literally killing half their body without them knowing."

"Fat will kill them, too. This way they looked good and my business thrived."

I took a step back and stared at the woman—vampire—in front of me. "You honestly think that knowingly poisoning people without their consent is comparable to extra weight? A person's weight doesn't change their value! A person's health doesn't change their value!" I narrowed my eyes. "Purposefully hurting people does, though."

"I was actually making a *difference*. Helping the hopeless. Making people happy with their bodies again."

"What about the lives you destroyed? The people you turned into vampires? Do their lives mean less to you?"

"Ask yourself, how did Thinner get so popular if people didn't want my help? If they weren't desperate for a solution? We were going international within a year. No one bothered to question a thing because we were filling a need."

"You were filling your bank account while filling people with literal poison."

She waved me off. "People fill their bodies with poison every day."

"Yeah, fair, but they consent to it. See the key word in all of this is *consent*."

She didn't respond, but I saw the truth in her eyes. She didn't think she did anything wrong.

I took a step closer. "Stop me if you've heard this one. A woman decides to start a company and begs her daughter to join. Drags her in blindfolded."

She shrugged.

I wanted to scream. "You're unbelievable."

"No, dear. I'm a businesswoman."

My finger flipped the safety off my gun. *Oops.* "How long did you think you could keep this up before someone caught on? Were you ever going to tell Carma?"

She leaned forward. "You don't get it, do you? People will believe whatever you need them to, as long as you convince them it's for their benefit."

"How did someone like you raise someone as amazing as Carma?" I shook my head. "She's so creative, full of light, would do anything for the people she loves. You took advantage of her. That's why you wanted me to keep my distance. So I couldn't interfere?"

She raised an eyebrow. A silent confirmation.

I studied her for a long moment. "You took the pills on purpose, didn't you? To get her to stay by your side and guilt her into working with you?"

"She was the best and I needed the best."

As the pieces clicked together, I swallowed hard, ignoring the wave of nausea at her confession. "Now you're going to take the best down with you."

She shook her head. "You wouldn't let that happen. She'll be fine. But I'm not confessing and damaging my reputation. I'm just another victim here."

She morphed her face into a perfect mask of devastation. "I didn't know the shakes were dangerous. Clearly my supplier lied to me."

I took a step closer. "Not going to work for me. You may be a businesswoman, but I'm a woman in love. And I'm willing to sacrifice everything for Carma. So try me." She shifted, and I held my gun directly at her head.

"I have rights. You can't do this to me."

"Want to take that bet?" I leaned close to her. "Because I killed the last vampire who attacked me."

She just watched me, waiting. At least this time she was smart enough to stay perfectly still.

"Here's what's going to happen: You're going to confess and name your accomplice. You're going to confirm Carma had nothing to do with what was going on. And you're going to go to jail for a very, *very* long time. When they say life sentence, it's not just fifty or sixty years for you. Oh, it's so much longer."

She growled.

"I'm going to spend my life protecting Carma as long as she wants me around."

"Stay away from—"

"No. You don't get any say in our relationship. I love her and I will do what I need to do to make sure she's happy and healthy. Even if that means shoving wooden bullets into your skin until you're screaming in pain."

She jumped at me and I shot her thigh, wincing at the echo of the explosion in the small cell. She wailed, gripping her leg as black blood spread across the thigh of her blue jumpsuit. Her fangs came out, but she sat down, gripping her leg. The wound wouldn't heal until she dug the bullet out.

"Confess. If you love your daughter at all, confess and save her. Or I swear to god I will make you and you won't like that."

She nodded once, then laid down, whimpering.

I exited. "She's ready to confess," I told the guard. "And she needs a medic. It was so weird; she got some wood stuck in her thigh."

"Pity," the guard said.

Chapter Twenty-Eight

CARMA'S ROOM WAS a combination medical suite and safe room, that was doing double duty as a makeshift cell. Jake was outside Carma's closed door, talking to Paris, my favorite woman from the research team. She was a little older than me, a little taller than me, and had a tan from summer days outside. Grade A eye candy. My "no dating co-workers" rule had prevented me from agreeing to a date when she'd asked a few years back.

"The team of the hour," Paris said. "I can't believe you two uncovered an oral-venom distribution site. I can't even believe one exists."

I smiled, although it didn't reach my eyes. "Be honest. Did you get emotional when you found out?"

"Cried a little," she sighed, then flashed a devastating smile that practically lit up the hallway.

Good lord. I looked over at Jake and saw him blink hard. Paris had that effect on people. "Did you meet with the doctors? What's going on with Carma?"

Paris's face turned serious and she adjusted her glasses, then looked at Jake. "You should take this."

I turned to him. "Tell me straight."

"You know once the virus enters someone's body after an

attack, we only have a few hours, at most, to save them."

A chill ran down my spine. "But this is super diluted, right?"

"Yeah. Which buys us time."

I looked between him and Paris. "But not enough?" I whispered.

Paris looked at her tablet. "Best educated guess without further testing, three months. Maybe six."

I looked at Jake. "Carma's been drinking the shakes for a year."

He nodded. "Yes." His eye met mine. "We can't reverse her."

"But we think we can keep her stable," Paris added. "We'll give her a choice as long as she has one, but she'll never be fully human again. It's hybrid or vampire or..."

"Door number three," I sighed. Permanent deanimation. "Does she know?"

Jake nodded. "She does."

"Can I see her?"

"Technically? No. But Paris was about to show me something on her phone, and we get better signal over by the window at the end of the hall. It will take about ten minutes, which is exactly the same amount of time until security returns from lunch." He slid his ID badge through the reader and unlocked Carma's door.

Paris pulled out her cell. "Jake, I have the most interesting thing to show you over by this window." She started walking in the opposite direction and Jake joined her.

I pushed into the room, smelling disinfectant and soap instead of strawberries. Carma stared blankly at a television hanging from a ceiling, her dark hair in a careless ponytail fraying at the edges. She looked over and froze.

"Is it okay that I'm here?" I asked, barely louder than her heart monitor.

She didn't respond for a moment, sucking the air out of my lungs. Then she nodded infinitesimally. She looked so young, so fragile in this room. Maybe it was the IV, or the hospital gown, or the hospital bed with stark white sheets.

Here, Carma was completely devoid of everything *her*.

"I want to ask you how you're doing, but that seems like a stupid question."

She brought her knees to her chest, folding her arms on top of the blanket covering her legs. "You know that song 'What A Difference A Day Makes?'"

"Dinah Washington."

"It just keeps playing in my head. But...with emo lyrics."

"I'm so sorry."

"They told me my mom's okay. Although she's a vampire now." She laughed without humor. Her hand covered her mouth, and she shook her head, then let her hand fall. "A vampire. If I hadn't seen it with my own eyes, I wouldn't believe it."

"I just saw her. She's adjusted well. She's safe." Technically.

Carma looked relieved. "I can't believe..." She rested her forehead on her arms. "I lost everything today. My family, my job..." she looked up at me, her eyes filled with tears. "You. Or at least the person I thought you were."

Without thinking too hard about what I was doing, I hurried to the side of the bed and sat on the edge. "I know

I'm probably the last person you want to see right now, but can I hold you? Just for a few minutes?"

She pressed her lips together and she frowned but nodded as the tears leaked out her eyes. I wrapped my arms around her, resting my head on top of hers. "I wish I could do something to make this better." I ran my fingers through her hair as she cried, trying to comfort her with touch instead of words.

"I'm scared," she admitted a few minutes later.

"You're not going to go through this alone," I promised. "The team is going to do everything they can—"

"No, I mean, I'm scared about being a hybrid. And I'm scared to start over without Mom. I'm scared for all the members." She shifted and I released her. She sat up and wiped at her face with her palms. "And I'm mostly scared that we can't fix us."

My eyes stung and my heart pounded so hard in my chest, I could hear it in my ears. "Carma…"

"I know why you did it, and I understand why you couldn't tell me. But you lied to me, Mina. And those lies had major consequences." She brushed her fallen ponytail out of her face.

I stood, turning so I was in profile but not brave enough to face her. "I was going to tell you who I was this morning. The secret beat me to it." I looked over at her, but she was looking at her chipped manicure as if it held all the answers. "Would it have made a difference?"

She bit her lower lip, and my heart splintered a little more. "I don't know."

There was a knock at the door and Jake opened it, poking his head in. "Security in two."

"Coming!" I promised, then looked back at Carma. "Paris and her team will take care of you, okay? Whether you want to stay a hybrid or turn full vampire. I would trust them with my life."

She nodded.

My chest was so tight I couldn't figure out how to push out enough air to talk. I rubbed the heel of my hand across my breastbone to try and loosen it. "Carma, I'm only a phone call away..."

Jake opened the door. "Thirty seconds, Summers. Move it."

Carma's gaze snapped to mine. "Summers?"

"My real name is Mina Summers." I turned to her and grabbed her hands and kissed both of them. "And I'm still in love with you, Carma Nicks."

"I'm sorry, Mina," she breathed.

Jake wrapped his arm around my waist and lifted me away, shuffling us toward the door. "You're not getting caught on my watch, Summers. Get out." He set me down and gave me a gentle shove.

I looked over my shoulder at Carma as the door closed, her green eyes glued to mine. Jake wrapped his arm around my back, and we moved down the hall only seconds before security stepped out of the elevator and we stepped in.

We let the doors close but didn't select a floor.

"We had a good run, Summers," he said.

"That we did, Robinson. So, what now?" His eyes met mine and I knew. The fissures in my heart turned into fractures.

Slowly, as if trying to make time last a little longer, he reached out for the elevator button and selected lobby. Then he waited, hand in his pocket, while I turned in my keycard and exited the lobby doors. And just like that, it was over.

Now I needed to go say the goodbye that would break my heart the most.

WHEN I ARRIVED back at my apartment, Sebastian was waiting for me next to the unmarked van. Ghosts could only stay with an active agent, and the moment I walked out the lobby doors of SHAP, my active agent status had been revoked. Sebastian hovered next to me as we walked into my apartment.

"If you knew how this would finish, would you have altered your course?" he asked.

Was it worth it? I closed my eyes for a long moment, remembering the smell of strawberries, the feel of her lips against mine, the sound of her heartbeat as I laid my head on her chest. I shook my head once.

He smiled. "Then it was worth it."

"I don't know what I'm going to do without you," I whispered.

"You're going to sit on that ridiculous armchair, you're going to find something that brings you joy, then you're going to write me letters so you can remember until we meet again."

I studied his face, trying to memorize the sharp cheekbones and slim nose. I wished I could take a picture, something to commemorate our time together, something tangible to frame. "Thank you for being the best of friends."

A woman walked over to us and explained they were ready to begin relocation. She motioned for her crew to give us a moment to say goodbye. Something inside me broke as they walked out.

Reggie stood by my side, openly weeping, as Sebastian took off his top hat and bowed to me as if I were royalty. "Miss Summers, it has been an honor and a pleasure."

"Sebastian…" I sucked in a shaky breath.

"We'll find each other again. I promise."

They wouldn't tell me where he was moved, as the locations of ghost agents were classified, but I would search the goddamn planet if needed. After all, I didn't have a job anymore. I had infinite time. And I had Reggie.

Sebastian lingered for one moment more, looking around the living room. "You are the person I love the most in this afterlife. Until we meet again." He gave me a sad smile before he turned and hugged Reggie. Then, they were gone.

I stood there, unable to do more than suck in sharp breaths through my nose as my fingers and toes went numb. I sank to my knees, unable to figure out how to keep standing. All the air in my lungs, the room, the planet, evaporated. I was drowning.

Sebastian's words bounced around the room. *Would you have altered your course?* Yes, everything.

But even as I rolled over onto my back and stared up at the ceiling, I knew that wasn't true. Because I would do it all again to go back to the morning after the fundraiser when I woke up in Carma's arms. The moment I buried my face in her neck and knew I was home.

Right before it all burned to the ground.

Reggie walked through my door—literally—and laid down next to me. "We'll find him."

I didn't respond. I just turned on my side to face him and burst out crying. The dam broke. Years of holding in stinging eyes and runny noses seemed to pour out.

Reggie, who had never seen me cry, *ever*, gasped and then tried to pat me. His ghost hands went right through. "Being dead es tan tonto." He sighed in frustration and then started humming.

I nearly choked when I recognized the song. "My Heart Will Go On"?

"Sí."

I rolled to my back and wiped my face off with my shirt. "You're ridiculous."

"Just so."

We both looked at each other and nearly smiled at the Sebastian phrase. "What am I going to do?" My voice shook with the admission that I *didn't* know what to do. "I lost everything." I turned my head to look at him.

"You haven't lost me."

"Who needs humans when I have ghosts, right?"

Reggie smiled at me, but it didn't quite reach his eyes.

Chapter Twenty-Nine

ME SPIRALING ALONE in my apartment lasted twelve days. Magnolia and Eliza had come by to drop off meals, but I greeted them at the door and didn't invite them in. I must have looked as bad as I felt, since Magnolia didn't even argue with me. She just kissed my cheek and left.

Belphegor—after what Amber had called "a harrowing five days" in SHAP's detention center—had been cleared of all charges, as Jake promised. The demon came by twice with plates of cookies and the second time I finally invited him in. I had forgotten the sound of my own voice and figured he'd be easier to tolerate than someone who actually cared about my well-being. He wouldn't make me cry with *feelings* talk.

"You look like shit," he said, settling into the orange armchair. "Also, where'd you get this? This would be perfect for our waiting room."

I frowned as I took a cookie. "Hell has waiting rooms?"

"Hell is *made* of waiting rooms."

Maybe it was time to get new furniture.

I finished a second cookie without saying anything. Belphegor looked around and sighed. "Go shower. You smell like the sulfur pit on a windy day."

I shoved myself to my feet and trudged to the bathroom.

Using water so hot it left my skin red, I scrubbed until some of the heartache washed down the drain. When I emerged twenty minutes later, Belphegor was finishing loading my dishwasher.

I stopped and stared at him. "What are you doing?"

He glared at me. "If Amber saw how messy this place was, she'd have a heart attack. I will not be responsible for that." He started the cycle then lumbered over to my fridge and looked inside. "Anthony's dropping off groceries for the Andrews later. Since you clearly can't take care of yourself, I'll have him get you some."

"Shit." I scrubbed my hand over my face. "I forgot. I'll go today."

"Good. Stop being a shitass before Amber tries to climb the stairs again to check on you. This pile of rocks needs to fix the elevator." As he slid past me, he stopped and patted my arm awkwardly. "A broken heart is the purest form of torture."

"You've had a broken heart?"

He pushed past me and moved to the door. "Just because my vocation is torture doesn't mean I can't fall in love, kid." He stood and eyed me. "Get your shit together and fight for your woman."

With that parting shot, he left without looking back.

Of all the people who might've succeeded at breaking through my grief, I hadn't expected Belphegor to be on that list. I looked around the apartment. The takeout containers were sorted into trash and recycling, the blankets on the couch neatly folded, the curtains pulled back to let in sunlight for the first time in days, and it clicked. I was not completely alone. It was time to get my ass in gear.

I picked up my cell and called my dad.

"Summers."

"Dad?"

He paused for a long moment. "Status?"

I straightened my shoulders. "I want in on the arraignments."

An email binged on my phone. "Details sent."

I pulled the phone away from my ear and opened the email. My eyes widened. "You planned this?" I gasped.

"I'd never make a plan with a demon," he said, thereby confirming it had been his plan all along. "Carma's arraignment at 3. Lucinda's 3:45."

When I hung up, a text was waiting for me.

Jake: *Pick you up in 30*

Chapter Thirty

J AKE STOOD NEXT to me as the council members filed into the hearing room for first Carma's then Lucinda's arraignments. In most cases, these hearings would've been done the day after the arrest, but because Lucinda had turned into a vampire and Carma had been at the mercy of the SHAP medical and research team, their stability was prioritized.

I was proud of myself. I held my professional mask in place as Carma was led in and asked to sit in the center of the room. This was simply the arraignment, so a SHAP judge would present the charges and ask for a plea. Since Lucinda's confession stated clearly that Carma had no knowledge of what was going on at Thinner, I didn't expect her arraignment to last much longer than the reading of the charges if any. Neither should go to trial.

I studied Carma, taking in her tied-up hair and demure black suit. There was nothing "Carma" about her outfit—no earrings, no coffin necklace, no skull brooches. Just efficiency. My stomach tightened.

We went through the opening bullshit, everyone introducing everyone else. Then Judge Murphy, a witch who could sense liars, looked over the file on her computer.

"Carma Nicks, you are being charged with transportation of an illegal substance over state lines on January 12th, 2021, where it's reported that you personally delivered shakes to the first ten members between Michigan and Ohio. How do you plead?"

Carma stood and looked straight at Judge Murphy. "Guilty, Your Honor."

Judge Murphy nodded. "As this is your first offense and you've been vouched for by former SHAP agent Mina Summers, the council sentences you to time served. Make sure to not have a repeat offense, Miss Nicks, or the council will not be so lenient."

"Thank you, Your Honor," Carma said.

"And Agent Summers?" Judge Murphy added, "Thank you for your and Agent Robinson's excellent work. You both will be sorely missed." She hit her gavel. "Case dismissed."

Carma and her lawyer, a werewolf who looked to be both forty and sixty at the same time, shook hands and walked out of the room. I rushed out after her. I had to speak with her, had to make sure she was okay. "Carma!" I shouted over the din of the crowd between us. She hesitated before stopping, then looked over her shoulder. Her face was completely blank.

I swallowed hard. Her attorney captured her attention and gestured to a nearby room. She walked in alone and I hurried in after her, closing the door. It was a small, but empty, meeting room.

She looked at me for a moment, then down at her low-heeled black pumps. "This is what they gave me for today. I hadn't brought anything formal."

"You look good," I rushed out. "How are you?"

She gestured to the hall. "Glad this part is over. Terrified for Mom. Not even sure…" she cleared her throat. "It's a lot to take in." She balled her fists up then released them. "I mean, I believed in ghosts before all this. And at the festival…"

My cheeks warmed at the reminder of the night we kissed. "Why did you ask me if I'd still…" *kiss you* "like you if you were a werewolf?"

"I knew something was off," she admitted. "I'm never tired, hardly sleep, and my heart rate is crazy low. I was afraid there was actually something seriously wrong with me, which I guess there was. I figured if you could deal with some ridiculous notion that I believed I was a werewolf, then you could deal with whatever was actually going on with me."

Carma laughed once then covered her mouth with her hand, then let it drop. "Little did I know they were real."

"Yeah." I picked at my cuticle. "They are mostly pretty cool. I know a few."

She lifted her shoulders. "SHAP started a support group for all of us."

"That's good!" I pressed my lips together. That sounded too overexcited. "I mean, I'm glad you have resources."

She looked down at her faded manicure. "I know this may sound ridiculous, but I don't mind. Being a hybrid, or whatever you want to call it." She ran her pointer finger over her thumb nail. "I mean, except the animal blood thing." She winced. "I was a vegan before Thinner."

"You do love animals."

"Yeah." She let her hands drop and looked everywhere but at me. "It's hard to navigate."

"I can only imagine. You know, I'm always here to help you through it."

Silence filled the space between us, pushing us further apart. Every part of my body hurt. My soul hurt. Was this what people meant by "lovesick?" This was horrible. Why would anyone ever want to do this?

"The judge said former agent?" Her gaze flashed to my face, but she didn't meet my eyes.

"I am no longer a SHAP employee."

"Because of me?"

I shook my head once. "Because of me."

"Because of us?"

I allowed my silence to answer for me. She looked at the door and shifted, and I knew she was preparing to escape. It took everything I had not to move to her, pull her into my arms, beg her to stay and stop this knife slicing between my ribs every time my heart dared to beat. I wasn't stupid. Desperate maybe, but not stupid.

"Do you regret it?" she asked.

I ran my hand through my hair. "I regret not being able to tell you sooner. Not discovering what was going on so I could save your mom." *Not holding you every moment we were together.*

The corners of her lips turned up as if she heard what I hadn't said out loud. She walked toward the door, pausing halfway there. "For what it's worth, I don't regret it, either."

I didn't know how to respond. Whether or not Carma regretted it didn't seem to change anything. She started moving again, and I leaned forward and put my elbows on my knees, holding my forehead. "I know I lied to you about who I was, I know we met while I was investigating you and your mom, I know everything fell apart in the worst way..." I cleared my throat.

She stilled.

"I can't imagine what you're going through. But...I want you to know I never lied about my feelings. I've never...said anything I didn't mean." *I love you, I love you, I love you. Please don't leave.*

"I know," she whispered.

"I wish it was enough."

She lifted her hand to the doorknob. "Me, too."

I knew the image of her looking back over her shoulder with tears in her eyes would stay burned in my brain forever. "What will you do now?"

She pursed her lips. "I have to stay near SHAP headquarters, but I think I'm going to look around for a haunted B&B. Start over somewhere and do something new."

I smiled even though my chest cracked wide open. "That would be really cool."

Carma smiled back, a genuine smile, and it was like a battering ram to what was left of my heart. I cleared my throat. "I'll walk you to your mom's arraignment?"

She smiled but shook her head. "I need a few minutes alone. But thank you."

And with that, she was gone. Taking my heart with her.

Chapter Thirty-One

LUCINDA WAS BROUGHT in with her hands and feet bound by silver chains and two vampire security guards. An electrified barrier was placed between Judge Murphy and the defendant's chair, a second between the chair and the audience. Unlike the resigned yet calm nature of Carma's sentencing, the room crackled with emotion.

People I recognized from Thinner packed the benches, all staring intently at the woman who brought them low. Rachel and Maggie sat together, not speaking, at the end of the front row. They both glanced up when I walked in, Maggie's eyes holding mine.

I mouthed, "I'm sorry."

She nodded once, giving me a concerned look. Then she glanced over at Carma, and back to me. Even now, she was trying to take care of me. I nodded, but this time I didn't listen, and I didn't go to Carma. She needed closure first, that much was clear.

Instead, I stood along the back wall, arms crossed, concentrating on not showing any outward sign of weakness. No nail chewing, no leg bouncing, no fidgeting. A molten ball of emotion lodged itself against my lungs as Judge Murphy began reading the list of charges.

"Lucinda Nicks, you are charged with knowingly acquiring, possessing, and distributing an illegal substance without proper permits, illegally dosing 714,364 people, creating a supernatural species without permission, endangering both supernatural and human lives, and three counts of homicide. We have a signed confession. How do you plead?"

Lucinda, who was standing, tilted her head to the side and smiled. An arctic chill ran down my spine. "Your Honor, I plead not guilty."

Lucinda's lawyer, a vampire, added, "Lucinda Nicks is revoking her confession on the grounds that she was coerced into writing it on the day she turned into a vampire. My client was not of sound mind or body."

The sounds of disbelief rolled over the audience, and Judge Murphy hit her gavel to call the room back to order. I pushed off the wall, but Jake's arm shot out in front of me. "Don't move," he warned.

"I won't let her do this."

Jake stepped in front of me, forcing me to meet his eyes. "This is Judge Murphy. Wait and see."

My jaw was clenched so hard, I was worried my teeth would crumble. "Fine," I spat. My muscles vibrated with fury, but I leaned back against the wall.

Jake returned to my side, positioning his cane across my ankle. I knew it would cost him—standing for so long without the benefit of his walking aid—but this way he could catch me if I did something dumb. He'd either trip me or hit me in the shins, which was just annoying enough to keep me in place. For now.

"Remember," Jake whispered. "This isn't exactly human

court."

I almost smiled.

Judge Murphy studied Lucinda, and I had been in her courtroom enough to know she was assessing for lies. "It's a bold move to reject the confession, Ms. Nicks. Are you sure you want to go to trial? Based on the audience gathered here alone, I have no doubt the evidence will be compelling."

Lucinda's lawyer responded. "My client, like her daughter, did not know the substance in the Thinner shakes was an illegal substance, nor did she know about the existence of vampires or vampire hybrids. Because this knowledge was kept from her—"

Judge Murphy hit her gavel. "Jess, your aura literally changes color when you're lying. You'd do better in the human courts. Lie again and I'll hold you in contempt."

The lawyer dipped her head and whispered something to Lucinda, who nodded. Jess straightened and smoothed her suit coat.

"Let me ask again," Judge Murphy said. "What does the defendant claim?"

"Not guilty. Ms. Nicks say she was coerced into distributing oral venom through Thinner by a supernatural crime syndicate."

The room erupted in gasps of disbelief.

Jake turned to face me. "This goes deeper."

"Fuck," I breathed.

Judge Murphy pounded her gavel again. "Order!" It took three tries before the room settled. "Lucinda Nicks, you will be held, without bail, while we review the details of this case. Guards, take the defendant away."

JAKE, SIENNA, AND I sat in my dad's office drinking his most expensive scotch. In another timeline, this would've been a celebration. Now, it was a devastation.

"How deep does this go?" Jake asked.

As if on cue, Dad walked in and tossed his suit coat across his desk. "Deeper than we think." He looked up at me. "You can't be part of it."

I threw back the rest of my drink. "Joy."

He turned to Jake. "Need you to finish this before you transfer."

Jake sighed and ran a hand down his face. "I figured. I want my niece protected."

Dad nodded. "Done." He checked his watch. "Tomorrow, we start hunting."

Chapter Thirty-Two

Three weeks later

B EING BUSY WAS like having a flotation device to help me keep my head above water. Jake and I tried to have a meal together once a week, but he'd had to cancel the last two because of work. Eliza was on a mission and couldn't get away, and Magnolia and I had gone to the movies twice, but we had *vastly* different taste, which made me just miss Carma more. I started hanging out in the lobby of my building just to have something to do.

Finding my new routine had kept me from spiraling more than I already had, but I was still trying to figure out what I wanted to do career-wise. Amber was trying to teach me how to cook, with mixed results. Reggie ran alongside me in the mornings, which was a habit that was growing on me. Even Doris had waved at me the other day. *Waved. At me.*

The nights were the hardest. I flipped endlessly through books, shows, and movies that didn't hold my interest. Now that I was finally allowed to have social media, since I no longer worked undercover, I found most of it pointless. I even tried a paint-by-number picture but spilled my brown paint and threw the whole thing away.

As the sun dipped down in the sky, I sighed. Another

night was here. In good news, with Mom and Isaac's small but beautiful wedding swiftly approaching, I had plenty of things to occupy me. Today, I was handwriting the place cards. There were only going to be about twenty-five people there, but I also had to teach myself calligraphy.

Reggie and Clint were locked in a fierce chess battle, although they were so busy making heart eyes at each other, the game had been going on for two days. I would be disgusted if I wasn't so happy for them. They hadn't found true love while they were alive, and it was inspiring to know there was a chance for them now.

Belphegor moseyed in with Amber on his arm. The demon held out a chair for her before sitting next to her. She had taken to visiting whenever George fell asleep in front of the television after dinner. We sat in companionable silence as she counted her stitches. Belphegor untangled her yarn and wrapped it around his large hand.

I smiled. It may be a weird group of friends—these ghosts, a grandma who liked to knit for demons, and an actual demon—but they had been my rock as I found the new me again. My found family, reminding me I wasn't as alone as I used to feel. When I finished the place cards, I reached over and snagged a real estate magazine that had been dropped off on one of the chairs.

"Thinking about moving?" Amber asked.

I shook my head. "Nah. I just like to look at houses I can't afford."

"Used to do that all the time," Reggie added. "Now I just haunt them."

I rolled my eyes. I admit I'd expected Reggie to search

for Sebastian high and low since he left, but after the first week he seemed to lose interest. I wanted to ask him about it, but I chickened out every time. I wasn't ready to deal with that loss yet.

As I turned the page in the magazine, I froze. I looked up at my companions, then back at the photo. *There's no way.*

"What's wrong, dear?" Amber asked. "You look like you've seen a ghost."

"The Blackburn House is for sale." Memories of Carma in my arms, telling me how she'd redecorate the outside if it was her bed and breakfast sliced through the peaceful facade I had created.

"Oh yes, Doris was talking about them downsizing and moving to Florida."

I took a picture of the page before remembering I didn't have Carma's number in my phone. I had replaced it with Eliza's number in case I tried to drunk dial Carma. I could send it by postal mail, but it'd take her a few days to get it. I moved to delete the picture when I remembered Carma had sent me a fundraiser to-do list from her personal email.

Scanning my inbox, I found her address.

Thought you might like to see this. Hope you're doing well. Mina

I attached the picture and hit send before I could chicken out. The back of my neck and my underarms were damp, as if I had just run a marathon. So much for being over her.

We all looked over when the front door opened, and I shot straight out of my chair when Jake walked in, looking exhausted. His tie was loose, and exhaustion lined his face.

He lifted up a paper bag and gave me a half smile. "Dinner? I know I'm like...two weeks late."

I smiled wide. I had missed my best friend. "Dinner sounds perfect."

I gathered the cards and the magazine, then followed him to the elevator Belphegor somehow managed to fix. While my instincts told me never to trust a demon or his handiwork, I knew he wouldn't put Amber or George in danger. I grudgingly respected him, and his love for the Andrews.

When we walked into my apartment, Jake stilled. "You got new furniture!"

I looked at the gray couch and yellow chair, the new additions to my living room. I shouldn't have been spending money without a steady income, but the small change helped make this place feel a little more like the new me. "I did."

"I like it." He set the bag on the new glass top coffee table while I moved to get plates and utensils. He set up the Lebanese spread, as if we had just dined together last week, and we began to eat.

"How goes the research?" I finally asked, unable to stand the silence.

He set down his salad. "It comes in waves. Somedays we're really lucky, then others we find nothing. I'm sorry I had to disappear. It's all...overwhelming."

"I get it."

He looked at the door. "Hey, there's something I wanted to talk to you about. It took me awhile to get things situated, but I got a new roommate. Lost the bet, after all."

"Bet?"

"You won fair and square. You got the food sample first, remember?"

Ghost bumps ran down my left arm, and I spun around and shot up from my chair, trying to blink the tears out of my eyes so they wouldn't blur my vision. Sebastian appeared, took off his top hat, and bowed. "Miss Mina. I'm ecstatic to see you finally resorted to sense and got rid of that godforsaken chair."

My hands flew to my face on a gasp. Sebastian leaned as close as he could, and I wished I could wrap my arms around him in a tight hug. Two tears streamed down my face, and he startled. "You're crying, love."

I laughed and sniffed. "I do that now, apparently."

Noise from behind him announced Reggie's arrival. The two ran at each other and hugged, speaking quickly in low tones. I turned to Jake and tried to form words, but no sound came out.

"It's weird, I'll give you that. But I convinced the board how vital Sebastian was to the case, and his residency was approved."

I moved to Jake and wrapped my arms around him in a tight hug. "Thank you," I whispered into his shoulder.

He put his arms around my waist and squeezed. "You ready for your mom's wedding?"

I released him and took a step back and smiled. "You know what? I'm actually excited."

"Good. Isaac is a good man."

"He is."

"You bringing a date?"

I rolled my eyes and went back to the armchair. Sebastlan moved to his spot on the couch, Reggie next to him. "Nope, unless you count one of these guys." I gestured to my ghosts. "Carma's not interested in continuing our relationship."

Jake picked up his salad and speared a tomato. "Never knew you to be a chicken, Summers."

I threw a piece of pita bread at him. "Watch it, Robinson. I know all your secrets."

He just winked at me.

Chapter Thirty-Three

*N*EVER KNEW YOU *to be a chicken, Summers.*

Jake's words echoed around my brain as I stared at the ceiling. It was only four. Too early to get up, too late to sleep. I wasn't going to spend my time chasing down a woman who didn't want me. It was disrespectful to both of us.

Why had I sent that email? She probably thought I was an idiot. Why wasn't there an unsend option? I could video chat with someone on the other side of the world with a push of a button—Mom and I managed a ten-minute Zoom for my birthday last year—but I couldn't unsend an email to my ex-girlfriend?

I pulled my pillow over my face and groaned. Then I heard my phone buzz. I sat up, confused. I didn't bother with do not disturb these days. There was no one who'd contact me in the middle of the night.

Flipping on the bedside light, I grabbed my phone and opened my texts. I recognized the number as soon as I saw it. *Carma.*

Carma: *Sorry, just saw your email*

Carma: *Wasn't ignoring you*

Carma: *Omg, I just looked at the time. I hope I didn't wake you!*

What did I say to that? It had been only like eight hours since I sent it and I hadn't even expected her to respond.

Me: *No need to apologize. Was already up. You okay?*
Carma: *Yes*
Carma: *No*
Carma: *Not really. But I will be*
Me: *yes, you will*

I stared at the three little dots so hard, I thought I'd burst a blood vessel in my eye.

Carma: *The Blackburn House has an open house tomorrow*
Me: *You should go!*
Carma: *I don't want to go alone*
Carma: *What are you doing tomorrow?*

I dropped the phone and laid back down on my pillow for a moment. "She wants to see me!" I said to no one. I sat back up and replied.

Me: *I'm completely open*
Carma: *Meet you there at 10?*
Me: *Sounds like a plan*
Carma: **heart emoji**

✕

I HAD BEEN less nervous when they airlifted me to the hospital. As I turned the corner to the Blackburn house, I nearly laughed. I was half an hour early, but Carma was already leaning against the patio. She had a parasol to block her from the sun, her polka dot, navy blue jumpsuit and orange sweater hugged every curve. She had a collection of bangles on her wrist with names and dates on them.

I don't know how it was possible, but she got more beautiful every time I saw her. "You look incredible."

She smiled so wide, it made me smile. "You, too." She leaned in and air kissed my cheek, giving me a quick, one-armed hug.

When she pulled back, I gestured to the bracelets that clattered. "Did you make these?"

She nodded. "They're the names and dates of every woman who was executed during the Salem witch trials. I wanted to honor them, especially now that I know witches are real. Even if these women didn't practice witchcraft."

"That's really cool."

"I'm weird."

"I like weird."

She searched my face. "Mina…"

I tensed, waiting for the "just friends" speech. Thankfully, the front door opened, and the Realtor walked out.

"You're early," he said. "But if you'd like to come in, we're ready for you."

"Wonderful!" Carma turned her most charming smile on him and he took a step back.

I know how you feel, dude. I followed her up the porch stairs and into the house that rolled out in front of us. It would need a few cosmetic updates and a handful of more serious upgrades, including the electrical, but as I watched Carma move through each room, I knew. She was all in.

I could see her designing each space, picture her with paint on her face and in her hair, sawdust covering the floor. She could start over here and go after her dream. I swallowed hard and fell behind her, needing a minute to collect my thoughts.

"You're early."

I startled as Sebastian appeared next to me. "What are you doing here?" I whispered through clenched teeth.

"I longed to see the inside of this house and thankfully, it's just within my tether."

Reggie appeared next to him. "He wanted to see how awkward you were being with Carma."

"Traitor," I grunted.

"So very awkward," Reggie surmised.

I sighed. "I don't know what's going on, okay? And I don't want to ask while she's doing her thing. I can wait."

The two of them exchanged a look.

"What?"

Sebastian nodded in Carma's direction. "Standing back here wasting your time with us isn't going to solve your problem."

I pinched the bridge of my nose. "I can't believe I missed you." I hurried after Carma, entering the uppermost bedroom in the house. It was small but cozy, with sloped ceilings and a small closet.

Carma stepped into the closet. "It's a decent size for a guest room."

I leaned in and looked. "Yeah, not bad." I stumbled as I was shoved by the door from behind and almost fell into Carma. I caught myself on the wall and spun around, only to hear the sound of a latch.

"You've got to be kidding me." I pulled my cell out of my pocket and turned on the flashlight app. Jiggling the handle did nothing. "Sebastian, Reggie, this isn't funny. How'd you even do that?"

"Been practicing," Reggie admitted. "Doors are easy now."

I ran my hand down my face. "I did this." I knocked on the door. "Let us out."

"After you both reach a satisfying conclusion about your relationship," Sebastian promised.

"You locked us in a closet to force us to talk about a relationship?"

"Yes," they both said at once.

"Exorcism."

Carma laughed softly. "Well, I did say I wanted a haunted B&B. I guess I should've known that would come with a side of ghosts. Are they friends of yours?"

"Depends on the day. I may sage these two out of this town."

She put her hand on my forearm. "Stop, it's okay. We can talk."

"Okay. Let's talk."

We were both silent. Then we both laughed awkwardly.

"I miss you," she whispered. "I almost call you every day."

"I miss you, too."

"I know the prudent thing is to ask if you'd like to try to be friends again?"

Friends. The word echoed in my brain. I struggled to get a lungful of air. "Friends doesn't work for me."

My voice was steady as I said it, even though my heart was pounding so hard my hands hurt. "I was willing to risk everything I had worked for my entire life to be with you, and that hasn't changed. I didn't know what I was missing until you came into my life. You unlocked something inside of me. So if only friends is what you want, then I'm sorry. I'm out."

Her only response was a soft gasp.

"I'm all in, Carma. I know I'm difficult and I have literally no experience with being in love, but I will do everything I can every day to make you happy. And if you're not all in, then I'll hug you when we leave, and we'll walk away. For good."

"Mina?"

"Yeah?"

"Are you done?"

"Yeah."

She moved so fast, I didn't have a chance to respond. I was in her arms, her mouth on mine in one single move. I gasped, wrapping my arms around her, digging my hands into her hair. I angled my head to deepen the kiss. All the pieces of my broken heart pulled together, delicately clinging to each other.

"I don't want to build a life without you," she whispered against my skin as she kissed my cheeks, the underside of my jaw, my neck. "Can we start over?"

"Yes. Please." I brought her mouth back to mine. In between kisses, I whispered to her. "My real name is Mina Summers. My parents are Jim and Beth. I'm technically an only child, but Jake is my brother. I like pineapple on pizza. I hate olives. I've never seen the new *Star Wars*. These two dumbass ghosts are my best friends."

She laughed and kissed me hard, shutting me up.

The lock releasing startled us back to reality. I gave Carma one more kiss then opened the door, taking a moment to smooth her hair before we stepped out, hand in hand. Sebastian and Reggie gave each other high fives, and I gave them the finger.

"You're welcome," Sebastian said.

"Exorcism," I teased. Carma squeezed my hand. "So, you going to make an offer?"

She smiled. "Definitely. What shall we do to celebrate?"

I laughed and shook my head in disbelief that I was about to ask her this. "Wanna be my date to a wedding?"

The End

Don't miss the next book in the Love Me Dead series, *Grim and Bear It*!

Join Tule Publishing's newsletter for more great reads and weekly deals!

Acknowledgements

This book almost didn't happen, so as I sit here writing the acknowledgments, I'm overwhelmed that it's officially done. Between my rare disease trying to take me out and basically all of 2020, I couldn't write a word. Then I stumbled across a musical called Julie and the Phantoms (Netflix), and it relit the spark that I thought had died. With the show came my fantom family, my fossil fantoms, and some of my best friends. As sappy as it sounds, thank you to the JATP cast, crew, writers, and Kenny Ortega for giving us something so special that it changed our lives.

Eliza, you gave me a place to daydream, and Ci you are the best hype-woman anyone could ask for. A huge thank you to you both. And to each and every one of our crew, who talk to me at three in the morning when I can't sleep, who fill my DMs with friendship, who have breathed new life into not only my books, but me as well: I adore you. Thank you.

All my love to Mr. Heather, who is my biggest supporter and has put up with me talking about fictional characters every day for the last decade. Your life could've been normal, but I'm so glad you decided to stick with me instead.

Thank you to Tule (everyone on the team and my fellow authors), and especially my editor Sinclair, for helping me turn these words into tangible magic.

Huge gratitude to my "brain trust": My alpha readers Janna Bonikowski and Erika Cooper, my translators Andrea

Véliz García and DCL, and my sensitivity readers Elyssa Mann, Jenna Walsh, and Eric Thomas.

Notable thanks to my writing team who talked me through the plot holes and didn't let me run away and start a llama farm (because allergies): especially Sarah and your songs, Shelly, Aliza, Sage, MK, Stacey, Fortune, Jadesola, Nan, Denise, Ieshia, Kelly, Mia, Elaine, Liz, Jen, and Kathryn. A very special thanks to Dana, who encouraged me to pitch to Tule and pulled me out of my own way.

To Keara and Jen for your daily pep talks, and to my sister Kate who reads everything I write to make sure I'm remotely sensical. To my hypopara sisters, my docs, and Krisztina who kept me from turning into a vampire.

To Hannah Leigh, for your amazing music and support. To my reader group, I don't deserve you, but I cherish you (shout-out to NP for the plot bunny). To you, my readers, for spending your most precious commodity—time—on my words.

Last but not least, to my family and friends, I'm so lucky to have you in my life. And to my grandparents, ja cię kocham. Thanks for all your support and unconditional love.

If you enjoyed *Blood Thinners*,
you'll love the next books in the…

Love Me Dead series

Book 1: *Blood Thinners*

Book 2: *Grim and Bear It*
Coming in June 2022

Book 3: *Dearly Departed*
Coming in September 2022

About the Author

Bold, Breathtaking, Badass Romance.

When she's not pretending to be a rock star with purple hair, award-winning author Heather Novak is crafting sex positive romance novels to make you swoon! After her rare disease tried to kill her, Heather mutated into a superhero whose greatest power is writing stories that you can't put down.

Heather tries to save the world (like her late mama taught her) from her home near Detroit, Michigan, where she lives with Mr. Heather and a collection of musical instruments. She identifies as part of the LGBTQ+ community and believes Black Lives Matter.

Follow her at www.HeatherNovak.Net

You can learn more about Heather's rare disease at:
www.Hypopara.org

AWARDS:

2021 BEQ Pride Magazine's 40 LGBTQ Leaders Under 40

2019 Writer's Digest Self Published E-Book Awards, Honorable Mention (Romance)

2019 Chanticleer International Book Awards: Chatelaine Book Award, First Place (Romantic Fiction)

2019 Write Touch Readers' Award Winner (Wisconsin, Romance Writers of America)

2019 New England Readers' Choice Winner (New England Chapter, Romance Writers of America)

Thank you for reading

Blood Thinners

If you enjoyed this book, you can find more from all our great authors at TulePublishing.com, or from your favorite online retailer.

TULE
PUBLISHING